# A LOTUS DREAM:

## The Life of a Stripper is More than Just Glamour and Ca$h

By:  Ralph M. Edgerson Jr.

ISBN 978-1-943159-20-8

The publisher would appreciate notification where errors occur so that they may be corrected in subsequent printing and/or editions. Please send comments to the publisher by emailing to deeprivers67@yahoo.com Printed in the United States of America

Ralph Edgerson Jr. was the youngest of three, born and raised in New Orleans Louisiana. He always had a wild imagination but didn't start writing stories and poems until high school. Impressed with his visual writings in class an English teacher introduced him to Journalism where he honed his skills even more. After high school Ralph thought of majoring in Journalism in college but life had other plans for him. He joined the work force and writing fell to the backburner of his mind. After meeting his soulmate in September of 1995 Ralph focused on family and his first born arrived in November of 2003. 2005 came and life again had other plans for Ralph but this time on a much greater level. Stripped from everything he knows; Ralph moved his family to Houston Texas for a new beginning but that didn't come without trials. Thoughts of the unknown and uncertain brought Ralph back to an old friend that allowed him to vent in a way of literary release, in 2006. It was just a way to occupy his mind for the time being, but the creation of the "Decisions" saga began without him even knowing it. Ten years had passed, and writing fell off again for Ralph as he focused more on family, but he still occasionally wrote poems. He met a poet on social media that really enjoyed his poems and she suggested he have them published. Ralph let her read over the short story "Decisions" he wrote ten years ago, and she immediately wanted to have the story published. In July of 2018 Ralph Edgerson became a published author and his five-star rated urban novel "Decisions" arrived. In June of the following year he had the second installment of his first book published and he hasn't stopped writing since. Ralph enjoys creating dramas that keep his readers enthralled in the storyline and hearing readers fascination with the story and the characters. What he loves the most is hearing the excitement from his children saying, "My father is an author.

Dedicated to "Essence", "Smiley", "Cashmere", "Mz Emerald", "World's Finest Chocolate", "Baby Doll" and so many more...ladies thank you for allowing me into your world.

INTRO

"The meaning of the Lotus flower comes from how it grows…it starts as a bud in a murky pond and grows, emerging from the muddy waters into a beautiful blooming flower. Create beauty and happiness in your life, no matter where your roots are."

The year is 2038 in the city of New Orleans, business is booming for big companies, new ventures are always available for those willing to put in the work and business moguls are dipping their hands in a little bit of everything. But that grimy underbelly of the city will always raise its ugly head just to prove it's still there. Join Stephanie Crawford on this rollercoaster ride into an industry that is often given a side-eye and watch as this timid creature blossoms into this raging force.

CHAPTER I

It was almost registration day at The University of
New Orleans and Stephanie Crawford's anxiety couldn't be
any higher than today because she was trying to figure out
how she was going to pay for schooling with a 50%
Academic scholarship. She tried every avenue she could to
get the funds she needed but working part-time at a fast

food pizza place, as a driver, wasn't covering her expenses. Stephanie knew she couldn't go to Doris, her mother, for help because she had enough issues just paying her mortgage, taking care of Stephanie's little sister Alisha and making sure her older brother Caleb is taken care of in prison. Her father, Calvin Crawford was pretty much nonexistent, only showing his face when he needed a handout for his heroin addiction. Stephanie was pressed for time because her deadline for her final payment was in two months and she was 28 hundred dollars short. She had no clue of how she was going to make that much in 60 days.

Stephanie went to the one person she knew, in her mind, was a true hustler that could help her make some money fast and that was her aunt Leslie. Leslie Wilson was a natural go getter when it came down to making money fast, be it legal or illegal, Leslie knew how to do it. She was Doris' little sister and the two really didn't see eye to eye when it came down to how Leslie made a living. Doris always felt that her little sister was wasting her talents, calling Leslie's way of living crude and tactless and she also faulted Leslie for being the reason her son Caleb was in prison. Stephanie called her aunt desperately in need of her help,

"Hey Teedy, are you busy? I need to ask you for a favor."

"Girl what you need? I ain't got no money", laughed Leslie. Stephanie told her aunt of her dilemma and Leslie was more than happy to help her niece out.

"Look, I'm picking up a package at the Port right now. Meet me at Saint Charles and Washington by the strip mall in like a hour, I may have something for you", stated Leslie as she got off the phone.

Stephanie knew The Port of New Orleans wasn't that far from where her aunt wanted to meet and rushed over there. She hoped it wasn't anything illegal she had to do to make the money she needed but at the moment Stephanie really didn't care. Stephanie's main goal was to become a Physical Therapist and she was going to do whatever it takes to get to that goal. As she was pulling in the parking lot her friend Keisha called,

"What you doing bitch?"

Keisha Warren been Stephanie's best friend since middle school and the two shared everything, from clothes to secrets.

"Sitting here waiting on my aunt to show up. Hopefully she can help me with this damn tuition money cause I don't know how I'm a come up with that 28 hundred", replied Stephanie.

Keisha suggested that her friend get in touch with her cousin Timothy Warren who is a chef at a Michelin star restaurant in New Orleans.

"Bitch no offense but yo cousin weird as fuck", answered Stephanie. Keisha laughed as she replied,

"But that nigga stays with money in his pocket and he recently told me they needed a hostess and a few waitresses for the restaurant." Stephanie was curious and asked,

"Why you didn't jump at it to make some extra cash?"

"Bitch! He my cousin but that nigga weird as fuck", replied Keisha. Stephanie just shook her head as she responded,

"But you want me to go work with him. Fuck I look like."

The two friends laughed over the phone as they gossiped about old friends when Stephanie's aunt drove up next to her,

"Girl I gotta go, my aunt here."

Stephanie got out of her car and greeted Leslie, "Hey Teedy."

"Don't hey Teedy me, trick what you want", replied Leslie as she opened the bed of her truck sorting through boxes.

Stephanie knew her aunt was a no-nonsense type of person and always wanted everything straight to the point. She began telling Leslie how she tried making enough money for school but working odd jobs just wasn't cutting it. Leslie sat on the tailgate of her truck, lit a cigarette and looked at Stephanie with a serious face,

"As long as a female got a pussy pointing to the ground, she should never be broke or in need of cash." "Teedy I'm not trying to be no damn prostitute, shit", replied Stephanie. Leslie laughed,

"Heffa you ain't even built to be a hooker, yo mama sheltered the shit outta you. I'm talking about finding you a financial supporter or a sugar daddy. Gotta be some lame ass nigga you know willing to pay for some quality time."

Stephanie started shaking her head because she wasn't ready to solicit herself for the cash she needed,

"Teedy I'm not trying to get no dude to give me money over a promise of sex that I'm definitely not willing to give up. I'm sorry, I can't do it."

Leslie turned around, grabbed a box out of the bed of her truck and handed it over to Stephanie,

"Good girl, cause I didn't want you to. Take this box and bring it to this dude name Kareem at Hard Heads Barber Shop. He knows you're on the way, don't take nothing less than 600 dollars and bring me back 75. After that we'll figure out how you gone make this money."

Stephanie just hugged her aunt, so grateful for the help, "Thank you so much Teedy, I really appreciate it."

Leslie got in her truck and as she was closing her door, "Don't thank me yet."


Stephanie quickly made it to the barber shop and asked the receptionist for Kareem when a tall handsome guy with dreadlocks walked up to her,

"Hey, I'm Kareem, you must be Lez niece. Come with me, I got your envelope in the office."

Stephanie was nervous as hell, but she followed Kareem to the back of the shop as he tried to make small talk,

"So, you always run trips for Lez, cause I never seen you before."

"No, this my first time doing this for her", replied Stephanie.

Kareem sat behind his desk as he shuffled thru his desk drawer looking for the envelope, he had for her,

"I like your locs, they real neat. How long have you been having them?"

Stephanie's palms started to sweat as she placed the box on Kareem's desk,

"I'm 20 now, so it's been like 8 years."

"Geez, you my nephew Semaj's age. You just a baby", laughed Kareem as he handed Stephanie a sealed envelope. She nervously tore the envelope open,

"If you don't mind, I'd like to count this." Kareem sat back in his chair with a smile on his face,

"No problem baby girl, it's all there. Tell Lez she needs to keep you on her team for real."

Her heart was beating out of her chest but as Stephanie counted the money, she realized instead of 600 it was 800 dollars in the envelope, she didn't say anything to Kareem and shoved the money in her pocket.

"We good", asked Kareem.

Stephanie nodded her head and started to walk out the office when Kareem stopped her,

"Hey tell Lez whenever she get some more straight razor kits, holla at me." Stephanie turned around puzzled,

"Razors?"

"Yeah, straight razors. Please tell me you didn't think this was a drug transaction. Baby girl, this is a box of straight razor kits", replied Kareem as he opened the box to show Stephanie.

She looked in the cardboard box to see 12 wooden cigar box shaped boxes that had etched in the wood the words "Premium Cutlery". Stephanie stepped back,

"Are you serious? A box full of razors." Kareem started laughing,

"You really thought this was something else. Baby, I may do some under the table shit but trust me, I don't mess around with anything involving drugs. I might smoke some weed every once in awhile but that's it."

Stephanie let out a sigh of relief as she walked out the office when Kareem told her,

"Hey, next time you wanna get your locs twisted or put in a style hit me up. I'll take care of you."

She headed to her car as she called her aunt to find out where she wanted to meet up. Leslie told Stephanie to meet her at Broad and Canal by the old burger place in 20 minutes. As Stephanie headed out to meet up with her aunt, she couldn't help but to laugh at herself over the fact that she was so nervous earlier,

"A box of razors? Really girl?"

She then got a call from her mother asking if she could pick up her little sister Alisha from track practice, Stephanie reluctantly said yes.

"Baby I would go get her, but my supervisor just walked in with a stack of paperwork and no one in accounting can leave until it's all finished", acknowledged Doris.

"I'm a go get her as soon as I finish dropping this stuff off to Aunt Leslie", stated Stephanie. With agitation in her voice Doris replied,

"Don't get yo self caught up in Leslie shit."

"Dang mama, it's nothing like that. She just had me drop off a box at a barber shop", responded Stephanie as she got off the phone with her mother and parked on the side of the burger joint.

Stephanie patiently waited for her aunt in her car after grabbing a shake and some fries, all the while pondering what she could do next to get the money she needs.

CHAPTER II


Stephanie was just about call Leslie when her little sister Alisha texted her,

"Hey mama said you coming pick me up. Coach just ended practice and I'll be ready in 15."

Stephanie told her sister she will be there in 20 minutes and just to wait in front of her school. She was getting a little impatient waiting on her aunt when Leslie finally pulled up right next to her. Stephanie jumped out of her car and leaned in the passenger side window of Leslie's car,

"Damn, you had to go change clothes and vehicles Teedy? I've been waiting here forever."

"Girl stop ya whining, I'm heading to a lunch date after this. Shit, I'm trying to see if this nigga trying to be your next uncle or not", replied Leslie. Stephanie laughed,

"Eww, I didn't need to know that" as she handed Leslie all of the money, she got from the barber shop sell. While Leslie was counting the money Stephanie stated,

"You said 600 but that guy gave me 800 for that box of razors."

"Look at you being all honest and shit. Why you didn't pocket that extra 200", asked Leslie. Stephanie looked at her aunt a little confused,

"Why would I take money from my aunt who is helping me out?"

"Well don't take it wrong but I knew he was gonna give you 800. I just had to make sure I could trust you with my money. Even family would turn on you behind extra cash Steph, always remember that", replied Leslie as she handed her 725 dollars.

Leslie then told Stephanie that she talked to a guy that manage a strip club, he was looking for a waitress and was waiting on her phone call to tell him when she could start.

"Now you not stripping there, you just selling guys drinks and Marcus said his waitresses make good tips there", stated Leslie as she handed Stephanie Marcus' business card.

Stephanie thanked her aunt as she rushed back in her car to go pick up her sister from school and Leslie informed her that she had another drop off she could have if she wanted it.

"Tell me it's not another box of razors this time. Had me nervous as hell, thinking I'm a mule", laughed Stephanie.

Leslie laughed as she told her it was just a box of designer shirts, she was dropping off to a convenience store,

"Ask for Samson and he is supposed to give you 500, bring me back 250." Stephanie agreed, loaded the box in the back of her car and headed to go pick up her sister.

Alisha was waiting with two of her friends when she seen her big sister pull up in front of her school.

"Allie I'm sorry, I was doing something for Aunt Leslie and I didn't know it was going to take that long", stated Stephanie as Alisha got in the car and waved at her friends.

"It's cool, I was chilling", replied Alisha.

"Mama probably still at work and won't be home til later. You hungry, you want something to eat", asked Stephanie.

"You buying, I ain't gonna say no", replied Alisha.

The girls went to Stephanie's part-time job to pick up a couple of pizzas before heading home when Alisha asked about the large box in the backseat.

Stephanie completely forgot about the drop off she needed to make,

"Dammit, this will only take a minute."

Alisha didn't mind cause she likes hanging with her big sister,

"I'm chilling. What's in the box?"

"Nothing, just something I need to drop off for Aunt Leslie", replied Stephanie.

"If I know Aunt Leslie like I do, it's something that's on that five finger deal she always running", responded Alisha.

Stephanie just looked at her little sister with a serious poker face,

"Mind yo business and get on ya phone or something."

Alisha started giggling at her sister's response as she started taking selfies of herself. Stephanie parked in front of the convenience store, got the large box out of her car and walked into the store looking for Samson.

Just like her first drop, she walked to the back of the store and waited in the office as Samson started getting the money, he owed her. The only thing was that they both could hear a loud commotion going on in the front of the store. Samson got up to see what was going on when he handed Stephanie her money,

"Hold on right here."

Stephanie waited in the office and counted her money when she heard a loud bang like a gunshot. She stooped down as she peeked out the office door looking down the hall to see if everything was ok. Stephanie seen a young guy running down the hallway and she crotched down in the corner under a large wooden desk. She heard the guy burst thru the office door and began rummaging through file cabinets next to the door. Stephanie stayed as quiet as she could, closing her eyes tight and hoping the guy doesn't see her. She could hear the guy scream to someone in the front of the store,

"I don't see it! Where is the monitor for the cameras?"

The other person just yelled back,

"Take all the damn computers fool and let's get outta here!"

The guy was standing right in front of the desk Stephanie was under, pulling computer monitors and PC's from the desk when one of the plugs wouldn't come out of the wall. Stephanie knew she had to unplug it or the guy was going to have to look under the desk and in turn find her hiding there. As he was pulling, she reached over right next to his foot, unplugged the wire from the power cord and he rushed off with the monitors in his arms.

Right when she thought she was safe, Stephanie eased from under the desk and went to exit the office. But she could see the two guys, a tall skinny black guy with a spider tattoo on his neck and a stocky white guy with long braids in his hair, hadn't left the store yet. She seen an exit door that led out the back of the store and Stephanie made her way to it while the robbers were occupied with something, but the sound of her phone ringing alerted them both. Stephanie knew they were coming and ran to the exit door as fast as she could when one of the guys shot at her but missed hitting the wall. They chased after her, but Stephanie pushed thru the exit door and ran out the back of the store. She ran to the main street and rushed in a near by nail salon as the two guys ran past the store front looking for her. Stephanie watched as the guys stood looking up and down the street for the female that sprinted out the back of the store when one of the workers for the salon approached her,

"You have to get out of here. We don't want no trouble."

Stephanie begged them,

"Please just give me a minute" when her phone started ringing again. It was Alisha looking for her sister after she heard the gunshots,

"Where are you?! I heard the gunshots and I ducked down in the backseat."

"I'm okay but Allie, I need you to stay put. I'm on my way to you right now", pleaded Stephanie.

She seen the guys race back to the store while she was on the phone and knew it was a perfect time for her to make her move. Stephanie left the nail salon, quickly walked up the sidewalk to where her car was parked, jumped in the car with Alisha and sped off looking in her rear-view mirror to see if anyone was behind her. As she was going down Claiborne Ave, she could see police cars speeding down the street on the other side when Alisha asked her what happened. Stephanie was shaking her head in disbelief,

"I was just in the back of the store when I heard a gunshot and I ran out the back exit."

"That is crazy", replied Alisha.

Still shaken and nervous, Stephanie grabbed hold of her sister's hand,

"Don't tell mommy cause she would lose here shit. This is between us and only us, don't tell anyone."


The girls made it home safe and after a long conversation with her little sister, Stephanie convinced Alisha that no one needs to know that they were ever by the convenience store. Alisha understood the amount of trouble her big sister would be in and agreed not to tell a soul. Stephanie sat in her room thinking about all that happened as she reached in her pockets, pulled out everything and laid it on her bed. She started counting the money when she noticed the business card her aunt gave her earlier,

"Shit, I was supposed to call him."

Stephanie looked at the card that read Marcus Jordan manager of The Rabbit Hole Gentleman's Club and laughed at herself,

"Really, The Rabbit Hole? I'm a be a waitress at a strip club called The Rabbit Hole."

She called the number and a young woman answered the phone,

"Stagelight Industries, how can I help you."

Stephanie let the woman know she was calling for Marcus Jordan about a position he had available and that he was expecting her call. The young woman put Stephanie on hold as she gave the phone to Marcus,

"Hello, this is Marcus."

"Hi Mr. Marcus, my name is Stephanie Crawford. I believe my aunt Leslie Wilson talked to you and you told her you were looking for a waitress. I was wondering if the position is still available", replied a professionally speaking Stephanie.

Marcus chuckled a little, "Please don't call me Mr. Marcus. Marcus is just fine with me but yes, I talked to Lez about you. Your aunt cool people and she said you got the look I'm looking for in a waitress. If you like, you can come over tonight and see how the place runs."

Stephanie agreed to meet with Marcus in two hours and he told her where the club is,

"The address is 322 Lafayette Street, we right behind the casino and when you get here tell them you're here for me.

They'll let you in and we can talk over what the waitresses do here."

She was curious as to what he meant by "what the waitresses do here" and she hoped it didn't involve her having to take off her clothes to get the job. Stephanie started to look in her closet for something to wear to the club when Leslie called her,

"Hey aunt Leslie, I was gonna call you."

"Don't say anything, all I wanna know is are you okay", asked a panic-stricken Leslie.

Stephanie was pleased that her aunt was concerned about her wellbeing,

"I'm fine Teedy. Where can I meet you cause I have something for you."

Leslie was thrown for a loop with Stephanie's comment,

"I'm not worrying about that right now but I do need to meet with you."

Stephanie agreed to meet with her aunt right before she was scheduled to meet up with Marcus,

"Let me get dressed cause I gotta meet up with Marcus at the club, he wants to show me the club and shit."

Stephanie went and took a shower so that she could get ready to leave. As she was putting her clothes on her mother walked in,

"Hey Steph, I wanted to tell you that I talked to one of my supervisors. He told me that he could get you a job with his fiancé's maid service to make some extra cash. It's called

NOLA Maids and they service almost all the hotels in the city.”

“Thank you, mama, but not offense. I’m not cleaning up behind nobody”, replied Stephanie as she applied her make-up. Stephanie continued,

“I’m actually going on an interview right now at a club.”

Doris looked at her daughter with a little concern,

“A club, doing what?”

“I’ll just be a waitress, the guy said his waitresses make really good tips and its right behind the casino”, answered Stephanie as she slid on her high heel shoes.

“Baby you going to an interview in some tight jeans, a low-cut blouse and heels”, asked Doris with a confused look on her face.

Stephanie laughed as she grabbed her purse to leave,

“Mama, I’m meeting a guy at a club, 8 o’clock at night about a waitressing job. I don’t think business attire is needed for this interview.”


Leslie sat patiently in her car waiting on her niece when she seen headlights come up behind her. Still a little uneasy about what happened at the convenience store, Leslie sat her .45 on her lap. When she seen in her review it was Stephanie getting out of the car the tension in her jawline relaxed and the grip on her pistol eased. Stephanie walked up to Leslie’s passenger side door,

"You gone let me in or do I have to stand outside the car and talk to you?"

Her aunt opened the door, Stephanie got in and handed Leslie the envelope with her cut from the money.

"I told you, I'm not concerned about this", stated Leslie as she asked Stephanie what happened at the store. Stephanie began telling her aunt the whole event and how everything went down.

"So Alisha was sitting in the car the whole time, did she see the guys", asked Leslie.

"No, she said she didn't see them at all because she was looking at her phone. She only looked up when she heard the gun shots", replied Stephanie as she told Leslie that Alisha knows not to say anything to anyone about them being at the store.

   Stephanie was adamant about not having her mother know that her daughters were anywhere close to that store.

"Alisha's smart, she won't say anything to get y'all in trouble", responded Leslie.

   Stephanie was confident that her little sister wouldn't say anything but she was a little nervous about the guys who robbed the store. She asked her aunt,

"Did Samson survive cause I only seen those two guys?"

Leslie's silence at first was almost a stinging response but her reply comforted Stephanie some,

"He didn't die but last I heard he was in really bad shape. They took all the security footage, so nobody knows what they look like but I got one of my patnas looking for them fools. Don't nobody shoot at my niece and get away with it."

"Well Teedy, let me get to this club and talk to Marcus. He said he wanted to show me around, so I could see what the waitresses do there", replied Stephanie as she got out of the car.

"Steph, do you have a gun with you?", asked Leslie.

With a puzzled look on her face Stephanie replied,

"No. Should I? I'm just going to a strip club for an interview."

"If you take the job, you'll be working late nights, going to your car at 3 or 4 in the morning and getting home when its pitch-black outside. You need a gun cause as you experienced firsthand these motherfuckers ain't playing", responded a very insistent Leslie.

She reached in her middle console of her car, pulled out a chrome .380 semi-auto and handed it to Stephanie, "Until you get your own, hold onto mine. Stephanie I'm serious, if you're gonna take this job you will need protection."

Stephanie listened to her aunt and took the gun because she knew Leslie had a lot more experience in the matter than she did.


Stephanie made her way to the club and parked across the street as she watched guys walk up to the club's bouncers standing out front. She sat in the car contemplating if this is what she really wants to do, the decision Stephanie made at that very moment would change her life tremendously, she just didn't know it yet. Stephanie procrastinated before reaching for her door handle when she received a text message from Keisha,

"Bitch, WYD".

Stephanie giggled as she replied, "Bout to see what this strip club life about."

It was less than 10 seconds before Stephanie's phone started ringing with Keisha on the line. When she answered the phone, Keisha didn't hesitate in asking,

"I know you fuckin' lying! Tell me you lying. You really about to start stripping?"

"I never said I was. I'm going in here for an interview to become a waitress girl", replied Stephanie as she laughed at her friend.

Stephanie told Keisha how her aunt introduced her to Marcus, who was looking for a new waitress and he wanted to meet her at the club to show her around.

"So, it's really a strip club, like girls in there naked and shakin' ass", asked Keisha.

"Girl, I don't know. I'm still sitting in my car right now, but I need to get my ass out and go talk to this man because he said his waitresses make really good tips. You know I need to make some extra money", replied Stephanie.

Keisha's response before ending their call made them both laugh,

"Bitch, you better tell me all the details tomorrow and don't do nothing strange for a little change."

Standing at the front entrance of The Rabbit Hole Gentleman's Club were two enormous bookends by the names of Ricky and Melvin. The guys resembled giants to the average sized person with Ricky standing 6 foot 6 at 300 pounds and Melvin wasn't that much smaller standing 6 foot 4 at 280 pounds. They were the club's official bouncers, and everybody knew they meant business when it came to what goes on inside or outside of the club. Ricky Boyd was a former CFL defensive lineman, born and raised in New Orleans with a heart of gold, he always looked out for the crew that worked at the club and watched over all the dancers. Melvin Stevens was a former Angola prison guard that ended up on the wrong side of the law after a prisoner died and he was blamed for it. He was later exonerated but the damage was done when it came to Melvin trusting the judicial system. Ricky and Melvin were laughing at a drunk customer that was stumbling down the street after leaving the club when Melvin caught sight of a dark mahogany princess walking across the street towards them. Melvin's eyes were fixated on this deep tone melanin goddess' thick hourglass figure adorned with a crown of perfectly placed dreadlocks. It was as if she was a beautiful Medusa and her locs were a head full of snakes because both bouncers were frozen in place when she stood in front of them. Ricky took the initiative and approached the chocolate eye candy,

"Hey lil mama, if you coming by yourself it's gone be 20 to get in but it's free for you if you got a date." Her luscious full lips parted a bit as she smiled at Ricky,

"No date tonight handsome, just me. But I am here to see Marcus Jordan, you can tell him Stephanie's here."

Stephanie waited outside with Ricky while Melvin went inside to get Marcus and the curious bouncer attempted to spark a conversation with Stephanie.

"So where have Marcus been hiding you", asked Ricky.

Stephanie looked over the massive muscular male species standing in front of her,

"He ain't been hiding me anywhere. This our first time meeting each other. I'm actually here for a waitress position at the club, if you must pry."

"My bad, my bad. Just making small talk. Since we may be working with each other, my name's Ricky", replied the bouncer as he extended his hand out to Stephanie.

She shook Ricky's hand and it seemed to disappear in his grasp as they cordially greeted one another,

"Stephanie, but everybody calls me Steph."

## CHAPTER III

Marcus stepped outside to meet Stephanie,

"So, this is the niece Lez been telling me about? How you doing mama, I'm Marcus."

"Hey, I hope she haven't been telling you nothing crazy", replied Stephanie with a smile.

Marcus escorted Stephanie in the club and couldn't help but to notice her alluring dimensions. He looked back at his two bouncers standing in the doorway and smiled because they were doing the same. Stephanie had never been in a gentleman's club, so the experience was a lot to take in. She seen a topless dancer performing pole tricks on an oval shaped stage, lit by an overhead spotlight, right in front of a long woodgrain bar. When Stephanie walked pass her the dancer, hanging upside down on the pole, reached out and pulled Stephanie to her. Stephanie was shocked but didn't resist as the exotic dancer caressed herself in front of everyone as Stephanie stood there on the stage. The performer managed to turn right side up while holding onto the pole with one hand, wrapped her legs around Stephanie and pretended to kiss her. Guys sitting at the bar began to throw dollar bills at them on the stage and Marcus took Stephanie's hand,

"Ok Diamond, stop harassing my company."

Diamond gave Stephanie a sexy smile and winked at her as she continued to perform on the stage.

"So, you sure you wanna be a waitress, cause it looks like you have potential of being a dancer", asked Marcus as he sat at the bar.

Stephanie laughed,

"Me, a stripper? I couldn't do it. Not that I have anything against it, cause they some talented people but I don't think I have what it takes to be that good."

"Well we gone focus on you being a talented waitress then", replied Marcus.

He went on to tell Stephanie what the waitresses do there, how much they get paid an hour and the hours she would probably be working. Stephanie was listening to everything Marcus was telling her, but she was amazed with the atmosphere in the club. As a novice to the lifestyle, she had a misconception of what or how a gentleman's club actually operates, thinking it's full of horny lonely men paying for sex and brainwashed or money greedy downgrade females dancing on a dirty stage. Stephanie seen an elaborate semi circle set up of leather recliners accompanied with square wrought iron side tables between every other chair. She noticed that the main stage, that had chairs all around it, was elevated just enough that when the customers sat at it they had to look up at the dancers on the hardwood floor stage that resembled a basketball court floor. The stage had a spotlight that always came on when a performer was up there, and disco lights lit the rest of the club with the exception of the bar that was lit up by white miniature spotlights. The presence of Fleur-de-Lis and Mardi Gras masks decorated the entire club in different colors or styles. Every time Stephanie thought she seen it all something else would catch her eyes, she noticed the waitress' uniforms were pretty much a low-cut corset, tights and heels.

"I see you're soaking it all in. You have any questions for me", asked Marcus as he handed Stephanie a mini umbrella and cherry decorated drink.

Stephanie took a sip of the drink and replied,

"Nice Rum Punch, when do I start?"

"Well how about you sit back and watch the waitresses in here to see what they do so you can get a good idea of how it goes. I don't wanna send you out to the wolves as a complete rookie. Hey drinks on me tonight", stated Marcus as he walked off to take care of some business.

   Stephanie did exactly what Marcus told her and studied everything the waitresses did in the club, from taking orders from the customer to interacting with either the dancers or crew. The performer that Stephanie encountered when she first walked in the club came sat next to her and handed her 10 dollars in ones. She was a little confused why she did and asked,

"Diamond, right? I think I'm supposed to give you money not the other way around."

Diamond laughed as she gestured for the bartender to give her a drink,

"That's for going with the flow when I pulled you on that stage. Those bar flies weren't dropping a dime but as soon as I wrapped my legs around you they started reaching in their pockets."

"I have a question if you don't mind me asking", stated a curious Stephanie.

"Girl, I'm an open book. Trust me you can't ask me nothing I've never been asked before", replied Diamond.

Stephanie let out a small grin as she proceeded,

"Nothing to serious but is it hard to make money in here? I'm considering becoming a waitress here. Marcus told me that the waitresses make pretty decent tips alone with their hourly pay. I would ask one of them, but they look really busy right now."

Diamond's answer intrigued Stephanie's curiosity even more on how much money she could actually make. She told her that the waitresses really make good tips because of the Casino, that a lot of times celebrities or even athletes frequently pop in and out of the club.  Stephanie thanked Diamond for talking with her and slid the 10 ones she was still holding onto in Diamond's garter,

"Thanks for letting me burn your ear up with my questions."

"No problem girl, welcome to the clique", responded Diamond as she kissed Stephanie on the cheek.

Stephanie continued to sit at the bar watching everyone in the club when the DJ came across the sound system,

"This ya boy, DJ Felt-Tip, on the ones and twos and fellas I'm a need you to dig deep in them pockets cause we got that pole acrobat coming to the stage. Get ready to enjoy the sexy and talented, Smiley!"

The sounds of a marching band drum cadence began when the curtains opened at the back of the stage revealing a gorgeous yet nicely toned exotic dancer dressed in a sequin two-piece string bikini and high glass heels. She seemed to walk up the stage as if she was on the runway, making every step count and when she made it arms length to the pole at the front of the rink she launched in the air. Smiley spun around the pole with her legs wide open like propellers on a plane, occasionally slowing down to give that signature smile at customers gawking at her. When she came to a complete stop, she dropped to the stage floor into a split and it was like a volcano exploded because dollar bills just flew in the air onto the platform. Smiley then amazed her onlookers by doing a handstand as she leaned against the pole spreading her legs wide open, resembling the letter T and more money made itself on the ring. Stephanie knew she wasn't gay by any means, but she couldn't keep her eyes off this exotic athlete performing on this dance field. Smiley simply demanded your attention with her acrobatic flips and turns on the pole as she exhibited her talents. There was at least 100 to 150 dollars on the stage and she hadn't even taken off her top yet. Smiley slid feet first off the edge onto an audience member's lap, straddled him as she rotated her hips and buried her face into the side of his neck. The gentleman was in glory as the sexy exhibitionist gyrated on him, but it all ended when the music stopped and Smiley slowly got off his lap.

Marcus walked up to Stephanie still in amazement of the talent in the club,

"You starting to look more like a customer than an employee."

Stephanie giggled,

"Nah, I'm strictly dickly. I just admire their skills; it takes a certain kind of person to be able to work that pole like that girl just did."

"Oh Smiley, yeah she's one of the best pole acts in the city but she not even our main attraction", replied Marcus.

Stephanie didn't know what to say because she couldn't imagine anything more attractive than what she just seen.

"I would like for you to come in the morning for the next week to train because it's slow in the mornings. That way you could get comfortable with the orders, the menus and moving around in the club", stated Marcus as he got a drink from the bartender.

"I believe I got it, but I understand some training would be good and greatly appreciated", replied Stephanie.

"Hey, I know this may seem a lil blunt, but I know you noticed our waitress uniform is a corset and tights. I ordered you a 32D for the corset and you can get your own tights or leggins", stated Marcus.

Stephanie was shocked that he got her bra size correct,

"How you figure you know my bra size?"

"If I don't know anything about a woman, I can look at her and tell you her bra size. I'm a bonafide titty man", replied a laughing Marcus.

The two continued talking when Marcus mentioned the other club that is being constructed,

"You actually came in at a perfect time because the company I work for is putting together a new club slash casino and I know my waitresses will make a killing there."

"A club and casino?", asked Stephanie.

Marcus told her that the company is remodeling an old but large paddlewheel boat into their new club and casino. He also mentioned that the boat would take hour long trips around Lake Pontchartrain during the day and night. Everything was sounding so promising for what's to come but Stephanie still had a nervous bug buzzing in the pit of her stomach because she never had a job like this before.

"Well I guess I'll be seeing you in the morning sir", stated Stephanie as she got up from the bar.

"Nah, you won't see me until later in the day, I don't do mornings. Eric will be here to get you started with your training and he'll have your uniform top, he cool people", replied Marcus.

Stephanie was leaving the club heading back to her car when Ricky stopped her,

"So, you gone just leave me and not even say bye."

Stephanie smiled at the buff bouncer as she continued to walk to her car and responded, "Bye Ricky."

Ricky smiled as he watched the "Chocolate Goddess" make her way across the street,

"Damn she's fine."

Melvin laughed as he stared at Stephanie walk,

"Say Round, she is outta yo league. That ain't one of them generics, that's top shelf right there. Remember your last relationship with a top shelf and how that ended?"


Stephanie got in her vehicle and headed home with anticipation that this new job will help her out with her financial problems. She was kind of excited about working at the club after talking to Marcus and seeing how the waitresses operate in there. She had already set a goal in her head to be the best waitress in the building and knew she had to work hard at it. As she got close to home, she thought about how much she needs to save so that she could pay for school. Stephanie literally calculated how much she had to make in tips just to break even and she thought about asking her aunt if she could run a few more errands for her also. Stephanie pulled in front of her mother's house and seen that all the lights were off except for the living room lights. She knew her mother probably waited up for her like she always does whenever any of her kids are out of the house. Stephanie walked into Doris sitting on the sofa with the most serious face,

"Hey mama, you didn't have to wait up for me."

"Where did you go today Stephanie", asked an angered Doris.

Stephanie was a little caught off guard with the question because she knew her mother knew where she went tonight as she replied,

"Mama I went to the club to talk with the manager about a waitress position, remember."

Doris stood up from the sofa and walked over to Stephanie still standing at the front door, looking her directly in the eyes. Her mother's eyes seemed to pierce through her spirit as Doris asked again,

"Don't play with me lil girl. Where did you go today with my daughter?"

Stephanie then realized what her mother was talking about and assumed that Alisha had told her about the convenience store incident, but she wasn't going to admit to it until she really knew. In all the excitement of being introduced to the exotic dance community, Stephanie forgot all about what had taken place hours before. She then got on the defensive and stated,

"Mama you told me to go pick up Alisha and that's what I did. You always assuming I'm doing something I have no business."

Doris was livid as she pushed Stephanie against the door,

"Stephanie Marie Crawford, if you gone stand here in my face and lie to me you can turn around and walk right out that damn door. What the fuck was you doing at that damn store?"

Right then Stephanie knew her mother knew what happened and replied,

"Mama I didn't tell you because I didn't want you to worry. I was in there and when those guys came in to rob the place, I ran out the back."

Doris was so upset at her oldest girl and told her that when she was looking at the news, she seen the report about the convenience store robbery. Alisha was looking at the news with her and mumbled, "It made the news" and at that point Doris started questioning her daughter. Alisha couldn't help but to tell her mother the truth about the incident.

"Stephanie, I don't want to know why you was at that store, but I need you to remember that your brother is serving time for dumbass decisions. All money ain't good money and fast money half the time end up to be illegal", stated Doris as she walked off to her bedroom.

Stephanie went in her room and began getting out of her clothes as she headed to bed but her mother's last statement kept ringing in her head. She couldn't sleep so she went in the kitchen for a late-night snack. Alisha walked in the kitchen,

"Steph, I'm so sorry. I didn't know mama heard me and she just kept asking me how did I know about that store. I tried not to tell her, but she was all in my grill about it. I promise on everything, I didn't want to tell her."

Stephanie let her little sister know it was ok and the two sat at the kitchen table eating some shortbread cookies. Alisha's curious teenage mind asked,

"So where did you go tonight? I heard mama tell you to be careful."

"None of your business, nosey", replied a laughing Stephanie.

The girls stayed in the kitchen talking about Alisha's next track meet that's coming up and of course boys. Alisha then asked her big sister,

"I know why I don't have a boyfriend but why you don't?"

"You don't have a boyfriend cause Doris would kill you. Why I don't? I couldn't tell ya, I guess dark skinned girls out of style this season", responded Stephanie.

She had a boyfriend three years ago, but the relationship became strained after he moved to Utah for school. Malcolm was Stephanie's first and they been knowing each other since middle school but didn't actually start dating until they were Sophomores in high school. Malcolm wasn't the top basketball player at Karr High, but he was good enough to get a full scholarship from BYU and Stephanie was his biggest fan. The two lovebirds tried to make it work but the 1500-mile distance, from Utah to Louisiana, was a bigger challenge than they expected, so they stayed friends, keeping in contact with one another. Stephanie's heart was always wrapped around Malcolm's pinky, but she knew he was living his best life in college. She attempted to date other guys, but they all were compared to what she use to have and it always ended bad, so Stephanie went on a hiatus when it came to dating. Stephanie was ready to call it a night when Alisha started doing Snap Chat videos with the hash tag

"Me and Big Sis Chilling" and "Melanin Strong Over Here".

## CHAPTER IV

It's been almost four weeks since Stephanie started working at The Rabbit Hole, she really was getting good at working at the club. She was doing so well that she started to get regular customers that looked for her to take care of them. The tips and pay weren't as big as she expected but along with running the occasional drop for Leslie, it really helped her to pay the remainder of her tuition. Stephanie's schedule was really about to be hectic with her going to school in the mornings and working at the club in the evening to late nights. But the end goal was all that kept Stephanie pushing to finish school, become a Physical Therapist and making a career out of it. Her birthday was in a few days and turning 21 was a milestone Stephanie embraced but really didn't have any idea of what she wanted to do.

"Steph bring these drinks over to Lance for me baby", asked Quincy.

Quincy was the lead bartender at night, Stephanie thought he was so handsome and was like putty in his hands when he would talk to her. The two would flirt through out the night but nothing really manifested from it. The most either ever did was go to breakfast after work but that was with the whole crew, a routine that seems to be an unspoken word.

"So, who gone pay me for these drinks and I want a tip too", responded Stephanie.

Quincy gave her his usual devilish grin,

"Just give it to him, I'm adding it to his tab but I got your tip plus more."

"Promises promises", replied Stephanie as she walked off to the section where Lance was sitting.

   Now Lance was an arrogant, flashy young guy that had 4 girls that worked for him in the club. He insisted that he was a businessman and he managed the four dancers that always brought him every dollar they made in the club. Stephanie have seen pimps before, and she knew Lance was no businessman and probably never studied for business management or business relations at any school. She made her way to where Lance was sitting, the designer cashmere cardigan sweater, gold link chains, leather pants and shined Stacy Adams simply screamed an overly egotistical attitude with a comical flare. Every time any female was in ears reach of Lance's voice, he would go into recruit mode as he talked with his understudies,

"Man, I'm like the Stock Market, ya heard me, always on the rise. Gas prices gone drop but pussy gone always be on the top tier, all they need is a manager to help them manage, ya heard me."

   Stephanie just leaned over the table, replaced the empty glasses with new drinks for Lance and his company as she just listened to the pimp logic he was spewing.

"Say Chocolate, when you gone let me take you out for real for real", asked Lance as he placed a 5 dollar bill on her tray.

"C'mon now Lance, I'm not trying to have your girls mad at me", replied Stephanie while backing away from the table.

Lance stood up watching Stephanie walk back to the bar,

"Man, fuck them! What's good."

Stephanie was taking an order from a customer when she seen Marcus walk in the club with two extremely business-like individuals, briefcases included. As Marcus was passing her, he whispered,

"After you finish with them, I need you to come help me out in the office real quick."

Stephanie nodded yes and continued to assist her patrons with a smile. As she gave Quincy her order she asked,

"Who are the suits that went in the back with Marcus?"

"Shid, yo guess as good as mine but they look like money", replied Quincy while making the drinks.

Stephanie brought her consumers their order and headed to the back of the club where the office was, to see what Marcus needed help with. When she opened the door, she found Marcus talking to the gentlemen, who both stopped talking and just gazed at her. One of the men, who was of a dark complexion with wavy hair, muttered out,

"Maldita chica, estás bien."

At that point Stephanie realized that at least one of them were of Latino descent and wanted to let him know she understood exactly what he said as she replied,

"Bien gracias papi."

The astonished gentleman sat back with a grin on his face just amazed at Stephanie's response as he replied,

"Look at you mami. Tu hablas español bien."

"Yes I do. 4 years of Spanish and two tutors, I better be able to speak it well", replied Stephanie.

Right then Marcus knew he picked the right person to aid him in his business meeting with his two companions.

"Ok I'm curious, what y'all talking about? Cause I failed French and Spanish in high school", asked the other suit in the room.

Marcus laughed as he agreed,

"Yeah, I wanna know too."

"That's our little secret. But what I can do is get you gentleman something to drink", stated Stephanie with the cutest smile.

Marcus just admired the way Stephanie was handling herself as he asked,

"So Alex, Luca, what would you guys like to drink?"

But before they could answer Stephanie said,

"Let me guess, a whiskey neat for you and a tequila with lime for you."

Alex stood up as he looked over at Marcus,

"Ok dude, where did you find her? I need her at every meeting from now on."

Marcus just smiled as he announced,

"That's my girl Steph, one of our top waitresses. This is what you get when you do business with Stagelight Industries."

Stephanie smiled revealing those cute dimples as she enjoyed the accolade of being acknowledged as one of the club's top waitresses, after only being there a month. As she set out to go get the guys their drinks Marcus whispered,

"Two things have Smiley and Diamond come back here when you bring the drinks. Also, what did he say to you?"

"He just told me that I'm fine and I said thank you daddy", replied Stephanie.

Marcus responded,

"Shit, he ain't lying."

Stephanie seen her little buddy Diamond on stage performing and entertaining the crowd with her extreme sexual gestures. Diamond knew how to get any viewer to do more than just be an onlooker and participate by sprinkling her with ones. Stephanie admired the drive Diamond had when she was performing and admire her even more when she found out that Diamond was working on her second degree in Computer Science. The two really connected since Stephanie been working at the club that even, Stephanie's best friend, Keisha has become close to Diamond too. Stephanie caught Diamond's attention when she was exiting the stage,

"Hey girl, Marcus wants you and Smiley in the office to entertain some potentials back there."

"Bitch, please tell me at least one of them are handsome. Last time Marcus ass had me sitting on an ogre's lap with sausage fingers and he smelled like a sour mop", replied Diamond.

Stephanie burst out laughing,

"No bitch, not a sour mop. Well both of them are kinda cute, especially Luca dark berry toned ass."

Diamond told her friend that she is going get cleaned up before heading to the office and that she'll let Smiley know their presence is needed. Stephanie agreed and got ready to bring the drinks to Marcus, but she really wanted to wait until the girls were able to join her, so that's what she did. She knew it wouldn't take long for the dancers to freshen up for the V.I.P. clients so she took the time to take a break outside with the bouncers, Ricky and Melvin.

"What you two knuckleheads doing out here", asked Stephanie.

Ricky was pleased to see Stephanie because he's been crushing on her since he seen her come in for her interview but Melvin's statement that she's out of his league stayed ringing in his head. Melvin turned around after pat searching a customer jokingly replied,

"Quincy know you out here with us commoners?"

Stephanie looked at Melvin with a sinister smile as she placed her hand on his chest,

"Now you know I had to come see Zaddy."

"Who me", asked a cracking voice Melvin.

Stephanie walked away as she replied,

"Boy stop, I was talking about Ricky" and gave Ricky a peck on the cheek.

The three laughed as Melvin couldn't think of a comeback for Stephanie when they seen a shiny silver SUV pull up in front of the club. A tall Asian guy got out of the driver side and went over to the back to pull out a large suitcase. As he walked to the back-passenger door it opened up and stepping out was an absolutely gorgeous woman. She was dressed down in a mid-drift cartoon character t-shirt, some grey sweet pants and flip flops but under all that you could still see she was an undeniable 10.

"Looka you, where you been Sunshine", asked a smiling Melvin.

The female turned around and it was if it was straight out of a movie, the way her long coal black hair just blew in the wind and she smiled when she seen Melvin's face. She walked up, hugged and kissed him on the cheek as she replied,

"My big teddy bear, I haven't seen you in like a month. I missed y'all."

"So you back in the city to perform tonight, Sunshine", asked Ricky.

She looked at Ricky and winked with a grin,

"I ain't here to hold the sidewalk down baby."

Stephanie seen it was time for her to get back inside and left the two-bouncers talking with the unknown celebrity she just encountered.

When Stephanie walked in, she seen Diamond and Smiley just coming out the back dressing room. She then told

Quincy to make the drinks she needed as she called the girls over to her. Diamond walked up next to Stephanie, smelling like a sweet peach and glistened as you could see her entire body was lightly oiled down.

"Damn bitch, if I was a dude, I would fuck the shit outta you", stated Stephanie as she laughed.

"I guess I'm just chopped beef then", replied Smiley who looked just as dynamic as her counterpart.

"Now you know I'm yo number one fan heffa, you always on point", responded Stephanie as she walked toward the office where Marcus was waiting.

As they got to the office door Stephanie told Diamond about the young lady Sunshine she seen outside.

"Oh, that's the club's money maker right there, it's about to get crowded in here", stated Diamond.

"For real? I've never seen her before. Is she really that good cause I've seen some talent in here", asked Stephanie? Smiley responded with strong conviction,

"If we were all chess pieces, me and Diamond are the Bishop or Rook but Sunshine is the Queen. Hands down but she's sweet as pie, real cool people."

   Stephanie opened the door to the office and all three-gentleman stood up as the girls entered the room. Diamond made a beeline toward Alex, a Caucasian guy with an ethnic flare about him, clean cut and a jawline that looks like it was chiseled from granite. Smiley rested her long soft legs in the lap of Luca who resembled a Colombian kingpin with his mahogany skin tone, immaculately sculptured goatee and thick wavy hair. Stephanie gave all the guys their drinks and whispered to Marcus,

"Sunshine just pulled up front and she said she's gonna perform tonight."

Marcus' eyes got really big as he heard the news of Sunshine's arrival. Stephanie wondered what was so exciting about this woman she seen out front and why everyone had nothing but great elation for her appearance.


Little did Stephanie know; Sunshine was and still is the headliner for The Rabbit Hole Gentleman's Club but she's more than just an exotic dancer. See Sunshine was a performer when it came to being on stage with props and all, she brought pure entertainment. She enjoyed being on stage and the excitement she sees on her voyeur's eyes during her routine is an adrenaline rush to her. Sunshine got her start at The Rabbit Hole and she was one of the first dancers there when the club first opened. She was born from an interracial marriage, her mother was a Filipino housewife, her father was a black New Orleans Native and Sunshine was unquestionably the epitome of fine standing 5'9" with the measurements of 34D-26-44. Her big brown slightly slanted eyes simply drew you in and her full luscious lips melted you down to the core when she would lick them. But Sunshine wasn't only a dancer, she was also a very talented tattoo artist that traveled all over the states leaving her ink mark on her customers. She had customers all over from celebrities, to athletes and hard down fans that would patiently wait for the opportunity to get some work done by the talented artist known as Sunshine.

Usually whatever city she was in, she would go on social media and announce that she would be performing at a gentleman's club after doing several tatts just to unwind. When you have over a million followers, the club you're attending is bound to be packed just to get a glimpse of the Exotic Diva Sunshine on stage. The crew enjoyed when she would come in the club, her personality was just like her name and everyone benefited because her presence brought in a lot of money. Melvin helped Sunshine's bodyguard get a few more bags out of the back of her SUV as he joked with her,

"Girl what is all this, you moving in?"

"Now you know I gotta be super extra but please be careful with that one, that's my baby Tiny", replied Sunshine.

"Tiny? This damn duffle bag is heavy, ain't nothing tiny in here", responded a confused Melvin.

"Tiny is her pet Boa Constrictor, fool", replied Ricky as he took the bag from a now frightened and froze Melvin.

Sunshine gave Ricky a peck on the lips as she admired his memory,

"Awww baby, you remembered Tiny. I still got Brutus at the apartment."

Ricky laughed as he asked,

"You still got that goofy turtle I got you years ago?"

Sunshine and Ricky had some intense history two years ago, but the relationship grew apart when Sunshine started to travel more for work. Ricky had no problem with her being a dancer, that's how they met, in fact he found it exciting and gratifying that his woman was attractive to everyone she came across. He knew that when she was on stage it was all a performance, strictly all for show and when she's off stage her main focus was all on him. The couple tried to make it work but when Sunshine started really traveling to different states and leaving Ricky behind, it went from a video chat or text everyday to them barely seeing each other when she was in town. But they stayed friends even though the relationship couldn't make it.

Marcus left his companions in the office with the girls to go see if Sunshine really was going to bless the club with her presence. He walked up to the bar where Quincy and the other bartenders were making drinks for waiting customers when he seen one of the waitresses standing by,

"You seen Sunshine come thru?"

The pre-occupied waitress let him know that she seen Melvin and Sunshine's bodyguard escort her to the back of the club. Marcus was elated that business was about to pick up because he knew the club's star was going to bring more clients in. He headed to the front door where he found the hostess cashing in customers and greeted them as they walked in,

"Thanks for coming to The Rabbit Hole, enjoy yourself."

Marcus peeked outside and was pleased to see a line forming as Ricky pat searched people coming in the club. He headed to the dressing room located behind the large stage to meet up with the main attraction and see what she has in store for her viewers.

"Hey Marcus baby!", shouted a half naked Sunshine as she applied lavender scented baby oil to her thick thighs.

The large colorful koi fish tattoo on her leg seem to be in 3D as she massaged in the baby oil. Marcus just stood their admiring Sunshine's magnificent body frame as she sat there conversing and laughing with her colleagues of the industry.

"Looks like people are flocking in to see you Shine, you always seem to pack this place", stated Marcus as he continued,

"After your first set, I have two guys I want you to meet. Trying to close this deal and you the perfect exclamation point."

"Boy, stop it. I ain't nobody. I'm just another stripper shaking her ass", replied a smiling Sunshine.

Some of the dancers close by laughed as they heard Sunshine's response to Marcus because they knew she was like an icon in the club, but she was also very humble all the same.

  Stephanie was serving her customers when one of her regulars indicated he needed her assistants over at his table.

"Hey Memphis, you need another Cognac and Grand Marnier", asked Stephanie.

Memphis looked at her and smiled,

"Now how you know I didn't just want to see that pretty chocolate face?"

"Cause you Memphis and you don't want for shit", replied Stephanie.

"Mane, you too fast for me baby girl, too fast. Gone fetch me that beverage gorgeous", laughed Memphis.

Memphis was the stereotypical version of what a person visualizes when they hear the word "Pimp". He came adorned with the brightly colored alligator dress shoes, the tailor made pinstriped suit, the freshly manicured long nails with a gold ring on every finger, the shoulder length permed hair, snake eyes and a mouthpiece that could only be challenged by the Devil himself. If given enough time, Memphis could con a scuba diver out of his air tank but if he likes you, you have a friend for life that will watch your back no matter what. Memphis wasn't a little guy either, his verbal skills were backed up by his stature that had him standing 6'9 at around 275 pounds. No one really ever approached him in a threatening manner but if they did, Memphis had the fortitude to physically overpower them if need be. But everybody seemed to respect the country twang talking Tennessee boy known only by the name Memphis. Stephanie gained his respect because he seen the drive in her but also, he seen she wasn't weak-minded by the least like the multiple girls he has working for him. Memphis noticed the club getting crowded and looked for one of his girls, gesturing for her to come to him.

"Hey daddy, you wanted something", asked a young brainwashed stripper.

Memphis looked her in the eyes with the coldest poker face,

"Bitch, I don't want for shit. But what I needs you to do is get this money in here mane. I needs you to be the example for the rest of'em."

The young broad put her head down,

"I'm sorry daddy. I'm a do better."

"Don't be sorry bitch, be careful. Now give Memphis a kiss", replied the calculating entrepreneur as he sat back and crossed his legs.

The young piece of tail did exactly what she was told, kissed Memphis on the cheek and went in search for her next prospect to make money off of.

Marcus went back to his office where Diamond and Smiley were entertaining the guys to let them know about the special exhibition that's about to take place in a few minutes. Alex and Luca happily took the dancers with them so that they could have some soft female companionship with them while they watch this attraction Marcus is so excited about. Marcus arranged for two V.I.P. chairs to sit directly in front of the stage, close enough where they could see everything but far enough where they weren't in the midst of the common patrons of the club. He made sure their exotic dates stayed close by if not on their laps to give them that added arousal. Marcus was always a businessman, making sure whatever client he was dealing with was completely satisfied with their experience. He went to Stephanie and pointed over to his potential business partners,

"Steph, do me a favor and make sure them two don't want for nothing. I'll get one of the other waitress to take care of your tables. Trust me I'll make sure you're taken care of."

"Marcus I got this, you just relax", replied a calm Stephanie as she smiled at passing customers.

Marcus just let out a nervous smile as he did what Stephanie instructed him to do.

The lights went low as a bright spotlight focused on the main stage, foggers began to set the scene for onlookers as the MC came across the sound system,

"It's ya boy, DJ Felt Tip on the ones and twos. We got a surprise performance for y'all here at The Rabbit Hole. After a long hiatus in Miami, she made her way back home, get them bank rolls out ya pockets cause it is time for the Exotic Diva Sunshine!"

The melodically instrumental sounds of The Art of Noise's "Moment In Love" began to flow through the speakers as the curtains at the back of the stage opened up. Thru the white mist of fog on the platform, the crowd could see a curvy silhouette standing still with their arms spread wide open. The image began its sashay toward the audience and the makeshift fog seemed to part like the Red Sea uncovering a glorious sight. There stood Sunshine, a golden cream-colored thoroughbred shinning in the spotlight's glare. She was perched atop some glass heels, leading up to a pair of Olympic track star legs that held up a perfectly round ass that resembled two basketballs accompanied by what old school cats call "childbearing hips". Her flat stomach led up to her plump oiled 34D's that sat under a gorgeous Asian face with African undertones. Sunshine remained still while viewers were astonished by how this beautiful woman could just stand there motionless with a six-foot albino boa coiling itself around her erotic body. Stephanie hadn't seen anything like what she was witnessing just now. She's watched all the other dancers act out on stage with their twerks and splits. Stephanie was amazed by Smiley's athletic feats of strength when spinning on the pole but never a complete performance as this. Diamond's ability to imitate sexual acts of masturbation on scene intrigued her but nothing like what was going on stage right now. Sunshine had captured her audience with smooth moves of elegance as the tall Asian bodyguard walked up to the stage and took her pet boa from her.

Sunshine grasped hold to the pole on stage and began an onslaught of moves like the Eye Opener to the Music Box and several others that tantalized her viewers. A guy walked up to the stage as Sunshine slid down the pole into a split and he pulled out a stack of ones from his pocket. The exotic diva laid on her back in front of the gentleman, staring deep into his eyes with her thick thighs spread wide open and he just let the ones rain down onto her. She then wrapped her legs around his waist, removed her top exposing her perfect teardrop shaped breast and erotically caressed herself in front of him. Other patrons walked up throwing money on stage in an attempt to get a piece of the interaction the first guy received, showering Sunshine in dead presidents. Stephanie was literally in awe at the talent when Smiley walked up to her,

"Like I said earlier, she is the Queen in here."

The speechless waitress couldn't do anything but totally agree with the statement as she went from a viewer to a fan in a 10-minute routine. After the performance was done, Stephanie couldn't help but to clap for Sunshine as she walked off stage with the biggest smile on her face. The professional dancer walked up to Stephanie,

"Girl did you just start clapping for me? That's too cute, thank you mama."

"When I see talent, I have to acknowledge it with respect, Sunshine you are the truth" replied Stephanie.

CHAPTER V


Stephanie woke up to her mother Doris and her little sister Alisha singing happy birthday to her early in the morning with a dozen balloons. The gesture was much appreciated but she was dead tired from the night before as she held the blanket over her head while Alisha bounced on her bed.

"Why are you jumping on my bed lil girl", asked Stephanie after Alisha pulled the blanket off her.

"Oh now that you 21, I'm a lil girl? Somebody thinks they grown grown", replied Alisha.

Stephanie could smell bacon cooking in the air,

"Mama fixing breakfast?"

Alisha just smiled, left her room and headed to the kitchen as she responded,

"Yup, go back to sleep witcha ole ass."

Right when Stephanie was about to get up Keisha texted her,

"Happy Bday Bitch! You ready 2 get turnt!"

Stephanie laughed cause her bestie seemed ready to celebrate the day, but she still didn't have an idea of what she actually wanted to do.

"Girl I'm just waking up", texted back Stephanie in her reply as she sat up in her bed but before she could put her feet on the floor Keisha texted back,

"Well me and Diamond on our way in a few, so get dressed."

Stephanie just wanted to lay back down, but it looked like everyone was more excited about her 21st birthday than she was, so she pulled herself together and began to get ready for some visitors. She sat in her room studying over some notes she wrote down from her last class making sure she was ready for the first quiz of the semester.

"Hey baby, you want some breakfast?", asked Doris as she stood in the doorway of her daughter's room.

"I'm a come get some, just gotta make sure I get these motor controls and therapeutic exercises down. Professor T giving us a quiz Tuesday", replied Stephanie.

Doris truly admired how hard her daughter was focused on completing her studies even though she's been working late nights everyday.

"Baby, you got this, no worries but are you going to spend your whole birthday studying? It's time to take a little time and enjoy yourself baby. You don't make 21 everyday.", stated Doris.

Stephanie understood where her mother was coming from and knew her friends were on their way as she closed her schoolbooks,

"Yeah I know mama, Keisha and Diamond on their way now."

"Oh ok, what y'all got planned?", asked Doris.

Stephanie just shrugged her shoulders as she didn't have an idea of what she wanted to do today.

The doorbell rung and Alisha rushed to answer it, when she opened the door, she found Keisha and Diamond standing there with a dozen roses. Doris heard about the stripper Diamond, but she never got a chance to meet her, until now.

"You must be Mama Dee. Stephanie and Keisha told me so much about you, it's nice to finally meet you", stated Diamond.

Doris stood there pleasantly surprised that the young lady that was standing in front of her was nothing like the mental picture she had. Doris thought she was going to see a half dressed female, with a rude demeanor, criminal intent, lack of manners and excessive amounts of meaningless tattoos all over her body. Diamond resembled "the girl next door" and was cute as a button.

"And you must be Diamond, really nice to meet you too", replied Doris.

Stephanie walked in the front room to her mother talking to her friends, still in her pajama pants and tank top. Keisha seen her and instantly started laughing,

"Heffa, I thought I said get dressed. I'm not going nowhere with you dressed like that. Where you think we going, Wally World?"

"Girl I was studying for Professor T's test Tuesday when you texted me, I'm bout to go get dressed", replied Stephanie as she headed to the kitchen for some of the breakfast her mother cooked for her.

"So Diamond, is that your real name or is that a stage name", asked a curious Doris.

Keisha put her head down as she responded to the question,

"Mama!"

As sweet as she looked Diamond replied,

"It's my real name, my mama said I was her precious gem when I was born. So, she gave me a stripper name, go figure."

Doris laughed at Diamond's statement,

"You girls want something to eat? I cooked up some breakfast just a while ago."

"Mama, you know I don't turn down your cooking", replied Keisha.

They all went to the kitchen to enjoy breakfast with the birthday girl.

After they all ate breakfast, the girls headed to Stephanie's room with Alisha following behind. Stephanie stood at her door staring at her little sister,

"Umm, where do you think you going? Bye Allie."

"Oh, it's like that? Turning 21 done changed you", replied Alisha as she went in her own room across the hall.

Stephanie started looking thru her clothes in her closet as Keisha and Diamond went over what they wanted to do for Stephanie's birthday celebration.

"So, it's your bday bitch, you got the day off and it is Saturday. What you wanna do today?", asked Keisha as she sat on the bed scrolling thru her Snap Chat.

"Girl I have the slightest idea. I know I wanna get back in bed but you heffas here", replied Stephanie.

Diamond started laughing as she pulled out clothes from Stephanie's drawers stating,

"One thing we definitely doing is stop by The Rabbit Hole tonight. Steph I don't know if you ever seen it but they have a special celebration for employee birthdays. Besides, Ricky would love to see you anyways."

"Ricky that big bear that be at the door, right? Now that is fine, Steph you haven't jumped on him yet?", asked Keisha.

"Yeah that's him. Diamond, I don't even look at him like that. He's cute and all but I look at him like a cousin", replied Stephanie.

"Shid, more like kissing cousin, if that was me", responded a laughing Keisha.

Diamond laughed at Keisha,

"Melvin goofy ass cute to you Keisha. But Steph got Quincy on the brain. That's why she can't see being with Ricky."

"Nah, it's not like that. Ricky fine and all but Quincy yella ass just sexy as hell to me. Now he can get it and if he keeps flirting with me he will", replied Stephanie.

Diamond changed the subject and started talking about what she wanted to do for her friends today,

"Look, before we go anywhere I have somewhere I wanna take both of you. So, Steph you need to hurry up and get yo ass dressed trick."

Stephanie did as she was told and put her outfit on while the girls laughed at Keisha making funny videos on her phone.

Leslie arrived at her big sister's house to drop off an unexpected birthday gift to her niece. When she knocked Doris answered the door,

"Leslie."

She looked at her big sister, smiled in contempt and replied,

"Doris."

"What you want Lez? Calvin crackhead ass ain't been around here in weeks and Steph bout to go out with her friends", scolded Doris as she stood in the doorway.

"Damn heffa, how you doing too? I was just passing by to give my niece a birthday card", replied Leslie.

Doris responded coldly to her sister,

"I'll give it to her."

"Dee what the fuck wrong with you? I know you still not blaming me for Caleb", asked Leslie.

Doris just closed the door in Leslie's face and walked away. Leslie went back to her car and drove off hurt that her own sister still believes that it was her fault that Caleb was in prison.

Just like Stephanie does now on occasion, Caleb Crawford ran errands for Leslie, and they made a lot of money doing it. Caleb use to take odd jobs on the side also for some of Leslie's customers, against Leslie's wishes. Leslie use to warn him that all of her customers aren't trustworthy and some of the jobs he did for them could bring unwanted attention from law enforcement. Caleb was young and naïve, but he thought he had everything under control when he started picking up shipments of firearms from one of his regular customers. Leslie only dealt with the guy when he had imported items that were hard to find in the states and would sell at a high price. She refused to move guns for him on several occasions. But when Caleb got word that the guy would pay him $1000 for every trip he makes, the youngster couldn't refuse. Once Leslie found out about the numerous runs Caleb was making with the arms dealer, she broke all ties with the guy because she didn't feel comfortable with the situation. She urged Caleb to do the same but all he could see was the amount of money he was making. It was hard trying to tell a 17-year-old, at the time, not to bring home $1000 for 2 hours worth of work. One-month Caleb made 10 grand running trips from New Orleans to Houston and back, he felt unstoppable. The only thing Caleb didn't know was that the ATF was watching the guy and anybody that frequently visited his establishment. It took them less than 6 months to build a case, raid the place and arrest everyone inside. He hadn't made it to his 18th birthday yet and was looking at federal time in prison. Leslie paid for top notch lawyers to take the case to avoid Caleb getting any prison time, but the Feds were pushing for all parties to receive no less than 20 years. Because it was Caleb's first time ever being arrested for anything the judge was a little easy on him and only gave him 10 years in prison for gun trafficking, he's set to be released early on 3 years of probation for good behavior.

Stephanie and the girls were laughing and joking as they were leaving her room to head out for the day when she seen her mother sitting in the living room with an envelope in her hand. She could see something was bothering her and told her friends she would be outside soon.

"Mama, you ok? What's in the envelope?", asked Stephanie.

Doris handed it to her daughter,

"Your aunt left that for you."

Stephanie opened the thick envelope to find a birthday card that read,

"You are destined for great things, don't let anything or anyone hold you back. Happy Birthday baby girl, love you Lez."

Inside the card was $500, a key card to The Bienville Hotel on Bourbon Street and a note that said,

"Enjoy your day baby."

"Aww, that's so sweet I gotta call her", stated Stephanie.

Doris started to walk away as she replied to Stephanie's statement,

"Don't get caught up in Leslie's shit. I don't need two of my kids in jail because they can't see she a damn con-artist."

"Mama, stop it. Aunt Lez has done nothing but good deeds for me. Without her I wouldn't have been able to go to school", replied Stephanie.

"But at what cost Steph? At what cost cause Lez don't do shit for free. She only being nice to you because of the shit she got Caleb in.", blared Doris.

As Stephanie headed to the door to leave, she hit her mother with the ugly truth,

"Mama you need to let that go. Caleb got in that trouble because his ass did what he did. He told me himself that Aunt Lez didn't want him making them runs. You knew he wasn't bringing home that kind of money doing something legal, c'mon now. Mama you can't keep blaming her for your son's screw-ups. He took his charge; he did his time and he'll be home next year and hopefully he learned an important lesson."

Doris watched her oldest girl get in the car with her friends and knew everything she had just said was all so true but couldn't get pass the fact that if her son wasn't with Leslie, he would be home safe instead of prison.

Diamond drove the girls to the New Orleans Lakefront Airport where she had a surprise for her friends.

"Girl why are we back here, you trying to kidnap us", asked Keisha.

"No simple. We bout to go see the city like never before. One of my clients been trying to get me to ride with him and when I told him that today is Steph's bday, he offered to take us all on a tour of the city", replied Diamond.

"Bitch, I am not getting in a small ass plane", blurted Stephanie.

Diamond laughed as she parked in front of a large building that read "Terminal" across the front of it,

"Not a plane, a helicopter and yes bitch you getting in."

Stephanie was nervous but excited all the same as she got out of the car,

"Diamond, girl I don't know about this. I never been in nothing higher than a skyscraper and I was jittery when I looked out the window."

"You never been in a plane Steph?", asked Diamond as she held open the door to the main building.

"No! If I can't get there in a car or bus, I don't need to go", replied a bug-eyed Stephanie.

The girls were all laughing at Stephanie's comment when the information clerk addressed them,

"Good morning ladies, how can I help you?"

"We're here to meet with Alvin Davi, he should have all three of us on the list of visitors", replied Diamond.

The clerk checked the ledger for the information she needed and picked up the phone,

"Hello Mr. Davi, your party just arrived…yes I will send them back to you right now."

The clerk walked them to the back of the building that lead outside to the tarmac where Stephanie first caught sight of a large black helicopter with gold stripes on it and a tall gentleman was standing out in front of it, checking the tail rotors. The guy walked up to them with a big smile on his face,

"Hey Diamond baby, so who is the birthday girl?"

Stephanie nervously raised her hand as she looked at the big vessel, she's about to get in. Diamond smiled as she told the pilot about how Stephanie has never been in a helicopter.

"Oh it's nothing to be scared about, I promise I won't bring us any higher than 1500 feet in the air. Anything higher than that and everything looks like ants", responded Alvin.

Stephanie's eyes were just stuck wide open as her imagination had her thinking 1500 feet is somewhere in the clouds. Keisha was ready as she opened the back doors to the helicopter,

"Well what we waiting for, let's get it. I'm ready to fly over the Empire State building."

"Ummm, you do know that the Empire State building is in New York right and we in New Orleans?", asked Diamond.

"First off, you ugly. Bitch, you knew what I meant", replied Keisha.

Everybody got in the helicopter, Diamond sat up front with Alvin as he started flipping switches to start the craft, while Stephanie and Keisha sat in the back, buckling themselves in. Stephanie latched onto Keisha's hand when the helicopter began to rise, the engine was so loud that no one could hear the other speak and that's when Alvin told them to put on the headsets that were hanging in front of them.

"Y'all ready for some fun?", asked Alvin as he maneuvered the craft up and pass a nearby hanger.

The helicopter flew over Lake Pontchartrain and curved around back over land; the girls were simply amazed at the view. The sight of seeing the tops of the oak trees that lined out neighborhoods were captivating as they could make out the location where they were in the city. Stephanie couldn't believe she was in a helicopter, her 21st birthday was really starting off better than expected and it was just getting started. She never thought she would be in a private helicopter seeing the city from a view that she could only imagine. They flew pass the Crescent City Connection, passed over the French Market and they all laughed as Keisha pointed out the Rabbit Hole down below them stating,

"Girl, I'm a work there one day, my name gone be Chocolate Thunder."

"More like Yella Girl, with ya light bright ass", replied Stephanie.

The pilot flew over the CBD, buzzed around the Superdome and followed straight down Canal Street back towards the lake where the airport was located.

"So Stephanie, how do you like the flight?", asked Alvin.

Stephanie was surprisingly satisfied, and her nervousness was gone but Alvin had one last trick for her before they headed back to the landing pad. As they approached Lake Pontchartrain, Stephanie noticed the helicopter descending,

"Excuse me, what's going on?"

Alvin started laughing as he seen the girls started to clinch hold to the handlebars in the cabin. The chopper dipped down just a few feet over the waters as the craft made a beeline towards the airport. Water splashed in the air, as the force from the helicopter blades carried the ship over the lake. The adrenaline rush was so intense that everything seemed to slow down as Stephanie watched how close they were to the water. Alvin pulled back on the lever and the helicopter rose straight up as if it was shot out of a rocket and Stephanie screamed. The aircraft then calmly hovered over the airport and slowly lowered, landing perfectly on the landing pad.

"Now that was fun", commented Alvin as he looked behind him at the girls still wide eyed from the conclusion of the flight.

"You trying to kill me man!", responded Stephanie.


Leslie was relaxing at Café Du Monde, drinking some coffee and enjoying a few beignets when her buddy Levi walked up to her table. Leslie had Levi search for the guys that robbed the convenience store that her niece was in. Levi told her that he had found the Caucasian with the cornrows but still haven't got any news on the guy with the Spider tattoo on his neck.

"Levi, I need them off the streets. They seen Steph's face and you know the streets talk", stated Leslie as she sipped her coffee.

"C'mon now Lez, you already know I'm a find him, calm ya nerves", replied Levi.

Leslie had the most serious look on her face when she responded,

"Were you calm when you was looking for them fools from that church shooting?"

"Lez, chill out. You know what that was and I know what this is. If I tell you I got it, I got it", replied Levi as he got up from the table and walked away.

Four years ago, Levi's daughter was caught in the middle of a rivalry that escalated into gunfire and she was fatally shot. He was distraught and torn up behind it because it was his only child, but Leslie made it her duty to find the people that did it. She gave him vital information that lead to the person that gave the order that killed his child and Levi took out some street justice on the killer. Leslie knew how much that meant to him and he always vowed to return the favor no matter what. She got up to follow behind Levi as he darted across the street, heading towards the St. Louis Cathedral and up St. Ann Street. Leslie felt bad bringing up the incident that involved his only daughter being shot,

"Levi wait up."

"Lez look, I told you I was gonna find them. Just be ready when I call you", stated Levi.

"I know you will, you always do Levi but let's take a break", replied Leslie as she held onto Levi's hand.

The two just walked thru the streets of the French Quarters like tourist as Leslie attempted to apologize to Levi through her actions. She knew how much Levi liked African art, especially African mask and they stopped by an African vendor's shop that had several extravagant mask.

"So tell me why you like these things so much because I don't see it", asked Leslie.

"First off, it's our heritage girl. Depending on the style, the color and even the shape or size, you can tell where the mask come from. The masks are said to ward off evil and possess the spirit of our ancestors", replied Levi.

Leslie was amazed at how much he knew about the origin of the African artifacts. She even laughed when he jokingly pointed out that some of them were made in China,

"See these are the real thing right here, even Africa gets China to make their shit."

"Boy you stupid, for real", replied Leslie.

She seen Levi staring at one large mask resting on the floor as the vendor attempted to show them some wooden animal figurines. While Levi was occupied looking at the figures, Leslie took it upon herself to check out the price of the mask. She was taken for a loop when she seen the mask was $100 and offered the vendor 80 dollars to take it off her hands, the vendor gladly excepted the negotiation.

"Now how you gone get that home, cause I parked all the way by Jackson Brewery and I ain't helping you carry it", stated Leslie as she smiled at her friend.

"Been a long time since I seen you smile Lez, looks good on you girl", replied Levi.

Leslie rolled her eyes and walked off as she ignored Levi's statement about her smile. Having the occupation, she has, Leslie has to hold a stern demeanor or people wouldn't take her seriously. But the thing is, a blind man could see the sexy under all the coarse exterior she portrays. The deep brown cinnamon tone of her skin was flawless, the hazel colored eyes simply sparkled when the sun hit it, her lips could boldly carry the ominous nickname of "soup coolers" and her body was curvier than an hourglass. As much as Leslie tried to hide it, men would compliment her on her image alone with statements like,

"Lez, you are too damn cute to be so damn mean" or

"Why haven't anyone snatch you up yet?"

But Leslie wasn't dumb by far because she knew when to use her lady wilds to get what she wanted when the "mean girl" act wouldn't work. She just needed to keep that act going now because she really needed Levi to find both of those guys before they find Stephanie.

CHAPTER VI

Stephanie was sitting in the backseat of Diamond's car still in shock that she was in a helicopter and took a tour over the city. Her day really started off with a bang, but her friends weren't finished with her yet as Diamond asked,

"Steph didn't you say you wanted to get a tatt on your birthday?"

"Yeah, but I don't know anyone that good to do what I want", replied Stephanie.

"Shit, I want one too", chimed in Keisha as she took a group selfie of the girls.

Stephanie wasn't new to getting a tattoo because she already had two, one small tattoo on her wrist of the eye of Horus and another on the back of her neck of the Ankh. She truly was intrigued with the meanings and meaningful tattoos were important to her because she felt if she's going to have something on her permanently, it better mean something. Keisha got on her phone,

"Hey Spice. You at the shop? yeah, me and my girls on our way right now. No, Diamond does not want your number. Bye boy."

Stephanie was curious to where they were going as Diamond was laughing with Keisha about the phone call she just had. The three drove thru the city singing to tunes on the radio until Stephanie's curiosity couldn't take it anymore.

"Ok, where are y'all taking me this time? Cause I am not getting a tattoo from some Rooty-poo ass artist", stated Stephanie as she sat in the back of the car.

"Bitch, did you just say Rooty-poo? Who the hell still says that? That's like saying fiddle sticks and green beans when you wanna curse", laughed Keisha.

"Dammit, you know what I mean. What I want takes talent and I ain't getting no anybody to do my tatt", replied Stephanie.

Keisha handed Stephanie her cell phone with a guy name Spice's IG page and a bunch of pictures of tattoos he has done. She was pleasantly surprised at his talent as she scrolled through his collection. Stephanie knew exactly what she wanted her next tattoo to be and wondered if he would be able to create it on her. After looking over his IG page she really felt he could master the task she desired. She agreed to meeting the guy and that was a good thing because Diamond was pulling in the parking lot. Stephanie looked up at the sign that read "Artistic Creations INC." and she started getting that nervous feeling again. Keisha was the first to walk in and greet the receptionist,

"What's up girl, where Spice ass at?"

The young lady walked the three friends to the back of the shop, passed a large game room with a pool table and passed workstations that housed tattoo artists working on customers. Stephanie could hear rock music playing from the back room they were heading to and wondered if this was the artist for her. Spice was sitting with his back to the door sketching at his drafting table when the girls walked in. When Stephanie entered the room, it was evident that this was the guy for her. Spice's walls were covered in Egyptian hieroglyphics, Japanese logographic kanji and an assorted collection of intricately designed flowers.

"Getcho ass up and greet me negro", blurted out Keisha as she walked up behind Spice.

Before he turned around, he stated as he laughed,

"Ain't nobody but Keisha Warren loud ass."

He wasn't the image Stephanie was expecting when he did turn around in his chair with a clean-cut baby face, button down slim fit Lacoste shirt, Polo khakis and some vintage deck slip-on shoes. Spice looked at Diamond with a sexy glare,

"Hey you."

"Keisha, he is too cute", stated Diamond as she walked up to Spice.

"Girl that nigga ain't shit", replied Keisha.

Stephanie just stood back and admired the artistry on the walls as Spice greeted her,

"So, you must be the birthday girl."

"Yes, that would be me. Hi, I'm Stephanie", replied the nervous birthday girl.

The two talked about what she wanted and whereas Diamond along with Keisha looked through Spice's portfolio. As Stephanie described her concept, Spice began sketching in his notebook, all the while listening to everything she mentioned and putting it on paper. By the time Stephanie was finished talking, Spice turned his notebook around and her mental picture was staring her in the face, exactly how she wanted it.

"Oh my God, that is beautiful. Now can you put it where we talked about is the question", expressed Stephanie.

"Baby girl I can tattoo this between your butt cheeks and they will call it a masterpiece", replied a cocky Spice.

Keisha looked in amazement of how pretty and detailed the drawing was as she asked,

"So where are you going to get it?"

Stephanie sat in the large leather tattoo chair, removed her top, took off her bra and showed her friends exactly where,

"The main part of the flower is going to be right below my breast on the top of my stomach, one leaf will reach the middle of my breast and the vines will outline under my breast. A perfect Lotus flower."

"Damn girl, you got some pretty ass titties!", stated Diamond after listening to Stephanie's explanation.

Spice couldn't do anything but look over his shoulder, while finishing his sketch and agree as he mumbled,

"You ain't never lying."

Ricky was at the gym getting a workout in with some of his old college teammates when one of them asked,

"I gotta know, how could you work at that strip club and not be bangin' a different stripper every night?"

"Dawg, it's not like that, trust me. You have a misconception of a dancer, those females are nothing like what you think", replied Ricky.

"Ok, you tell me. Cause all I see is ass and titties", countered his workout partner.

Ricky went on to tell them how out of all the dancers at the club, only a few are staying with only being an exotic dancer. He mentioned how a lot of them are really going to school and even a couple are working on their second degree. Ricky talked as if he was talking about his little sisters and how proud he is of them when he told his friends about a few dancers who started modeling. How one of them started working on creating her own business, in selling her own clothing line for the dancers. He had to remind them of his ex, Sunshine, who is a well-known tattoo artist and exotic dancer that continues to be featured in several magazines. Talking about the girls gave Ricky an extra boost as he began pumping the weights on the bench and his friends just listened. He went on about the amount of respect he has for them and the talent it takes to be on that stage.

"C'mon now dude. It don't take talent to shake yo ass", commented one guy.

Ricky just shook his head and laughed a little as he thought about how much strength it takes to lift up on them poles as he replied,

"Well let's go find a vertical pole, not a horizontal pull-up bar and I wanna see you lift yourself up to the top, only using your hands. Then we can talk about strength."

As the guys continued their conversation, they noticed an old buddy make his way into the gym.

"I know that's not Denver's number one D-end Devin Daniels, blessing us common folk with his presence", stated Ricky.

Devin was a year behind Ricky at Texas A&M and a lot of the tricks of the trade he learned, he learned from watching Ricky perform on the field. Ricky was always proud to see one of his teammates make it to the big league, especially one that played at his position.

"Big bro! Man how have you been? I haven't seen you since our Texas days", stated Devin as he hugged his old teammate.

"Man, I been watching you ever since you got drafted and I always tell people, they call him Double D because if you don't he is gonna get your QB", replied Ricky.

The two almost forgot that they were supposed to be working out in the gym as they reminisced about school days.

"So, what you doing in the city? I figured you would be in Denver living it up like a king", asked Ricky.

Devin told him he came in town to help take care of some family issues and he's heading back to Colorado after that.

People in the gym started to recognize Devin and a crowd started to form around them. Ricky noticed all the people gathering around them and he wasn't one that was used to big crowds like that so he excused himself.

"Double D, I'm a let you get to it. But come over to a spot where I'm a bouncer, The Rabbit Hole, I got you", stated Ricky as he prepared to leave.

The two exchanged numbers and Ricky left to get in the showers.


Doris was doing a little dusting when her phone started ringing. When she answered it, a recording stated,

"This is a collect call from Caleb at The Louisiana Federal Corrections Facility, if you accept all charges please press one."

Doris happily accepted the call as she called out her son's name,

"Caleb? Hey baby."

"Hey mama, how y'all doing", replied Caleb.

Her eyes started tearing up as Doris talked with her son,

"How have you been baby? You been keeping yourself busy?"

"As busy as prison could let you, mama. But I do have this volleyball tournament to referee in like five minutes", chuckled Caleb.

Doris really didn't like that her son was making fun of being in prison. She began to tell him about his baby sister Alisha's track meet coming up soon and how excited she is to travel to Baton Rouge for the state championship.

"My baby sis gone run all over them", stated Caleb as he asked where his other sister Stephanie was on her birthday.

Doris told him that Stephanie was with her friends "running the streets" enjoying her day.

"Damn, I wanted to talk to her", replied Caleb.

Doris then angrily told Caleb about his aunt Leslie's visit and began blaming her for him being in prison. She started to rant and rave about how it should be Leslie in jail and not Caleb.

"Mama I'm a need you to stop talking and listen", stated Caleb.

Doris' son then dismembered all his mother's accusations and took total credit for him being arrested. He then went on to tell Doris how Leslie even acquired a lawyer for his case to try and get him off. Everyone in the family could see that the reason Caleb was in prison was all his fault except for his own mother. Doris like many other mothers refused to see that her child would be capable of breaking the law or guilty of a crime but after listening to Caleb take blame for his actions, she started to believe the masses. Caleb then started telling her how he's going to be home right before his birthday next year. He even mentioned that he knows his birthday is in October, but he really wants a Thanksgiving meal for his birthday dinner. Doris laughed as she listened to him give out full details of the list of dishes he wanted for the event.

"Boy you really expect me to cook all that", asked Doris.

"I'm a help you cleaned the dishes", laughed Caleb.

"You have one minute left", announced the automatic recording.

"Well mama, looks like it's time for me to go. Tell Allie she better whip they ass in that championship, tell Steph I said happy birthday. Love you, mama", stated Caleb as he got ready to hang up the phone.

"I sure will baby. Mama loves you Stanka", replied a tearful Doris.


Leslie laid on her sofa looking at old sitcom reruns on TV when she received a call from Stephanie.

"Hey Teedy, I just wanted to thank you for the card", stated Stephanie.

Leslie could hear a loud buzzing sound coming from the background as she replied,

"You're so welcome babygirl. What is all that noise though?"

Stephanie then told her aunt that she and her friends are getting tattoos for her birthday.

"It's your friend's birthday too", asked Leslie.

"No Teedy, they just copying off of me today", laughed Stephanie.

Leslie then heard a knock at her door, but she wasn't expecting anyone. She told Stephanie to hold on as she checked to see who it was and when she noticed through the peephole it was Levi, Leslie told her niece she'll call her back later. Leslie opened up the door to Levi standing there with two to-go plates from Triangle Deli and a six pack of beer. She looked at him with a serious look,

"Boy what do you want?"

"To come inside and chill with my homie", replied Levi.

Leslie looked at the bag and walked away,

"One of them plates better be smothered chicken with mac and cheese on it."

"Of course, what else would I get you from there", replied Levi.

He walked over to the kitchen, after closing the door and sat the plastic to-go containers on the countertop. Levi couldn't help but to noticed Leslie was walking around in a white tank top and a pair of boy shorts. He tried not to make it obvious but Leslie was just too fine not to stare at her as she walked around in the kitchen. She bent over to feed her pet cat Fluffy and Levi could see the print of her pussy peeking out right under her big round ass.

"Girl stop mooning people, damn", jokingly stated Levi as he slid Leslie her plate.

She took her plate and went to the living room where she was looking at TV,

"Nigga, you coming or you staying in the kitchen."

At that point Levi couldn't help but imagine what that body looks like completely naked. He has always playfully flirted with Leslie but behind closed doors at this moment he's ready to risk it all. Levi sat on the couch next to Leslie as she was flipping through the channels and he literally sat there admiring Leslie's beauty.

"Lez honest question, why don't you have a man", asked Levi.

After finding a movie she wanted to look at on TV responded,

"Cause you niggas ain't shit. Why, you trying to be my man now Levi? I'm a need more than a plate from Triangle."

Leslie noticed how silent Levi was to her comment and instantly knew something was wrong,

"Say bruh, you and me cool but I ain't looking for no man right now."

"But what if a man looking for you? I've seen people waste their lives, doing what they call grinding and hustling, only to be lonely and miserable. What's the point of having it but having no one at the same time", replied Levi.

Leslie was listening to what Levi was saying but didn't want to admit he was right,

"I thought I let in Levi and not Dr. Phil, can you stop preaching to me and eat yo food, damn."

Levi let out a small grin and continued to eat his food while they looked at TV. The two enjoyed their meal and each other's company as Levi continued to make Leslie laugh at his jokes. Leslie has always been comfortable with Levi but today seemed to be different. In the six years she's been knowing Levi, she has seen another side of him today and that side is actually appealing to her.

"Ok, so you asking these questions. Why don't you have a woman", asked Leslie as she sat back on the sofa waiting on his response.

Levi gathered the empty containers from their meals and walked off to the kitchen. His nonresponse had Leslie curious now and she really wanted an answer.

"Hold up, I can answer your questions, but you can't answer mine", asked Leslie as she followed Levi in the kitchen.

Levi put the empty containers in the trash and grabbed two beers from the refrigerator as he replied,

"Because I haven't found a woman to challenge me yet but I'm trying to see something now."

Leslie looked in Levi's eyes and for the first time seen a very sincere stare. She took a sip from her beer and just walked away as Levi stood in the kitchen adoring her sexy.


Stephanie and her friends stood in the mirror just amazed at the artistic work Spice created on them. Keisha had him do a heart on her wrist with a rose wrapped around it, Diamond got the Chinese logographic kanji of the words "Respect, Love and Honor" on her side by her ribcage and Stephanie's Lotus flower tattoo was everything she expected it to be with it's vibrant colorations of detail. Stephanie went to Spice and hugged him so tight,

"Thank you so much Spice, I love it. I really do love it."

"You are so welcome baby, happy birthday. But if you don't get yo half naked fine ass off me right now, girl we gone have some problems", replied Spice as he laughed.

Stephanie couldn't do anything but blush when Keisha replied,

"Nigga you know you liked it, probably got a chubby. Lemme see it."

Spice covered the girls tattoos up and walked them to the door when Diamond invited him to The Rabbit Hole later tonight,

"Come through, I'm not working tonight but I may have to get you a lap dance."

Spice told them he would definitely try to come to the club later as the girls left to go to dinner.

"Girl, Spice can get it with his sexy ass. That boy had me all kinds of aroused when he was doing my tatt", stated Diamond as she started up the car.

"He is good with his hands, but I thought he was about to suck my titty at one point, how close he was to them", responded Stephanie.

"And you would have let him bitch", replied Keisha as they all laughed.

The girls all were singing in the car to the tunes on the radio as Diamond drove to their next stop of the festive day. As the car pulled into the driveway of Drew Orleans Food & Spirits restaurant, the valet opened the door to the car and escorted the girls to the front door. The restaurant was gorgeous and eloquent but with a casual feel to it. Stephanie heard of the restaurant but never been inside of it and the visual was astounding as everywhere she looked, she seen something beautiful. Black carpet with gold fleur-de-lis covered the entire eating area, wooden columns reaching up to the 20 foot ceiling framed out the restaurant, twisted wrought iron railings connected every column and every 20 feet from the entrance you could find an old fashion street lamp post with the name of a New Orleans street sign attached. The hostess walked the girls to their seats as the waiter arrived,

"Hi, I'm Jessie and I'll be your waiter, let's get you young ladies some drinks."

Keisha ordered everyone's drinks as they all sat down. Stephanie was still amazed at the beauty of the place as she looked over the menu.

"So, what y'all getting cause I have no idea what to order", asked Diamond.

Keisha nor Stephanie had an answer for her as they looked over the menu, but Keisha's response was comical as always,

"Bitch where is the kid's menu cause I ain't paying 20 dollars for chicken."

"Girl, I was thinking the same thing but that crawfish etouffee stuffed catfish sounds so good though", replied Stephanie as she pointed it out on the menu.

They all contemplated on what they wanted to order as Jessie arrived with their first round of drinks. He placed them all on the table as he asked if they were ready to order. After the girls put their dinner order in, Stephanie had to tell her friends how she really feels as she stated,

"I just want you barbies to know I really enjoyed today, y'all have went far and beyond of what I was expecting. Thank you."

Diamond reminded her friend that their night is not over after dinner and that she has a surprise for her at The Rabbit Hole. Stephanie was curious of what her friend had in store for her at the club, but she didn't question it. Keisha started taking photos of her friends as they celebrated Stephanie's birthday with a few drinks. The girls were really enjoying themselves when the food came out and were blown over with the presentation of their meals. The crawfish etouffee stuffed catfish was a complete hit with all three of the ladies.

Levi was still chilling at Leslie's house when he dosed off to sleep as his friend sat watching one of her favorite old movies. Leslie herself got comfortable and laid up against Levi's shoulder as she looked at TV. The feeling really felt good to Leslie because she hasn't had a man in her home in a long time, let alone one that she's comfortable with enough to be this close to. Levi realized he had nodded off and got up so he can head home but Leslie's statement stopped him cold,

"So, you gone come all the way over here, tell me all this nonsense about me needing a man, feed me, get me all relaxed and leave? I never took Ronald Levi Sweed for a duck."

He turned around and replied,

"Who you calling a duck?"

"Oh my bad, I meant to say Fuck Boy", responded Leslie as she stood up in front of Levi, looking him up and down.

Levi let out a devilish grin, reached down under Leslie's soft round ass, picked her up and her legs instantly wrapped around him. She looked him in his dark brown eyes and stated,

"You done went this far, no sense in stopping now."

The two embraced into a passionate kiss as Levi walked back towards the sofa and laid Leslie down. Her soft skin felt like silk as Levi caressed her thick thighs while kissing her luscious lips. Levi's arms simply cradled her body as Leslie could feel every inch of his muscular frame pressed against hers. The feeling of goosebumps traveled through her as Levi's hands moved all over, arousing her completely. Leslie tugged at his shirt, pulling it over his head and off, tossing it on the floor. The sight of Levi's pure masculinity was pleasing to her as she reached down into his pants to find a moderately large harden staff awaiting her. She grasped hold of it and the muscle jumped in her hand, Levi looked at her with a smile. He sat up on the sofa, Leslie straddled him, and he took off her top, revealing a lovely set of breast that he couldn't help but to kiss. The erotic moment had just begun when Leslie stopped him,

"I can't do this on this damn sofa" and went to the bedroom with Levi following behind her.

As Leslie entered the room her shorts and underwear dropped to the floor, so did the rest of Levi's clothes. She sat at the foot of the bed with Levi standing in front of her, with his harden manhood staring her in the face and Leslie did what she wanted to do the first time she grabbed hold of the monster. With one hand wrapped around his man muscle and the other caressing his six pack, she let him enter her mouth all the way to the back of her throat. Levi could feel himself reach pass the back of her tongue and the shock of her not gagging aroused him so that he tried to push in deeper. She sucked and stroked him so good that he couldn't take her oral pleasure much longer. Leslie got aggressive with the dick, placing her hands on his hips and making him fuck her face. The sight of seeing his dick slide in and out of Leslie's soft lips almost brought him to that explosive moment but when Leslie looked up at him with those big gorgeous hazel eyes he had to pull out. Levi then pushed her on the bed, parted her legs and the image he seen was utterly delightful as he knew he was about to devour Leslie's pussy. He started slow as he licked her moist clit, tasting her delicious juices and feeling her body shiver while he occasionally sucks on her. Leslie enjoyed his mouth service as Levi's licks began to circle around her clit while he took two fingers and slid them deep inside her. The pussy juices seemed to cover his fingers like the glaze on a donut as Levi sucked on her clit until it swelled in his mouth. The glorious feelings flowed through her body as Levi tongue fucked her into an orgasmic squirt that filled his mouth. He knew it was time to fill her up as he climbed on top of her, Leslie braced herself as she felt the head of his dick part her lips and press forward. It was as if she could feel ever groove and vein slide inside of her while Levi adjusted his hips and pulled her closer to him. He began slow stroking as he took his thumb and rubbed her clit, teasing her close to another orgasm. The faster he thrust, the more he rubbed her clit, until the rubbing stopped and both hands were on her hips while he pound away. Leslie didn't expect anything less from Levi's athletic prowess as he effortlessly flipped her over onto her stomach and continuously tickled her G-spot with his stiffened appendage. The performance came to an end when Leslie's juicy pussy gripped and squeezed Levi's dick into a spasm like explosion.

CHAPTER VII

Stephanie and her girls walked up to the club to find Melvin talking with two guys that were trying to get in. Ricky greeted them as he was standing watch at the entrance,

"Now look at all this sexiness here. Where y'all coming from?"

"Hey Ricky baby", replied Diamond.

The girls stood outside talking to Ricky, telling him about their helicopter tour and about Stephanie's new tattoo. Ricky tried his luck,

"So Steph, when can I see your new tatt?"

"Stop trying to be slick, yo ass trying to see some titties", replied Keisha.

"Don't do my teddy bear like that", responded Stephanie as she smiled at Ricky.

Melvin walked up escorting the two guys he was talking to earlier and a frightening chill went through Stephanie's soul. One of the guys with Melvin had a spider tattoo on his neck, the exact tattoo Stephanie seen at the store robbery. When the second guy walked by he glanced over to Stephanie and did a double take as his facial expression screamed, "I think I know you" but he said nothing. Stephanie knew she recognized them both and when the white guy stared at her, she knew he recognized her too. The butterflies in her stomach were moving around with cast iron wings on. Diamond seen that her friend seemed a little troubled,

"Steph, you ok?"

Stephanie's worried face misrepresented her response that she was fine, she was far from it. Diamond couldn't figure out what was wrong and announced to her friends that she believes it's time for some shots. The trio walked in the club, headed straight to the bar and Diamond had Quincy pour up three Jager's. Keisha and Diamond down their first shot with no problem but Stephanie was still holding hers as she scanned the club looking for the two guys that came in right before them.

"Girl, where is your head? You've been in another world since we got here", stated a concerned Diamond.

Stephanie just took her shot, smiled and nodded yes while trying to enjoy herself with her friends. Her fears came face to face with her while she was sitting at the bar talking with Keisha as the white guy she seen outside walked up and stood next to her. He ordered two drinks and turned to Stephanie,

"I know you probably hear this shit a lot but don't I know you from somewhere?"

Stephanie swallowed her heart as she remembered the last time she seen this man was when he was chasing and shooting at her. She let out a nervous grin as she replied,

"You don't look familiar but I'm a waitress here so maybe you seen me here."

The guy just agreed to her statement as he shook his head yes and walked off with his drinks.

"Who was the white chocolate you was talking", asked Keisha.

"Nobody, he thought he knew me", replied Stephanie as she noticed the two guys were talking to each other while looking directly at her.

She knew she had a problem when she seen the white guy whisper in his counterpart's ear and the guy's eyes got big as a silver dollar while looking at Stephanie sitting at the bar. Stephanie told her friends she'll be right back and headed to Marcus' office in the back of the club. As she was walking, she could feel eyes following her every move and that scared feeling covered her like a blanket. Stephanie walked into the office and immediately pulled out her cell phone to call her aunt. She was so nervous that she could barely hold her phone in her hand while the phone rung,

"C'mon Lez, pick up", cried Stephanie.

The phone would ring so much that the answering service came on, Stephanie would hang up and call right back, desperately needing to talk to her aunt. Leslie finally answered her phone with what sounded like sleep in her voice,

"What girl?"

Stephanie's response,

"That spider tattoo is here with his friend!", completely woke Leslie up.

The petrified young woman could hear her aunt moving around frantically as she asked a series of questions,

"Where are you? Did they see you? Are they still there? What do they have on?"

Stephanie answered all of Leslie's questions and then was told something she didn't expect as her aunt informed her to stay in the club until she calls her on her cell. Stephanie's nervous voice cracked as she stated,

"Lez, I don't know about this."

"Have I ever led you wrong? Trust me Steph", replied Leslie.

Marcus walked in his office to Stephanie sitting in a chair fiddling with her fingers. Before Marcus could get out one question, Stephanie made up an excuse that she needed to check on her little sister home alone. Marcus told Stephanie that someone was waiting for her in the hallway and she almost collapsed from fright. She peeked out the door to find Quincy standing there with the biggest grin on his face and a rose for her. The sight was so welcomed that she ran out the office, hugged Quincy so tight and kissed him.

"If I get all that for a rose, what would I get for this right here?", asked Quincy as he handed Stephanie a small box.

She was surprised that he got her a birthday gift and when she opened it, it was everything she could ask for. In the box Stephanie found a thin gold necklace with a flower charm at the end. She looked at the flower and was pleasantly shocked as she asked,

"Is that a lotus flower?"

"Yeah, I got it because it reminds me of you", answered Quincy.

Stephanie couldn't do anything but smile as Quincy stood behind her to put the necklace on her and kissed her on the neck. The feeling sent chills down her body while Quincy hugged her around her waist. Stephanie could feel his whole body pressed against hers as she leaned into his chest.


    Leslie was getting dressed when she woke up Levi,

"Hey, get up! We got work to do."

Levi sat up in the bed, getting his head together, asking what they had to do that was so important he had to get up in the middle of the night.

"I'll tell you in the car", replied Leslie as she threw his shirt to him.

Levi knew it had to be something serious the way Leslie was fussing around in the room. He was putting on his boots when he told Leslie,

"I need to stop at my crib real quick."

"We don't have time, we need to get to The Rabbit Hole like now", uttered Leslie.

As Levi got up to go to the front door, he reminded her of his skills,

"If you need me to do my part, I need to stop by the crib first. It's on the way."

The two rushed out the door and headed to Levi's apartment to grab his equipment while Leslie told him what Stephanie told her. Levi was driving to his place listening to everything but planning out actions in his head as he pictured the landscape of the scene. He knew the club always had two bouncers out front standing at the corner and the parking lot was across the street. Leslie was jittery with nervousness as Levi ran inside his apartment and quickly came out with a large duffel bag in his hand. He sped off to the club and ran down to Leslie what they were gonna do because he didn't want her to be shocked or surprised as things escalate at the club. Leslie wanted to be involved because she felt it was all her fault that Stephanie was in the predicament she was in but Levi was reluctant to give her the greenlight.

"Look man, just cause I let you pin my legs behind my head. Don't mean you gone treat me like some fragile female. I'm getting my hands in this, if you want it or not", stated Leslie.

Levi was shaking his head in disbelief of the statement he just heard,

"Really bruh, we gone talk about this right now?"

He reached in the duffle bag, that was in the backseat, pulled out two black hooded sweatshirts and handed one to Leslie,

"Put that on with yo crazy ass."

Levi knew if he didn't let her come with him, she would come anyways, and he needed her to be completely with the program. They were almost there when Levi stated,

"Lez don't act different with me after this. We've hit some licks together before but nothing on this level. Shit, you the first person I've ever let roll with me since my row-dog Reem."

"As long as my niece is safe, we gone be good", replied Leslie.

Stephanie finally came out the back of the club with Quincy and sat at the bar with her friends as Memphis walked up to her.

"Now you lucky it's your birthday Steph, why you ain't introduce Memphis to this pretty tender here", stated Memphis as he lightly held Keisha's hand and kissed it.

Diamond laughed as she pulled Keisha to her side,

"She's forbidden fruit Memphis."

"If it was good enough for Adam, who am I to judge", replied Memphis as he sat next to Stephanie at the bar.

The girls laughed while Memphis entertained them with his classic Mack banter of catch phrases and sly remarks. Stephanie almost forgot about the two guys that were sitting in the club literally "eye fucking" her from across the room. There was no one on the stage when Marcus walked up on it with a chair in his hands. The crowd looked at him a little strange but then the DJ came across the sound system,

"This ya boy DJ Felt-Tip and today is a special day here at The Rabbit Hole. It's one of our own birthdays and she needs to get her sexy chocolate self up on this stage right now. I need my ladies to please escort Stephanie to the stage for her Rabbit Hole gift set."

At that very moment a spotlight singled out Stephanie sitting at the bar, 10 dancers walked up to her and had her follow them to the stage where Marcus was still standing. The crowd roared as they watched Stephanie step up on the platform with the dancers and sit in the chair that was next to the pole. Marcus handed a pair of handcuffs to Smiley who was on the stage with 9 other dancers and she gently cuffed Stephanie to the dancing pole with a smile as she asked,

"You ready?"

Stephanie was totally lost as to what was about to take place, but she knew one thing, she was about to be part of the show. The DJ started playing a throwback rap song by Luke, "Its Your Birthday" and when the beat dropped so did the dancers' clothes. 10 extremely gorgeous half naked exotic dancers took turns dancing on Stephanie's lap and some like Smiley even hoisted themselves up on the pole and slid down on her. Guys just threw money on the stage as dancers performed and Diamond didn't want to miss out on the fun as she took Keisha's hand as they went up to the stage. Diamond had a band of ones she split with Keisha and the two began to shower the dance area with ones as the audience cheered. Stephanie couldn't help but to laugh as she seen her friends enjoying the show. All the dancers finished their performance and Smiley removed the cuffs to let Stephanie up from the chair. Stephanie was so comfortable up on the stage for some reason that she grabbed hold of the pole and climbed up to the top. Her friends were all stuck in amazement as they watched her slide down the pole as if she had been doing it forever. Stephanie spun around the pole performing simple tricks she had seen other dancers do every night she was at work. The guys in the audience didn't let one trick go unseen as they cheered for more and threw more money on stage. Diamond reached out for her friend to get down but instead Stephanie pulled her up with her. To Diamond the next thing came naturally as she went into performance mode and grasped hold of the pole to pull herself up in the air. Spice walked up to Keisha standing in the crowd,

"You never told me your friend was a dancer too."

"She's not but she damn sure know how to work it. GET IT GIRL!", shouted Keisha as she threw the last bit of ones she had left.

Diamond slid down the pole and stood behind Stephanie as she attempted to be as sexy as possible for her audience. She put her hands around Stephanie and began to squeeze on her breast as Stephanie reached behind her to squeeze on Diamond's ass. Stephanie felt so free that she let her dreds down, pulled her top off and unhooked her bra to take it off too. Diamond quickly cupped Stephanie's breast, hiding them from the parishioners and began walking her to the back thru the curtains.

"Girl you was about to show all yo goodies tonight", laughed Diamond as she handed her friend her bra.

Stephanie still full of adrenaline responded,

"That shit was fun; I couldn't help myself."

The girls laughed as Stephanie got dressed so she could go back up front when one of the dancers came with a plastic grocery bag full of money. Stephanie was a little confused as to what all it was for and Diamond told her that all of the money that was on stage was for her birthday. The birthday girl was so pleased that the dancers would do that for her, but Stephanie understood the hard work they do. She sat down, began quickly counting the money up and when she was finished gave every dancer that was on the stage with her a share of the money. Stephanie looked at Diamond with a smile and stated,

"If I'm eating, my girls gotta eat too."

Diamond just smiled back so proud of her friend's generosity and they both went back up front to meet up with Keisha.

   Keisha and Spice were sitting at the bar having a drink when Diamond walked up with Stephanie close behind. Spice bought all the girls some drinks as he complimented Stephanie on her performance,

"Steph, you looked like a professional up there. You been practicing?"

"No, I've just been watching the girls every night I'm at work and tried it out for the first time", replied Stephanie.

Right when everybody began to get comfortable at the bar, Stephanie's phone began vibrating and when she looked at it she knew she had to answer. She excused herself to the bathroom as she answered,

"Hey Teedy, I'm here."

"We out here. I will see you when you come outside, no one will touch you", replied Leslie.

Stephanie walked out the bathroom and the "spider tattoo" met her at the door as if he was waiting on her. She just eased pass him,

"Excuse me"

and walked back to her friends to tell them she's ready to call it a night. Stephanie went to Quincy and told him that she will be at The Bienville Hotel on Bourbon Street when he gets off of work. He smiled at her and told her he will definitely see her there as soon as he leaves the club.

Everyone started to head to the exit as Stephanie told her co-workers goodnight and thanked Marcus for the fun time on stage.  Marcus joked with her telling Stephanie that she is always welcomed to changed job descriptions and become a dancer. Stephanie walked out the door heading to the car when Ricky stopped Keisha and Diamond to ask them where they're going afterwards. Stephanie didn't realize she was walking by herself until she heard a man's voice call out to her,

"Say lil mama, where you going?"

When she turned around all she could see was that ominous "spider tattoo" staring at her. Stephanie's feet seemed to sink into the asphalt as she couldn't move an inch with the tall black guy standing in front of her and his white partner just steps away.

"You know I know you right", stated the guy as he slowly stepped towards her.

It was as if Stephanie's throat had closed on her because her mouth was open but not one sound came out. The white guy had an evil smile as he responded to his friend,

"She playing dumb now, she must think we stupid stupid."

Stephanie backed up into the car as the two guys advanced towards her but right at that moment two hooded dark figures with black bandannas on stood behind them. The gleam from the street light shinning on a chrome .357 caught Stephanie's eye but the sound that came after dropped everyone to the ground but the two dark figures. A loud boom went off and the unexpecting white guy simply dropped to the ground as his brains poured out in the street. Stephanie couldn't believe what she just witnessed but what she seen next had her completely stunned. The other hooded person walked up to the black guy laid out on the ground and commenced to beating him with a wooden bat. The batter viciously swung their instrument of destruction, hitting the victim in the back, legs and arms. The sound of the bat making contact with his limbs were gut-wrenching as clacks of bone breaking filled the night air. In the distance Stephanie heard police sirens moving closer and closer to where they were. The hooded batsman then kneeled down next to the thrashed casualty, grabbed him by the shirt and firmly stated as they pointed to Stephanie,

"See that girl right there? She is off limits. If you see her walking up the street, you go the opposite way. If I ever see you near her again, you gone end up like yo friend over there. You bet not say shit to nobody. Am I understood?"

The hooded figure stood up, stared Stephanie in the eyes and didn't say one word but she knew exactly what the message was as she looked into those hazel colored eyes. The hooded villain made one more defining move and swung their bat one last time, striking their victim in the spine with a devastating blow. The two dark figures darted down the street into the night and disappeared as Ricky ran over to Stephanie's aid. Melvin pulled out a chair that was right by the front entrance and Stephanie sat down still in shock as to what just took place. Her friends were frantic, moving about like chickens with their heads cut off but Stephanie sat in the chair calm and collected. Three police cars came screeching to a halt in front of the club as a crowd began to form outside completely traumatized at the horrific scene in the street. The officers immediately came out and moved the crowd back off the street, trying to preserve any salvageable evidence. Everyone could hear an ambulance coming up the street, lights swirling through the dark skies reflecting off the buildings. One guy made a comment,

"They don't need paramedics; they need a coroner. That white boy dead as a muthafucka and ole boy look like he on his way, somebody fucked them up."

Diamond squatted down in front of Stephanie,

"Baby are you ok?"

Stephanie just nodded her head yes as she sat there quiet and watched as the police scurried around looking for any sort of clues. Marcus came out and sent Diamond inside with her friends,

"Bring Steph and Keisha to my office, if the police need to talk to y'all I'll send them in."

Diamond went inside with her friends and couldn't believe the conclusion to the day.


The car was quiet as Levi raced down the street, pulling off his sweatshirt and instructing Leslie to do the same. He parked in front of an old abandon house that had two hoopties parked in the carport and stated to Leslie,

"You gone follow me, we gotta get rid of this stuff."

Leslie agreed as she jumped in the driver seat and waited for Levi to drive off. Leslie has threatened people before and even had to draw a gun on a few but this was her first time ever inflicting pain on another person intentionally. She didn't know if she was scared or that her nerves just got the best of her because she couldn't stop her hands from shaking. Leslie knew Levi's past; she knew he was known in the streets as a certified hitman and even helped Levi when he was looking for his daughter's killer a few years ago. But that was all hearsay, she never been in the midst of an actual hit firsthand and the sight of seeing that man's head open up turned Leslie's stomach. She knew in her heart it was a necessary evil because if those guys could they would have hurt Stephanie and Leslie was not letting that happen. Levi exited Interstate 10 at the Michoud Blvd exit and the only lights that were back that way came from the headlights of their cars. It was so dark back there that when Levi parked his car and turned off the headlights it was as if the night swallowed the vehicle. Levi instructed Leslie to park her car at the dead end of the road and to leave all the stuff in the backseat. He had Leslie remove all her clothes except for her underwear and he did the same as he quickly threw all of the clothing in the backseat. Levi went to the trunk of the hooptie, pulled out two gasoline cans and began covering the car in the flammable liquid. He lit a match and threw it in the window, igniting the interior of the car instantly. Levi got in his car and the two headed back to Leslie's house as Leslie watched from the rearview mirror the image of her car become engulfed in the flames.

"I usually dump cars on Almonaster but I've been catching NOPD back there a lot lately, so I couldn't risk it. But in the morning, I'm a need you to report your car stolen", stated Levi as he cruised onto the Interstate 10 heading west.

Leslie sat there silent as she tried to get control of herself. But nausea started to take hold of her as images of brains scattered on the concrete filled her head. The feeling became unbearable when Leslie uttered,

"Levi, stop the car. Please stop the car."

He pulled over to the shoulder of the Interstate and Leslie pushed open the car door as she leaned out, head down. Levi could hear Leslie empty out her stomach onto the concrete and cringed to the sound as he asked,

"You good?"

Leslie just sat back as she tried to catch her breath and calm her nerves. At that moment, Levi realized that was her first time experiencing someone's life being taken. He knew that was the whole reason he didn't want to involve Leslie in the first place but she was so persistent. Levi just put his hand on Leslie's thigh,

"C'mon, lets go home."


Quincy walked in the office with two officers that wanted to talk to Stephanie about what happened outside. Stephanie was sitting quietly in the corner of the office, with a bottle of water just resting in her hand, when the detective approached her. Stephanie looked up at the officer standing in front of her with those big brown eyes and gave him a forced smile.

"Hey honey, my name is Detective Jason Babineaux, I won't keep you long. I just have a few questions for you. But first, are you ok? Do you need me to get you any medical assistance?", stated Babineaux.

Stephanie just shook her head no as she prepared herself for the detective's questions. Babineaux got a chair and sat next to her as he started his interview,

"So, can you tell me a few things? Did you know the two guys? If you can recall, what exactly happen out there?"

Stephanie looked over to the other detective talking with her distraught friends as she started off,

"I actually talked to one of the guys, the white guy, at the bar cause he thought he knew me. We had a quick convo and he walked off. When me and my friends were leaving, the other guy came up to me outside."

At that point Stephanie started to shake nervously as she thought about what happened next.

"It's ok Stephanie, take your time. Tell me what happened", replied Babineaux.

After taking a sip of water Stephanie continued,

"The black guy walked up to me, I guess he was just trying to flirt but before I could say one word two guys came up behind them and they shot that guy in the head."

Detective Babineaux could see that Stephanie was in distress but he needed more information from his witness as he asked,

"Did they say anything to them? Did you hear them say a name?"

Stephanie shook her head no as she continued to tell the detective what took place after the gunshot. Babineaux listened to every detail as Stephanie told him about the guy being beat with a bat in the middle of the street and jotted down everything important in his little notepad.

"They didn't say anything to you", asked Babineaux.

"It was as if I wasn't standing there the way they beat him. One of the guys looked me in the eyes but he had a bandanna around his face, so the only thing I seen was his dark brown eyes. That shit scared the hell out of me because I thought I was next, but they ran off up the street", replied Stephanie.

The detective wrote down a few more points as he told Stephanie to stay in touch with him if she could remember anything else and handed her his business card. Stephanie asked if it was okay if she leave because she just wanted to get out of the club, Babineaux thanked her for the help and told her that she was free to go. She made eye contact with Quincy and he immediately came over.

"Can we please get out of here", asked Stephanie as she grabbed hold of Quincy's hand.

Keisha, along with Diamond, were finished talking to the detective that was questioning them and they both were ready to leave. The group left the office heading toward the front door, the club was eerily quiet with no one in there and they could see police lights sparkling from the wide-open front doors. Stephanie stepped outside with her friends and the first thing she seen was the New Orleans Coroner's van parked in the middle of the street. The crowd from the club was standing behind the yellow caution tape as Quincy walked Stephanie to the car.

"I can't go home tonight because I don't want to have to answer a bunch of damn questions", stated Stephanie as she got in the car.

Diamond suggested they all go to her apartment, but Stephanie told them she still has a hotel room. Stephanie looked at Quincy,

"I would really like if you could still come but if not, I understand."

Quincy agreed to meeting her at the hotel. Diamond drove off as Stephanie looked out the window at the blood-stained concrete. Everyone was completely silent in the car when Stephanie made the comment,

"What a way to finish off a birthday celebration"

and put her head down into her hands. Keisha turned and seen her friend in the backseat just totally upset as tears began to drop onto her cheek.

"Baby as long as you're safe is all that matters. Whoever went after them had nothing to do with you", stated Keisha.

Stephanie just sat there quiet because she knew that what happened to those guys had all to do with her. In one way she felt guilty, but she knew that those guys would have hurt her if given the chance. Stephanie thought about how those two guys robbed a store, shot a clerk, shot at her and then chased her to cover-up their crime. After awhile she started to realize they were some bad men that just received a little street justice. Stephanie also knew the hooded batter that stared her in the face was Leslie and she was so grateful that her aunt was there to save her. Diamond pulled up in front of The Bienville Hotel and the valet opened their doors to let them out. Stephanie's two friends stood back as she headed to the door,

"What are y'all waiting for? I'm not staying in this hotel by myself."

Diamond was a little confused,

"I thought you wanted Quincy to come over. You don't need me and Keisha here."

"Yeah girl, I love you and all but I ain't sharing yo nigga with you", replied Keisha as she tried to get a smile out of her friend.

Stephanie rolled her eyes at Keisha,

"I don't wanna be by myself in a hotel with him either, not after today."

The trio went inside, Stephanie got the room and they all headed upstairs as Stephanie texted Quincy the room number.

CHAPTER VIII

Stephanie woke up to Quincy gathering his things as he was getting ready to leave the hotel room.

"You leaving already", asked the half sleep Stephanie.

"You had finally fell asleep good and I gotta get home", replied Quincy.

She sat up in the bed, watching him put on his shoes and replied,

"But everybody else sleep and I wanted to show you my new tattoo" as she pulled her shirt off along with her bra.

Quincy stood there and admired the beautiful sight of Stephanie sitting on the bed with those plump 38C's just staring at him. He walked over, placed his hand in the middle of her chest and softly let his fingers slide down across Stephanie's new tattoo. Quincy then realized why Stephanie liked his gift so much last night,

"Looks like I got the right gift for you."

"I like it when you touch it though", acknowledged Stephanie.

Quincy leaned in and kissed her as he reached down between her legs grasping a handful of her plush pleasure pocket. Stephanie shifted her hips, pressing down onto his hand and the warmth of her could be felt up to his wrist.

"Keep kissing and palming my pussy and I won't let you leave", stated Stephanie as she leaned back onto the headboard of the bed.

Quincy took that as his cue that it was time for him to go or he'll end up staying much longer than he anticipated. With one more passionate kiss, he walked out the door and Stephanie was left there with her sleeping friends. She looked out of the bedroom into the living room to see Diamond and Spice asleep together on the sofa bed, while Keisha was curled up with a blanket on the loveseat. Stephanie was so grateful for her friends and for all that they did for her on her birthday, but the conclusion of her night kept haunting her. She went in the bathroom to take a shower and clear her mind as the hot water just seemed to wash away all the hounding memories of last night. Stephanie thought her mind was playing tricks on her as she seen a shadow go pass the foggy shower curtain as she asked,

"Hello?"

"Girl it's just me, I had to pee and don't use up all the hot water I wanna take a shower too", answered Diamond.

Stephanie peeked from behind the curtain and jokingly replied,

"Guess somebody gotta wash all that Spice off of them."

"No you didn't. I see you washing away all that Quincy juice", responded a laughing Diamond.

Stephanie let her friend know that her and Quincy never got a chance to do anything intimate except for kissing because she fell asleep earlier. Diamond laughed at that fact that her friend fell asleep on Quincy, but she also understood her friend had a rough day. Stephanie stepped out of the shower as Diamond got undressed to get in,

"Damn Diamond, you just gone get naked all up in my face like that?"

"Bitch stop acting like you ain't ever see me naked before", replied a laughing Diamond as she got in the shower.

Stephanie went in the bedroom laughing at her friend's remarks as she got dressed so they all could get ready to leave the hotel.


Leslie woke up to Levi sitting on the end of the bed looking at the early morning news of the event that took place at the club.

"One person was shot and killed as another was brutally beat in an apparent gang retaliation in front of a gentleman's club late Saturday evening. Witnesses told NOPD officers that the two assailants were dressed in black hoodies with bandannas around their faces. Surveillance cameras caught the criminal act that occurred in the middle of the street and detectives are investigating the footage but there are no suspects as of yet", reported the newscaster.

Leslie didn't know if she was glad, they said there was no suspects or scared that they would find a lead. Levi got up and headed to the bathroom when Leslie asked,

"Do you think they seen anything on the video footage?"

"With them saying it was a gang retaliation, they guessing now and they don't really know", answered Levi.

Hearing that from him was a bit of a relief for Leslie as she hopped out of the bed and went to her kitchen. Levi came behind her to remind her that she needs to call the police about her car,

"Just tell them you just came outside, and somebody must have stolen your car, cause it's gone."

Leslie got on the phone and did exactly what Levi told her. Her nerves was bad after getting off the phone as she went back in her bedroom with Levi following her.

"C'mon now baby, everything is fine, no need to stress", stated Levi as he tried to sooth Leslie.

She believed Levi as she laid across the bed but being caught wasn't her worries, it was the fact that she had a hand in taking a life.


Doris was getting herself ready to head to church with Alisha when she heard a knock at the door. She was in the kitchen pouring herself a cup of coffee when she heard Alisha answer the door and the voice Doris heard annoyed her to no end. As she walked to the front door all she seen was her daughter standing there talking to her father. The unwarranted visit agitated Doris tremendously,

"Calvin, what you want?"

Calvin Crawford, the kids' father and Doris' estranged husband stood there in tattered clothes holding a teddy bear as he caught sight of Doris. He stepped back from the door as he replied,

"Doris, I just came by to give my baby girl a present and to wish the birthday girl a happy birthday."

Alisha wanted so much to invite her father in but just by the smell alone that was rolling off him pushed her away from the idea completely. Doris then reminded Calvin that Stephanie's birthday was yesterday and not today as she motioned Alisha to go back to her room. Calvin stood there with nothing else to say as his stance staggered a bit like his balance was off tilt. Doris with complete disappointment in her eyes just closed the door and walked away. She couldn't stand seeing the man she was so madly in love with five years ago fall so far down to the bottom. Calvin Crawford wasn't always a homeless addict, he used to be a hardworking postal worker. Calvin, like a few of his other co-workers, dabbled in smoking marijuana as a recreational thing but when one of his associates introduced him to lacing his weed with heroin, things began to fall downhill. He went from working 70 hours a week to barely covering 32 hours a week and blamed it on everyone else but himself. Calvin got to the point where he was spending days in search of his next hit instead of working to provide for his family. Doris knew something was wrong, but she refused to admit it to herself because she loved her husband and the father to her children so much. When Calvin was fired from the post office, after being there for 12 years, he blamed it on them making pay cuts and laying people off, but he didn't tell his wife that he failed a random drug test. When Doris found out she was furious but instead of giving up on him she tried desperately to get him help and back on his feet. For awhile it actually looked like Calvin was turning his life around but one day when Doris came home early, she found that her husband had taken the TV's, the kid's gaming consoles, emptied the savings account and took the car. After hearing about what happened Leslie searched for Calvin for her big sister and a week later found him in a rundown motel with a female dope fiend with only a few hundred dollars left. Calvin had destroyed whatever love Doris had left for him after that incident. The kids still loved their dad but knew he wasn't welcome back in their home, especially because they knew they couldn't trust him not to steal anything. Leslie use to use him for hard labor unloading trucks for little to nothing and just like a heroin addict Calvin would break his back for a few dollars. Now Calvin lives under the Claiborne Avenue bridge in a makeshift tent, standing on the corner asking for hand outs to get his next fix.

Ricky woke up thinking about Stephanie as he picked up his phone, but he didn't want to bother her early in the morning. He laid in bed scrolling through his IG when he came across a video Keisha posted last night of herself in The Bienville Hotel room and he seen Stephanie in the background with Quincy. Discouraged a little at the sight he mumbled to himself,

"I guess she's alright."

Ricky got out of bed to get his day started as he went in the kitchen to get some breakfast. After pouring himself some cereal, getting comfortable on the sofa and about to dig in there was a knock at the door. Not really in the mood for company and just wanting to relax in his apartment Ricky reluctantly went to see who it was at the door,

"Who is it?"

"Open the door and find out", replied a recognizable female voice.

When Ricky opened the door, he found Sunshine standing there looking as sexy as ever in a pair of tight grey sweats and a midriff matching hoodie.

"What you doing here, bighead", asked Ricky.

Sunshine walked in with the usual pretty smile she always carries as she responded,

"Well it's nice to see you too. Just came over to check on you cause I heard about what happened at the club last night. Marcus told me you was outside when all that shit went down. You good?"

"I'm good, that shit was crazy last night but it had nothing to do with me", replied Ricky.

Sunshine sat down on the sofa and made herself comfortable with Ricky's bowl of cereal as she started eating it,

"You don't have to go into work today at the gym?"

"Nah, I don't have any clients today so today will be a complete lazy day", replied Ricky.

The clients Ricky was referring to was the ones that workout with him at the gym because he's their Personal Trainer. Ricky been a Personal Training since he stopped playing football a few years ago. The money is good and the clientele is plenty for Ricky, who deals with customers from the normal house mom that wants to lose that "baby weight" to professional athletes that are in search of a good workout to stay in shape in the offseason. He really wanted to be alone this morning but after sitting with Sunshine, Ricky kind of enjoyed the company as they sat on the sofa looking at cartoons like two little kids.

"So, since you ain't doing nothing today and my day is free, how about you let me do a tatt on you", stated Sunshine.

Ricky thought about it as he laughed out,

"I am not gone be yo guinea pig ma'am."

Sunshine got up giggling as she went to the front door and told him she'll be right back. Ricky was relaxed on the couch waiting for Sunshine to come back inside when he received a phone call from Detective Babineaux,

"Good morning Mr. Boyd, I don't mean to call you this early, but I had a few questions for you about last night. Me and my partner looked over some surveillance footage of last night's incident. While you and the other bouncer Mr. Stevens were talking with the young women in front of the club, the two unknown suspects darted right pass y'all from the side of the building and that's when they fatally assaulted one victim before brutally beating the other. Before Ms. Crawford and her friends exited the building, did you see anyone snooping around that didn't look like they belong or drive by that looked suspicious who fit the description that night?"

"Detective Babineaux I wish I could help you because what they did to them men was horrible. But I seen so many people throughout the night that I honestly couldn't just pick out one specific person or persons that just stick out as suspicious", replied Ricky.

Detective Babineaux thanked Ricky for talking with him as Sunshine walked in with her case of tattoo equipment. Ricky got off the phone as he asked,

"You was serious about this tattoo thing? What you trying to do bighead?"

Sunshine just smiled while she started to set up her material and cleaned up the wooden dining table. She told Ricky to think of what he wanted his sleeve to look like and to be ready to not go anywhere no time soon because she wanted to do it all in one day. He chuckled at the thought of getting a full sleeve, but he knew Sunshine was the only person he trusted to do it. Ricky thought about what he wanted and then said,

"I want something that shows my heritage and journey breaking the chains of slavery."

"Nuff said, I gotcha", replied Sunshine as she put on some latex gloves.


Stephanie walked in her house after Diamond dropped her off and notice everyone was gone,

"Peace and quiet, finally."

She went in her room, got undressed and snuggled under her covers to get some shut eye but it was short lived when her cell began ringing. Stephanie was agitated until she seen the name that came across her screen, it was her ex Malcolm calling her. She quickly answered and all she could hear was Malcolm singing happy birthday to her in the worst singing voice ever. Just hearing his voice made her smile,

"Thank you but you are late sir."

"I know baby and I'm so sorry about that. We had a late game yesterday and by the time I got home I knew you was too busy partying", explained an apologetic Malcolm.

Stephanie scolded Malcolm as she told him she was never too busy to talk to a friend and told him to come up with a better excuse. The two enjoyed each other's conversation as Stephanie told Malcolm about her new job at the club, her first time in a helicopter and how she made a bunch of money dancing on stage for her birthday. He was shocked that the quiet girl he used to date back in high school had the guts to actually get on stage with 10 other strippers. Stephanie told him everything but the bloody ending because she didn't want all the questions in fear of saying something incriminating over the phone. She then told Malcolm about her new tattoo and just like Ricky last night, Malcolm asked when he can see it. Stephanie laughed as she denied that access with an excuse,

"I don't think you ready to see all of this, besides you gotta wait til it heals."

"I show you mine if you show me yours", replied Malcolm.

Stephanie burst out laughing at his response telling him that use to work when they were younger but not anymore. They continued talking as Malcolm let her know he will be coming in town in a few months and would love to see her while he's there. The two agreed to make an effort to see each other while Malcolm's in town and Stephanie was actually bubbly with excitement to see him. She got off the phone with Malcolm to attempt to get some sleep, but she heard her family coming inside and knew that idea went out the window when Alisha walked in her room. Stephanie was laying in her bed with the covers over her head when Alisha plopped herself right at the foot of the bed. Alisha sat there silent until she asked,

"Steph, you sleep?"

"Really Allie? How you expect me to be sleep with you bouncing on the bed", answered Stephanie as she sat up.

Alisha then went on to tell her big sister about their father coming over before they left for church. Stephanie wondered why he would come to the house but when Alisha told her he came over to wish Stephanie a happy birthday, the older sister just shook her head in disbelief. Alisha was just nine years old when their father finally left to be a fulltime addict and still had a glimmer of hope that he would return. Stephanie on the other hand seen the problems and heartbreak Calvin brings to the family when he's in the house and knew his presence would be disastrous. She could hear her mother rummaging around in the kitchen with the sounds of pots and pans clanging together as she asked,

"How did mama take him coming here?"

Alisha told her sister that she expected their mother to go off the deep end, but she was actually composed and calm before closing the door in his face. Stephanie reluctantly went to go check on her mother because she didn't like seeing her upset over the disappointment of the love of her life, but she wanted to be there for her. She sat there quietly in the kitchen as Doris began preparing things for Sunday dinner.

"Hey honey, your brother called for you yesterday to wish you a happy birthday like right after you left. Did you enjoy your day?", asked Doris.

She sprinkled a cup of flour in a large skillet to make a roux for gravy as she attentively listened for her daughter's response. Like she did with everyone else that asked her about her birthday, Stephanie told her mother with excitement in her voice of the adventure she had with her friends. Doris was pleased that her oldest girl enjoyed herself, but that irritating thought of Calvin came back as she told Stephanie,

"Your father came over this morning to wish you happy birthday."

Stephanie made her mother laugh as she replied,

"I guess him and Malcolm both high because Malcolm called me this morning singing happy birthday."

Doris just fiddled around in the kitchen as she enjoyed her daughter's company while she prepped things for dinner.


After the police had left her house, taking a report of her car being stolen, Leslie got in her truck and headed to her sister's house to check on her niece. She tried to put the night behind her, but it was still too fresh and she knew she had to see if Stephanie was going thru the same thing. Leslie was almost at Doris' house when she received a text from Levi,

"I don't wanna sound corny or nothing, but I can't get you out of my head. Can I see you tonight?"

With the whole "Bonnie and Clyde" episode that took place last night, Leslie almost forgot that she had an extremely pleasurable sexual experience with him. She read the text like three times before she replied,

"You sure you ready, cause I need a serious stress reliever."

Levi just sent back a tongue, an eggplant and raindrop emoji with the words "Round Two" to her phone. Leslie didn't think a guy could make her smile with a simple silly text, but it did and it kind of made her feel better.  She pulled up to her sister's house and as she looked at the front door Leslie let out a big sigh because she was preparing herself for the usual Doris attitude. Leslie rung the doorbell and her bubbly teenage niece Alisha answered the door,

"Hey Auntie Lez, mama and Steph in the kitchen."

"Hey Allie baby, how you been big head", replied Leslie as she kissed her niece on the cheek.

Doris came out from the kitchen, walked up to her sister and gave her an embrace Leslie haven't felt from her older sister in a long time. Leslie was baffled at her sister's behavior, but she didn't question it as she just hugged her sister back.

"This yo second time coming over here in one weekend. You miss me or something", asked Doris as she smiled at her little sister.

Leslie just smiled back and told Doris she just wanted to see how Stephanie enjoyed her birthday. Doris sat down with her little sister and what she did next caught Leslie off guard like the hug. Doris sincerely looked Leslie in the eyes as she began to apologize for her actions of aggression.

"I was blaming you for a lot of stuff and I had a long talk with my son, and myself. Caleb knew what he was doing, I knew but I was looking with blindfolds on and putting the blame on someone else instead of myself. Baby sis, I'm so sorry for how I've been acting, and I truly hope you accept my apology. I love you Lez", stated a wholehearted Doris.

Leslie just hugged her big sister so tight that all the bad blood between them dissolved into nothing and was replaced with nothing but love for one another. Stephanie walked out the kitchen immediately telling her aunt about all that she did for her birthday. She went in full detail of the whole day but when she got to the part of the story about her getting a new tattoo Doris eyes got big.

"Steph, you got another tattoo", asked Doris.

Stephanie tried to ignore her mother's question, but it was kind of hard with Doris giving her the usual "stare-down" to get answers. Stephanie raised her tee shirt to show her mother and aunt the new tattoo she got as she explained to her mother the meaning of it. She knew that was going to be the first thing her mother wanted to know, was the meaning behind the tattoo. Doris had no problem with her children getting tattoos, but the artwork had to mean something, it couldn't be a flagrant work of nonsense. The mother of three felt that if a person was going to permanently mark their body that if they were to do so that the markings had to have a deeper meaning than just permanent ink. After hearing Stephanie's explanation, Doris jokingly responded,

"Girl you get anymore tattoos, we gone have to find you a stripper name."

The three women laughed the comment off but in the back of Stephanie's mind she already had an idea of a good name she would use if she became a dancer, but she kept that to herself. Leslie was enjoying being at her sister's house and there not being any animosity or arguing going on as she sat there talking with Doris. As she watched her big sister leave the kitchen to change out of her church clothes, Leslie took the opportunity to ask Stephanie if she was ok after last night's events.

"Teedy, I had a good time yesterday and I want to thank you for the hotel room because that was the perfect ending to a wonderful night", stated Stephanie as she stared Leslie straight in her eyes with confidence all over her face.

Leslie knew right then and there that everything was okay with Stephanie and that they need not talk about the situation anymore.

Sunshine was putting the finishing touches on the full sleeve she just completed on Ricky's arm and pulled out her cell phone to make a video for her Gram followers. Making sure she was nicely focused on her artwork, all the while rubbing his arm down with some moisturizing ointment, Sunshine made the statement,

"Another bad creation y'all, the ABC's of Sunshine."

Ricky went to the full-length standing mirror in the corner of his living room to check out the finished product and was greatly satisfied with what Sunshine had created for him. Starting at his shoulder was a family tree with his mother and father's names. Under the family tree was his high school, college and CFL football jerseys followed by a dragon and tiger intertwined. Finally, below the mystical animals was an open scroll that read "Loved by Many, Hated by Few, Respected by All" and entangled throughout the entire tattoo starting at his shoulder was a broken rusted slave chain that ended at his wrist. He couldn't believe how detailed she did every part of the tattoo, from the leaves on the family tree, the scales on the dragon and even the realistic look of the chains. Sunshine could see the amazement in Ricky's eyes as he looked over her work,

"So, you like it?"

"I love it, thank you so much for this one", responded Ricky as he kissed her.

As Sunshine was putting away her equipment she playfully stated,

"Now I take payment in cash, dinner or ass. Which one you got for me?"

Ricky laughed while pulling his tee shirt off over his head and replied,

"I'm fresh out of money and I know you don't want any cereal."

Sunshine walked over to Ricky as she looked over his massive muscular frame, looked into his golden brown eyes and stated,

"I definitely don't want any cereal, sir."

Ricky picked Sunshine up in his arms as she wrapped her legs around him and the two engaged into a passionate kiss. Ricky walked over to his solid wooden dinning table and laid Sunshine on it. He began to undress her, all the while continuing to kiss her lips and neck as she did the same. Sunshine leaned back onto the table when Ricky positioned himself between her legs, staring down her freshly waxed plump pussy. She smiled after he slowly fingered her and licked her sweet juices off his fingers. He put his head down between her thick almond color thighs and took a long lick to her clit. It's been years since the two have been intimate but the feel-good feelings began rushing back when Ricky took Sunshine's clit into his mouth.

"Dammit baby! You just gone eat me like I'm yo dinner, right on the table", mumbled Sunshine as she reached down and grasped the back of Ricky's head.

The more his tongue twirled and flicked against her swollen clit, the more erotic the moans that came from her until the moans turned into words. Ricky could hear her whisper words of gratitude and pleasure as she whispered,

"Yes baby, right there. You like that pussy don't cha? Damn you got me wet."

Sunshine tried to hold on but Ricky's perfection at what he was doing brought her to her first gushing orgasm as she came in his mouth. He stood up and Sunshine immediately started kissing him while recovering from her electrifying climax as her clit thumped repeatedly. Ricky pulled her closer to him by her hips, placed his hand on her chest, laid her back down on the table and slowly slid his harden manhood in her moist warm tight tunnel. To Sunshine it felt like the dick wouldn't stop coming as she reached to place her hand on Ricky's stomach to slow him down from entering her any deeper. He knew it been awhile since they been in this position, so he took his time as he easily slid in and out all the while picking up the pace with every thrust. Ricky got a good grip onto Sunshine's hips, so that she couldn't run away from him and began an onslaught of lunges deep inside of her. The pleasured pain of his massive swollen shaft filled her up as she could feel every inch of him and she uttered,

"Baby, you in my stomach. I'm a be good, I'm a be good."

The words just amped Ricky's aggression as he pounded harder until the room filled with the sounds of skin slapping together and Sunshine's moans turning into erotic screams.

Ricky himself tried to hold back but looking at Sunshine's immaculately framed body, how her plump titties just jiggled with every push and how her walls were squeezing around his dick as if she was milking him, Ricky couldn't hold on anymore. He pulled out of her soaking wet hole and began stroking himself as he came all on Sunshine's flat stomach, she could feel nothing but thick warmth spill on her. She jumped down off the table and made her way to the bathroom to take a shower when Ricky made the comment,

"Maybe next time we can actually make it to the bedroom."

Sunshine looked over her shoulder and smiled at him as she entered the bathroom.

CHAPTER IX

It's been two weeks since the gentleman's club incident and when Doris found out that her daughter was in the middle of the whole thing, she was livid. Stephanie assured her mother that she was not harmed and that the only reason she didn't tell her in the beginning was because she didn't want her stressing over it. Doris wanted Stephanie to quit working at the club, but Stephanie was definitely not doing that, especially now that Diamond is training her to be a dancer. Stephanie saw the potential to be able to pay for her schooling without relying on any financial aid, help from her mother or help from her aunt. She was determined to make this decision work out in her favor. Ricky and Sunshine was a complicated relationship where he wanted a committed relationship, but Sunshine strictly wanted a fuck buddy. Ricky wanted to deny her of that but once he looked into her big brown eyes, it was a wrap and he would fold every time. Sunshine knew that their relationship wouldn't last with her busy schedule but was content with just having a piece of Ricky when she could, she felt having a piece of him was better than having none of him. Diamond and Spice became undeniably the cutest couple anyone could come across as Stephanie and Quincy were the close runner-ups. Leslie and Levi have become a complete item, to the point where they have exchanged house keys to each other's residence. She was really nervous for a few days but Levi continued to comfort her that everything would be fine and she finally relaxed. Marcus was in his final stages of finalizing the Grand Opening of the Stagelight Casino and Gentleman's Club with the surprising assistance from Stephanie's business savvy with investors.

Stephanie was leaving class for the day with her bestie Keisha when she received a text from Quincy telling her that he wanted to meet up with her. Keisha could see the smile just appear on Stephanie's face as she read the text,

"Bitch that must be Quincy the way you cheezin' and shit."

"He wants to hook-up today before we head to work", replied Stephanie.

Keisha started putting her backpack in the backseat of her car as she asked,

"So I guess you heading over to his house then?"

Stephanie sat in the car quiet for a few seconds before she answered,

"I've never been to his house before, we always hook-up at a hotel. He's been to my house once, but we've never made it to his."

Keisha stayed silent but wondered why her friend has never been to her boyfriend's house before since they've been together. Stephanie told her that Quincy lives almost an hour away and that he said he doesn't feel comfortable with her driving that far by herself. Keisha found it strange but if her friend was cool with the arrangement than she's comfortable with it also.

"With me going to school and work five days a week plus training with Diamond on my off days, we hook up when we can", stated Stephanie as she texted Quincy back.

Keisha assured her friend that she had her back,

"Girl, you don't have to convince me about y'all. If you happy, I'm happy. Besides, we have a break from school coming up and maybe you could spend that week at his place. You hoes could play house all week."

Stephanie thought about it and really thought it would be a great idea she'll run by Quincy. The two headed to Stephanie's place so that she could meet with her boyfriend later when Diamond called Stephanie with some good news. With excitement in her voice Diamond stated,

"Hey chick, you sitting down? Look I talked to Marcus earlier today. He and Eric are getting ready to hold an open audition for dancers in two weeks because they need dancers for the club and the casino. So, we got to get to work trick, I'm a need to get you right."

"Wow, so we really doing this? I don't know if I'm ready Dee", replied Stephanie.

Diamond assured her friend that she will have her more than ready before the auditions arrive. As always Keisha was ear hustling the whole conversation as she drove up to Stephanie's house and reinforced Diamond's statement that their bestie is ready for the challenge. Stephanie thanked both of them for the encouraging words and made her way inside to get her stuff together so that she could meet up with Quincy in a few.

Leslie was relaxing at home when she got a call from one of her regulars that a package was waiting for her at a warehouse. She was always cautious when it came down to picking up or dropping off packages ever since Caleb was pinched for illegal gun running, so she did what she always do and that's call Levi to check out the creditability of the information. Leslie found herself trusting Levi more and more, the closer they became. Levi went over to check out Leslie's tip on the pick-up but when he got there, he seen an old associate at the warehouse,

"Mook, what's going down witcha boy?"

"Levi I haven't seen you in a minute. Where have you been hiding", replied Mook.

Levi and Mook caught up on old times, reminiscing over past days of running the streets hustling, fallen friends and incarcerated ones. Back when Levi was a "corner boy", he and Mook worked for an old Vietnamese convenience store owner that distributed narcotics to all New Orleans east. The two were a force to be reckoned with as teens but after Mook's girlfriend at the time gave birth to his first son, he stepped away from the lifestyle. The guys talked a little more about the old days when Levi remembered why he was originally there,

"Say dude, did you hear anything about a special package that's suppose to be picked up today? A dude called my friend about a pick-up."

"Oh you here for Lez package, let me go get it", replied Mook.

Levi waited for his old buddy to come back as he texted Leslie that everything was fine with the pick-up and that he'll bring it over later. Mook came from the back of the warehouse with a large box on a dolly when he made the statement,

"Man, I'm glad you came early, I can go visit my son at the hospital before I head home."

Levi was a little concerned that his friend's child was in the hospital and asked why. Mook started telling Levi about the murder and assault that happened two weeks ago in front of the gentleman's club. He told Levi that the man that was beaten with a bat in the middle of the street was his oldest boy and that he still has one more surgery to go through. Levi stood there in total disbelief of the six degrees of separation that connected them all as Mook told him that the police still have no clue who it was or why.  Levi then sent his old friend on his way,

"Well I definitely don't wanna hold you up any longer, go check on yo boy and if you need anything please hit me up."

Mook told Levi he will keep in touch with him after helping him get the large box in Levi's trunk and rushed off to the hospital. Still completely caught off guard over what Mook had relayed to him, Levi made his way to Leslie.


        Ricky was working out with one of his clients at the gym when Sunshine walked in. Ricky's client lost all concentration as the sexy Sunshine dressed in white yoga pants and a tight-fitting white tank top greeted Ricky with a peck on the cheek,

"Hey you."

He smiled and returned the kiss on the cheek as he continued to encourage his client to push through his last set of reps. Sunshine saw that her beau was more focused on his work than talking with her so she excused herself to the treadmills in the back of the gym.

"Man, you just gone let her walk off? That's Sunshine, Another Bad Creation Sunshine, the fine as hell Sunshine. Like I follow her on IG and Snap and you just let her kiss you and walk away", stated the confused customer.

Ricky laughed at him sitting there breathing heavily as he sat on the work bench. The guy grabbed his towel off the floor and as he wiped the sweat that was dripping from his face he replied to Ricky's laughter,

"You laughing cause you know you need to be over there with her and not here with my ass. I'm done for the day anyways, so get to getting. You can tell me the details on our next meet."

Ricky let his client leave and he himself headed to the showers to get ready to leave. The thing Ricky didn't tell his client was that he was really trying to wean himself from Sunshine and the only way he knew how was to just stay away from her by being busy. After all this time from the first time they were together, he still had deep feelings for her, but he seen that the feelings weren't mutual. Sunshine merely wanted the relationship to stay casual with the occasional sexual encounter and what man wouldn't want an arrangement like that with an exotic dancer. Ricky knew all of his friends and associates would look at him crazy if he was to walk away from such an appealing agreement, but he truly wanted more out of a relationship.

As he left out of the locker room and headed to his car, he received a call from Sunshine,

"So, you gone leave and not even say bye or see you later?"

Ricky could hear that she was still running on the treadmill by the heavy breathing as he replied,

"My bad, I got some errands to run before I head to work tonight."

"Well can I see you before you go to work tonight, I have to catch a flight out to Orlando in the morning and I need some dick to hold me over", replied a giggling Sunshine.

Ricky shook his head no as if she could see him as he stayed silent over the phone until he responded,

"Practice breathing in through your nose and out through your mouth so that you can catch your breath, it will help you last longer while running."

Just from that response Sunshine took that as a defining no and politely thanked Ricky for the informative instructions as she got off the phone. Ricky felt that was the end of what he considered was a strained relationship anyways and made his way home to relax before heading to the club. He respected her and himself too much to let them continue what he felt was a meaningless encounter.


     Stephanie finally made it to the hotel where Quincy was and immediately headed to the room, he had texted her. It was as if he could sense her when he opened the door, standing there with nothing but a pair of basketball shorts on, he kissed Stephanie passionately and grabbed her bags as they headed inside. She was excited to spend some alone time with him before they both went to work as she relaxed on the bed, kicking her shoes off. Stephanie brought up the idea of her spending the week with him on her break from school and Quincy's response was very promising,

"Now baby that right there sounds like a plan. Let me make sure my schedule is completely free cause I wanna spend it all with you, no interruptions."

Stephanie smiled like a little schoolgirl thinking about spending nights with him. Quincy took it upon himself to start removing Stephanie's top, caressing her breast and reaching down between her thighs rubbing her summer warm pussy. Just from those two moves he made; Stephanie knew it was time to get some much needed sexually curricula activity going. She reached down and grasped hold of a skin covered baseball bat that sent chills down her back thinking about how that manly instrument is about to fill her up. The two began kissing one another, tongues twirling around and hands stroking every inch of them. Quincy laid back on the bed and pulled Stephanie up to his head gesturing for her to prop herself on his face, she had to oblige him of his request. She stood over him positioning herself directly over his face and lowered herself down until her clit rested right on his lips. Quincy slowly slid his tongue out as it slowly slid pass her moist lips deep inside her and licked up, her juices instantly began dripping down his chin. He focused on one spot as his tongue twirled, twisted and flicked against her throbbing clitoris. Stephanie attempted to hold onto the wall while Quincy continued his journey of devouring her soaking wet juice box. She literally was straddled on his face and to keep her secured there Quincy wrapped his arms around her thighs as he sucked on her clit. She reached back, wrapped her soft hands around his hardened meat and began slowly stroking it, while he continued to ravage her pussy. Stephanie so desired to return the oral pleasure she was receiving that she turned around so that she was face to face with the monstrous snake. She started at the base, licked up to the shiny helmet and inserted the entire thing until it pressed against the back of her throat. The gag sound that came from her excited them both and she went back for more as the saliva in her mouth spilled down his shaft. She stroked as she sucked and could feel him thrust his hips, pushing himself deeper in her mouth, so she moved her hands while he fucked her throat. He could feel the pleasure was getting too intense and knew if he didn't stop this pleasurable voyage would be over before it started. Quincy climbed from under his sexy lady, keeping her on her knees, knelt behind her and slowly inserted his man meat into her soaked pussy. Stephanie inhaled deeply as she could feel every inch of him slide in, from every vein to every rigid curve of his dick as her juicy walls envelop it all. He began with a slow grind while holding onto her hips pushing deeper every time, he goes in. Stephanie started to push back into him, and Quincy knew she wanted him to pick up the pace, so he did exactly that as the sound of skin slapping could be heard outside of the hotel room. He flipped her over onto her back, pressed her legs wide open and plunged his dick deep in her that she could feel him press against her stomach. Quincy began really pounding away and the orgasmic pain Stephanie was going through was welcomed like she was Quincy's lowly cult follower. The two continued their naked escapades until they both collapsed from explosive orgasms and just laid there covered in sweat.

After talking with Levi over their newfound information of the club incident, Leslie headed to see Doris at her office. Ever since Doris apologized to Leslie that Sunday afternoon, the two always tried to make an effort to meet up for lunch or after work. Leslie really enjoyed reconnecting with her sister, to the point where it became the highlight of her day sometimes. Dealing mainly with nothing but males all day it was refreshing to have a meaningful conversation with another female. Leslie walked into the Orleans Parish Medical Center's lobby and seen one of Doris' co-workers,

"Hey Ced, long time no see. How have you been baby?"

"Hey Lez, I've been good. Girl you look good as always", replied Cedric Daniels.

Cedric was standing in the lobby talking with his nephew Devin when Leslie walked up to them and Devin couldn't take his eyes off her. Leslie and Cedric been knowing each other since high school, he was the main reason Doris received the promotion to head accountant over purchasing at the Center. Leslie always returns the favor by giving his brother Kareem first dibs on any special packages she could find for him. The two talked for a brief moment but Leslie had to get to her sister and Cedric was heading out the door with Devin, so they gave each other a hug as they said their goodbyes. Cedric's nephew just smiled when Leslie walked away to the elevator and couldn't help but to ask,

"Now that right there is one sexy ass woman, who the hell was that?"

"She's way out of your league nephew, trust me you not ready for her. Besides she's my age or maybe older, let's go fool", laughed Cedric as they walked off.

Leslie met Doris at the elevator and the two made their way to the cafeteria for a late lunch. Doris knew she still had a long wait before Caleb would be able to come home but she couldn't stop talking about her son's arrival. Leslie was anxious too because she had a new business opportunity in the works that could be the beginning of her turning all her illegal shipments into a legal and profitable business. She felt obligated to Caleb to have it all complete by the time he's released from prison and they both could run the company together. Leslie ran the idea by Levi earlier because she wanted him to join her with the company and he was a little reluctant of the venture but he also knew that the type of business he's in is not suited for older men. She wanted it to be a surprise to the rest of her family, so she kept it all a secret. Leslie asked her sister how Stephanie was doing after the club incident and if they heard anything back from the police. Doris told her that the police are ruling it a gang related attack and that Stephanie was never in any immediate danger, that the attackers were focused on the two guys. She said that the young guy in the hospital told detectives that he never got a chance to see their faces and that it happened so quick that he didn't have a chance to turn around. Doris not knowing her sister was just fishing for info of the situation, but Leslie was truly concerned about her niece's mindset. The two sat in the cafeteria while enjoying a hearty salad and later parted ways as Doris headed back to work.

Ricky was fixing himself something to eat when he got a call from Marcus,

"What's up Ric? Shit is moving fast with the new casino and I wanted to run something by you. The casino part will have its own set of armed guards, but I need someone I can trust with the security of the girls and I was wondering if you wanted to be head of security with the club part. You will have a group of guys, you'll oversee, you'll be in charge of the schedule and no event goes through without your approval when it involves any of the dancers. What ya think?"

Ricky was completely caught off guard because he never expected Marcus to offer him the position, figuring Melvin would get the job because of his experience. He thought briefly about it and quickly said yes to the challenge but had one request that he be there during the interview process to check out the potential bouncers he'll be working with. Ricky wondered what his co-worker Melvin would think about him being the head of security at the new place, but Marcus informed him that his buddy will take over being in charge of security at The Rabbit Hole when the casino opens. Right when Ricky was getting off the phone with Marcus, he heard someone banging at his door, the banging was so hard that Ricky thought someone was trying to kick his door down. He grabbed his gun from his bedroom and immediately walked to the front door.

"Who the fuck is it", shouted Ricky as he focused a black 9mm at the door.

"Ricky, open the damn door! You know who it is", replied a recognizable female voice.

When he opened the door, there stood a very angered Sunshine who pushed her way passed Ricky into his apartment. Confused to why she's at his place and a little frustrated, Ricky asked,

"What the hell wrong with you?"

"Bitch don't play stupid with me; you know exactly why I'm here. That was some bullshit you pulled at the gym and you know it was foul as fuck. If you don't wanna fuck with me anymore don't make up fucking excuses, brushing me off like I'm some basic bitch!", shouted Sunshine as she paced back and forth.

Ricky calmly walked up to Sunshine and his massive frame just seemed to block out the sunlight that was beaming through the patio window. She looked into his eyes and seen that he was very serious as he calmly but sternly responded,

"First off watch who the hell you calling bitch, I ain't one of those females in the locker room you can easily intimidate."

Ricky stood there directly in front of Sunshine as he explained his reason for brushing her off at the gym, why he felt their relationship wouldn't go any further than where it is now and that he wanted more than what she was willing to offer. Sunshine was still upset of the fact that he just walked away from her at the gym and deep down she knew he was telling the truth about the future of the relationship they had but her stubbornness wouldn't acknowledge it. She stood there with her hands on her hips, furious to the idea that a man would tell her no and it was evident that Ricky really didn't care how she takes the information as he went on. He let her know that they will always be friends and that she will always have a place in his heart but that he had to move on from what he felt was a dead-end relationship. Sunshine placed her soft hands on each side of Ricky's face, kissed him ever so passionately and stated before walking out of his apartment,

"Whoever she is, whenever y'all meet, I really hope she makes you happy. Damn, I'm a miss that dick."

Ricky just shook his head as he laughed at her comment and watched her walk down the hallway to the elevator.

CHAPTER X

Diamond, Smiley and Stephanie were training at the studio for the auditions when Keisha walked in to watch her friends. When it came to perform on stage Stephanie knew she had two of the best exotic dancers in New Orleans teaching her. The athletic part of the performance was easy for her, being that Stephanie trained in the gym all through high school and partially in college but being sexually appealing all at the same time was the true feat. Handling tricks or stunts were all under Smiley's level of expertise but having the ability to seduce anyone watching her dance is all Diamond. While in the "Teddy Cleaver" pose, suspended in the air like a sultry butterfly, Diamond explained to Stephanie,

"One of the main tricks of the trade is eye contact. Your client is focused on your body and what you're doing with it but if you make eye contact with them, make sure your eyes tell them that you want them and them only. This is all an act, a fantasy that you must create for them in their head. Once you get in their head, you got full control."

Diamond performed a quick skit as she showed Stephanie what she meant by eye contact, while the other three women sat there and watched. The whole time Diamond created eye popping tricks she made sure to focus on each one of them as if she was dancing strictly for that one person. As talented as Smiley is, she herself was taking pointers from Diamond's performance and was caught up in the whirlwind of sexual prowess she poured out on the stage. Diamond slid up and down the pole effortlessly as if she was attached to a rope in the ceiling. Her lotion covered legs simply glimmering as her toned arms raised her up and down, all the while looking every person watching her in the eyes, like she wanted to undress them all. She gracefully placed herself on the stage, crawled to them like a lioness prowling her prey before spinning to her back and snapping her legs wide open as she caressed her plush pussy. Stephanie was paying attention to every detail, such as Diamond's hand placement, the arch in her back, the extension of her legs and even how she landed from the pole onto the stage. Keisha already had respect for dancers in the industry but just then had a newfound respect for the art of an exotic dancer and shared her excitement by cheering as she stood up,

"Get it bitch! Get it!"

Diamond smiled as she stepped down off the stage and went to thank her friend for the applause. After watching Diamond's act, Stephanie could feel the pressure of making sure she does everything right during her audition but her best friend and future co-workers had her back all the way with encouraging words. Stephanie and the girls left the studio for the day to go grab a bite to eat, Keisha still talking about how she was floored with Diamond's erotic spectacle, they all looked forward to relaxing the rest of the day before having to head to work later.


Levi and Leslie were meeting with a realtor about a building Leslie had been looking at on Tchoupitoulas Street when Levi got a call from an old friend. He stepped out while Leslie looked over the floor plans and debated over the asking price with her realtor. As Leslie was signing the paperwork with the realtor, Levi came back inside,

"So, you really getting the place babe?"

"Looks like I actually am", replied a smiling Leslie.

They all left the building and as Levi was getting in the car, he told Leslie that the phone call was from his old buddy Mook who told him that his son got out of the hospital today. Levi always wanted to stay up to date on any news about the young man's condition, but he also wanted to stay informed on any news about the assault. Levi knew he had to stay ahead of any situation that arise, if any but he felt that everything was going smooth. Leslie was so excited about starting her own legit business soon that the club incident fell to the back burner, besides she had confidence that Levi had it all under control. The two headed back to Levi's apartment, which is actually around the corner from the building Leslie's buying and relaxed looking at TV. Leslie laid there in Levi's arms on the sofa and couldn't imagine a better feeling. Levi sat there enjoying the moment as well when he jokingly stated,

"Girl, you making me soft. Usually I'm out somewhere turning corners but I'm here watching this do it yourself show."

"You can go if you want to, I'm a chill here", replied Leslie.

Levi chuckled at her response as he grabbed two handfuls of Leslie's breast,

"And leave all this?"

The gesture was met with Leslie making herself even more comfortable in Levi's arms as she started to realize that they both have changed since their relationship grew. She couldn't believe that the one person to get pass her stern demeanor would be him, but it was a fitting match. Most men couldn't handle Leslie's temperament because they felt she was "too manly" for them and she used their feelings to her advantage.  Levi on the other hand broke through the façade she had created for so many years and found the true Leslie, they complimented each other.

Ricky pulled up in the parking lot across the street from the club when he seen Melvin getting out of his car. The two usually like to get to the club before any of the other employees just so they can do a security check of the building. While they were doing their walk-through Melvin congratulated Ricky on his new position,

"Made me proud to know you was getting the spot over there and not some outsider."

"I really thought you would have though", replied Ricky as he unlocked the front doors of the club to let in a few employees.

 Quincy walked in with a few of the waitresses and Melvin couldn't help but to clown around,

"Where's you better half? She's usually following right behind you", referring to Stephanie.

"We not that cool bruh, stop playing with me", replied Quincy as he walked off behind the bar.

Melvin was caught off guard with Quincy's response and didn't let it go unchecked,

"Nigga who the hell crawled up yo ass, cause I'm not the one you wanna come at."

Ricky tried to deescalate the situation between the two by standing in front of Melvin and cracking a joke,

"C'mon now Melvin, dude weighs as much as your left leg. Let him have his little moment."

Melvin thought about it and walked off to the front of the club but made himself clear with a loud statement,

" Niggas taking my kindness for weakness cause I'm always laughing and happy but I will slap the taste outta ya fucking mouth bitch."

Ricky just gesture for Melvin to go outside as he attempted to keep Quincy behind the bar, but Quincy knew he didn't want any of Melvin.

"Say dude, you good", asked Ricky as he sat at the bar.

Quincy just ignored his question and continued prepping the bar for the nights opening. Ricky noticed that the bartender wasn't really in a talking mood, so he left him to his duties and headed outside with his bouncer buddy. Melvin was sitting on a stool in front of the entrance doors talking with a police officer that was just patrolling the area when Ricky came outside. Ever since the incident that happened in front of the club, NOPD have been making sporadic stops and just checking out the club for anything unusual. After talking with Ricky and Melvin the officer left which gave Ricky a chance to check on his friend,

"Say round, you good?"

"Man, I'm Gucci. I just had to let it be known to that fool that I'm not the one he wants smoke with", replied Melvin.

Ricky understood exactly where Melvin was coming from as they left Quincy inside to his own vices while they stayed outside of the club.

Doris was leaving work when she got a call from Leslie to meet her on the corner of Tchoupitoulas and Josephine but was very vague on the reason for the meet. She knew her sister was usually in that area because of the ports, docks and warehouses she frequently visited, so she obliged her and agreed to meet her there. Leslie and Levi patiently waited for Doris to arrive so they could show her what they were up to.

"You sure you want me here when Doris gets here? I know I'm not the most welcomed face someone wants to see when they pull up", stated Levi as he leaned against the car lighting a cigarette.

Leslie did something Levi haven't experienced in a long time and that's someone comforting him by telling him that his presence is much needed and welcomed. He let out a little grin while he admired his woman's strength and sexiness, but her compassion was winning him overall because most people only see a criminal when they see him. Levi was truly attempting to turn over a new leaf and Leslie's new venture could be exactly what does it for him. He tried before but was brought back to the dark side when his daughter was murdered and all he could see was revenge. Now with all of that in his rearview, a new beginning is in store for the newly reformed street thug but he's not oblivious to the fact that he could go back to what he's been used to for over two decades. Doris had finally made her way to the address Leslie had given her and the smile on her little sister's face was a definite sign that she was about to enjoy what's next. Leslie walked up to the car,

"Took you long enough, come over here, I got something I wanna show you."

"Girl, you do know there's traffic out here around this time right", replied Doris.

Leslie just took hold of her sister's hand and walked her to the front entrance of the building that still had the "For Sale" sign on it. Doris was still confused to why she was there until they all walked inside and she seen a large sign on the floor that read "Wilson & Crawford Shipments Inc." Leslie stood there proud as she announced to her sister that she is starting a delivery service company for her clients but this time she's going legit and when Caleb is released from prison he will be her partner.

"Lez you really doing this all by the book, no more scams or under the table transactions?", asked Doris.

Leslie just nodded her head with the biggest smile as she interlocked her fingers with Levi's,

"Sis, I'm doing this all by the books I promise. We all deserve this second chance and Caleb needs something positive to come home to, something he can call his own. I owe him that."

"You don't owe him anything Lez but I'm so proud of you sis", replied Doris as she hugged her little sister.

Melvin was at the front door standing watch when three young women walked up to him. Ricky had just stepped outside when one of the women asked if Quincy was working the bar tonight. Neither of the guys ever seen the women before at the club and Melvin answered,

"I believe he is."

The bouncers let the ladies in, and they headed straight to the bar. Diamond and Smiley were sitting at the bar talking about the upcoming dance auditions happening Monday when they seen the three females walk in. One of the women stood at the end of the bar and shouted to get Quincy's attention,

"Hey Q baby, fix us your special!"

When he turned to see who was calling him, it was as if he had just seen a ghost and Diamond recognized that look from anywhere. She knew that whoever this woman is that she is a female that Quincy never expected to see at the club or never wanted in the club. Diamond nudged Smiley to see the event she just witnessed, and it only got more interesting the more they watched. Quincy stuttered as he asked,

"Ba ba baby, what y'all doing here? I thought you was going to the reggae spot."

"Nah, we all agreed to come hang out here and partake in some of those free drinks you always mentioning to me. Oh, and look at some naked ass", giggled the young woman.

Smiley realized that Quincy personally knew the women just from the way they all talked to him but the icing on the cake was when one woman leaned over the counter and kissed him on the lips, right then Smiley knew it was more than platonic. Smiley is a scanner; she can look over a person and find the smallest detail the average person may overlook. She grasped Diamond's hand in excitement when she asked,

"Bitch! Does that heart tattoo have the letter 'Q' in it?"

Diamond then pointed out the wedding band on the woman's left ring finger. The dancers completely forgot that they were at the club working as all the clues they seen point to their friend's boyfriend actually being a married man. Stephanie was clueless to what was going on in front of her friends' eyes as she walked up to the bar to place an order for her customers. Diamond tried to get her attention, but Stephanie's attention was all focused on her beau as he made the drinks she needed. Smiley figured the all-out blunt direction was the best way as she walked up to Stephanie to tell her what they just seen but before Smiley could get out one word the young woman with the heart tattoo walked up to Stephanie.

"Hey, your name is Steph or Stephanie right", asked the woman as she waited for a response.

Stephanie was puzzled to who the woman was and how she knew her name as she acknowledged the question with a question of her owns,

"I'm sorry and who are you?"

Smiley tried to intervene, but Stephanie wanted to know who this mystery woman was that knew her name. The female so sarcastically replied as she went thru her cell phone,

"It's understandable if you don't know me but I sure do know who you are. My name is Tracy and you have been texting my husband some really provocative pics lately. I just wanted to make sure you knew who I was before I got outta hand with you."

Stephanie became very defensive when Tracy accused her of having dealings with her husband and Quincy tried to intercede but when Tracy showed her screenshots of nude pics, Stephanie knew the "husband" she was referring to. Tracy was very polite but undeviating from expressing how she felt about finding out that her husband was having an affair with a waitress at his job. Stephanie was completely caught off guard trying to fathom the fact that the guy she grew to trust would do such a thing. But then all the other things became relevantly clear as to why he would never want her to come to his house and that he would always meet her at a hotel. Stephanie tried to apologize for the affair as her eyes began to well with tears, but Tracy let her know that it wasn't her fault,

"Nah, I could see from the text that you didn't know me, nor my kids existed so don't apologize. Just know that I know who you are and NOW you know who I am."

Diamond and Smiley both escorted their friend away from the situation to the locker room as they could hear over the music glass breaking accompanied with aggressive shouting. Stephanie couldn't believe she was caught up in a deceitful web spun by Quincy as her friends attempted to console her. The feeling only got worse the more dancers began to come in the locker room talking about the three women that had to be put out the club for trying to fight Quincy at the bar. Stephanie just put her head in her hands as she quietly stated,

"I can't believe that nigga played me like this, fuck."

The club had finally closed for the night as Marcus locked the front doors while Ricky and Melvin stood watch over the last few employees walking to their cars.

"Anybody call and check on Steph, cause I don't know what to say to her", asked Marcus.

The two bouncers just stood there shaking their heads no because neither of them knew what to say themselves. No one wanted to look guilty because they all knew Quincy from work but really didn't know him personally being that he didn't talk about anything but work when they were together. Ricky took the responsibility of calling Stephanie when he got in his car but was met with an immediate answering service, so he left a concerning message for her. He thought about calling Diamond or Smiley to check on her, but he didn't want to seem like he was prying into Stephanie's business. Ricky was almost home when he got a text from Stephanie saying,

"Thank you, I'll call you tomorrow."

He thought nothing of it and made his way to his apartment when he got a call from Melvin. As soon as Ricky answered his phone Melvin started telling him about what he found out about Quincy from one of the dancers,

"Dude now I know why he was acting like a little bitch earlier today. Q's wife went thru his phone and found text messages from a few different females in his phone, but Steph's text stood out because it was naked pics, freaky text and about times they hooked up. I'm guessing she confronted him about it and then he came to work pissed."

Ricky was listening to the whole thing but couldn't get out of his mind how distraught Stephanie must be after finding out that her so-called boyfriend unwillingly made her a side chick. He wanted to reach out to her again after hearing the full details but didn't want to be bothersome since he called her already. But the thing is, Stephanie sat on the floor of her darkened room covered in her own tears and was in desperate need of a caring shoulder to cry on.

## CHAPTER XI

Dancers all over the city and surrounding areas all packed in The Saenger Theatre on Canal Street. They all were there with their contestant number taped on for the audition and the opportunity to work at the Stagelight Gentleman's Club. Marcus was at the auditions with Eric, the newly appointed manager of The Rabbit Hole, to see the potential exotic performers when he seen two familiar faces. Stephanie was nervously waiting with Diamond for her turn to show off her talents on stage when Marcus walked up to them.

"So, you really going through with the audition? Just a bit of advice, don't get in your head, just relax and let it flow out. If you're as good a dancer as you are a waitress, you gone kill it", stated Marcus.

He continued to encourage Stephanie to do her best as they watched other dancers get themselves ready. The crowd of dancers varied from every category, from slim to BBW, from little people to basketball player height, from every race and even from female to male. Stephanie never realized how many dancers there were in the city auditioning and was a little overwhelmed with the idea that she might not get rewarded a spot at either one of the clubs. She sat there in her seat, with her head down, going over her routine when Diamond nudged her. When Stephanie looked up, she seen Sunshine walking with two other girls.

"She did say she was working with some new prospects for the club", stated Diamond as she was referring to the two ladies following behind Sunshine.

Stephanie just nodded her head in agreement but noticed how the judges of the event were all looking at Sunshine's protégés. She told Diamond that those two dancers are now the standard that everyone else must meet. Diamond assured her friend that she's a very good dancer and that she will surpass the judge's expectations. Stephanie felt she was a good dancer but didn't think good was enough to get in. They sat there watching the other performers put on an exhibition for the judges, noticing the novice from the pros and the artist from the frauds. Diamond's critique of the dancer's stance, form and even choice of music all had Stephanie thinking she's going to step on stage just to fail. Stephanie never really seen herself perform on stage, only thru the eyes of her friends and those compliments were not enough for her confidence. She watched as one of Sunshine's students walked on stage with a smile, told the judges her name and then head straight toward the pole in the middle of the platform. The little white girl was all bubbly with smiles, like a bobblehead doll but when the beat hit in the music she chose the smile disappeared and that bobblehead turned into a vixen. The sheer elevation the dancer produced shocked even Diamond, her sexuality poured out on stage as she carried out every stunt with ease and they watched attentively as she executed her 90 second performance without a flaw. Sunshine stood there like a proud mama as the performance came to an end and the audience applauded the show they just witnessed. Stephanie's nerves began to climb when one of the judges called her number over the sound system because she was the next act up. She started walking to the stage, but everything just seemed to go in slow motion and the only thing she could hear was her heartbeat. Diamond watched as her friend made her way to the judge's panel and could hear the whispers from other dancers wondering who is this new girl. Stephanie's heart was racing as she waited for the music to begin and as soon as the guitarist solo began, Diamond knew that everyone who didn't know the new girl was about to find out. The instrumental of the song "When Doves Cry" continued to play as the guitar solo sped up more and more.  The judges along with a lot of people in the theater haven't seen anyone dance off such an old school song in awhile. Stephanie climbed up to the top of the pole but when the guitar solo stopped and the beat of the song hit the speakers, she stunned the entire crowd. A simple release dropped Stephanie to the stage floor in a thunderous split. She then rose tantalizing the judges with erotic moves and sensual gestures unlike anything they've seen on that day. But the young woman on stage had so much musicality in her choreography that the rhythmic sounds of the classic song was welcomed with open arms. Sunshine looked as Stephanie produced a seamlessly perfect performance and knew this waitress was true competition for her two students. Sunshine watched while Stephanie continued her exhibition as she reached over her head and pulled herself up the pole and amazed everyone as she flipped upside down, only holding on with one hand. She then slid down, still hanging in that same position, legs spread wide open, facing the judges and spent around the pole landing on her feet. Stephanie remembered her friend's advice, purposely seduced every judge with her eyes as she continued her extravagant performance and all the while caressing her thick toned chocolate frame for everyone to enjoy. Diamond realized her friend was just about finished with her act, stood up to see Stephanie's final stunt and she didn't disappoint. Stephanie finished her presentation with a barrage of drops, twists and flips without touching the floor once, captivating her audience including the judges to the point of a standing ovation. The job was done, and she dropped to a curtsy towards the judges as she walked off the stage. Sunshine made her way over to where Diamond was and tried to find out how this waitress stayed under her radar until now. Diamond was so excited for her friend that she ran to her and hugged her so tight while the crowd still were clapping for her. Sunshine walked up to the two and congratulated Stephanie,

"Girl you did that. You came with that fire."

Stephanie thanked her as they walked off to wait for the judge's decision of the contestants. But no matter what the decisions was, for Diamond, the concerned look on the face of the industries proclaimed Queen was all the gratification she needed.


Doris and Alisha both went over to Leslie's new building to help her with a little clean-up project. She was so excited and proud of her little sister that Doris was more than happy to spend her off days helping Leslie.

"So, mama I get to be the receptionist at aunt Lez new shop right", asked Alisha as she checked out herself in the mirror.

Doris laughed at her youngest child as she informed her that the decision would be all up to her aunt but knew that Leslie wouldn't let Alisha work at her shop. Alisha was determined to have a new gig with the upcoming family business, so she resulted in using her brother as collateral,

"If I can't get Aunt Lez to say yes, I know Caleb gone let me work there."

"You already got a job, go to school and bring me home good grades", replied Doris.

The teenager wasn't trying to hear any sort of defeat in her quest for her first job as they pulled up to the building and seen Levi walking out the front door with a wheelbarrow full of trash. Levi waved at the two in the car as he dumped the debris in a large trash bin and made his way back inside. He must have told Leslie that they were outside because she ran outside to meet up with Doris and Alisha,

"Hey y'all, you ready to get dirty cause it's nothing but dust and dirt in there."

They all headed inside, and Alisha immediately noticed that this clean-up project was way more than she expected. Leslie knew her little niece wasn't trying to get her designer jogging suit dirty, handed her 20 dollars and sent her to the corner store,

"Allie go grab us some waters and bring me back my change."

The teen welcomed the task as she quickly headed out to grab everyone something from the convenience store up the street. Leslie took the time to show her big sister her vision of what the new delivery business would look like while they cleared out debris from the building. Doris was so proud of her sister's accomplishments and how she's changed things around but the phone call she was about to receive would bring her joy over the top. Alisha walked in with cold bottled waters and chips for everyone when Doris' cell began to ring, she looked at the number and realized it was Caleb calling from prison. After accepting the call Doris quickly called out her son's name,

"Caleb, hey baby."

"Mama, you do know I'm not a baby right", replied Caleb.

Doris just ignored his statement and continued to tell her only son that no matter how old he is he will always be her baby, right along with the rest of his siblings. Caleb laughed it off and started to ask his mother what plans she had for next weekend. Doris thought nothing of the question and started running down her normal list of tasks she usually does on the weekends. Caleb then asked,

"Well can you come pick me up that Friday so I can help you with all of that?"

Caleb's mother just stood there stuck on the phone speechless but everyone in the room could hear Caleb on the other end calling out to her,

"Mama, mama, mama you there?"

Leslie took the phone from a tearful Doris as she answered Caleb and found out the news her sister just heard that had her frozen in place.

"Boy we all coming get you, you best believe that. Stretched limo and all the Ramen noodles you can eat", replied a laughing Leslie.

Caleb made sure to let his aunt know he doesn't want to see not one more pack of noodles as long as he lives. He told his aunt the good news that he just received from his lawyer, that the judge and parole board reviewed his case and granted him an early release. Leslie was so excited to hear that her nephew would be back home sooner than she thought as she handed Doris back her phone. The clean up project had a whole new purpose for Leslie now because she wanted to have the building ready for when her nephew got back to the city. She wanted him to be able to show any and everyone it is possible to turn a negative into a positive with a little help. The process for a new beginning for her, Caleb and Levi were set on a fast track now.


Stephanie was chilling with her small circle of friends at Diamond's apartment, in the east, discussing what's next for the newly hired exotic dancer. Her performance was so good that the judges unanimously voted for her to be apart of the dancers hired by Stagelight Inc., the company in charge of the gentleman's club side of the casino.

"We gotta come up with a good stage name for you Steph", stated Smiley.

Keisha and Diamond blurted out a few tag names that didn't appeal to Stephanie at all. But after a numerous number of failed names got scratched off the list, Stephanie settled for the stage name "Chocolate Dream". Diamond's boyfriend Spice came over to drop off some smoothies for the girls when he asked,

"What y'all all huddled around plotting on?"

Diamond thanked her beau for the delivery with a kiss and explained to him the dilemma they were working on. Spice looked over at Stephanie and like a light switch going off in his head he replied,

"That's easy, her name should be Lotus."

Stephanie thought about it and the more she said it in her head the more attractive the stage name "Lotus" became for her. After Spice walked off to the kitchen Keisha pointed out a problem with the new name Stephanie fell in love with stating that people may confuse it with the bug locust instead of the flower lotus. Spice heard Keisha's concern and walked back in the living room with the girls and with an event announcer's voice replied,

"Coming to the stage, we have that erotic and exotic flower, Lotus."

Everybody heard the announcement and fell in love with the name along with Stephanie. She finally had the perfect name and Smiley started to show her a great way to get some publicity before she even touches the stage. Stephanie was amazed when she seen Smiley's paid social media sites and the amount of people that pay her for personal pics or videos. Diamond even showed her the "premium" site that Spice manages for her stating,

"Girl unless it's a video call half the time he answers the DM's and the guys be thinking it's me talking to them."

"Stop it! He's cool with you doing that", replied Keisha as she scrolled through Diamond's "premium pics".

Diamond called for Spice to come in the living room with them, he assured them all that his lover's paid sites don't bother him one bit and even pointed out that some of the newer pics he captured himself. Stephanie truly admired Diamond and Spice's relationship, especially after dealing with the lie she thought was a blossoming relationship with Quincy. Except for placing drink orders at the bar, she hadn't spoken to him since his wife came to the club that night. He was just another guy on the street to Stephanie and she kept her distance from him as much as she could. Smiley pulled Stephanie off to the side while Keisha and Diamond were looking through some potential risqué pics to post on her IG page.

"Steph I wanna ask you a favor", whispered Smiley.

Stephanie was all ears for her friend as Smiley began to tell her that she was going on a trip to Tijuana to have breast and buttocks augmentations done there. Stephanie was a little confused as to why her friend would do that to herself but didn't want to judge her in anyway. She felt that Smiley had a perfect body frame in her eyes but listening to how excited Smiley was about the adventure and how she wants to come back looking amazing, Stephanie couldn't crush her ideas with doubting questions. Smiley began to tell her what favor she needed from her,

"I'm a be gone for like three weeks and I just need someone to check on my mama for me. I would ask Diamond but she's hell bent on me not going all together to get the surgery and I don't need nobody judging me right now. This is something I wanna do, for me."

"Girl you gone come back with watermelon titties and two basketballs in your back pocket", jokingly replied Stephanie as she hugged her friend.

The two went back in the living room with the other girls as they all relaxed watching a movie when Stephanie got a phone call from her mother.

Ricky sat in Marcus' office going over resumes of probable candidates for his bouncer crew, disappointed in some of the potentials because of their views of the business, when this massive muscular figure walked through the office door. He recognized the guy from the gym he frequently visits with his workout clients and Ricky knew the guy had a very strong presence. Ricky was looking for guys that had intimidating looks about them to work with him at the new club, but he also wanted someone that would look after the dancer. He knew that most people have a misconception of the dancers that perform, and most men look at them as objects and not human beings. Ricky needed men that would not only protect the interest of the club but also protect the performers and treat them with the respect that they deserve. He wondered if Tyson, the large gentleman sitting in front of him, was the caliber of bouncer he was looking for. Tyson greeted Ricky with a firm handshake as he took a seat in front of the office desk and they both went over his previous employment.

"So, Tyson, I see you use to work at the cabaret on Bourbon. What made you leave there, cause I know they bouncers get paid good over there", asked Ricky.

Tyson put his head down, like he was embarrassed to give the reason but replied,

"I broke a customer's arm after he got a little too physical with one of the girls. I tried to explain to management that the guy was harassing and grabbing on one of the dancers, before he even took a swing at me. But they wasn't trying to hear it and let me go, even after a few of the dancers came to my defense."

"Hey, I'm a bouncer so I understand the situations we get into and management seem to turn their backs on us when shit goes wrong, especially shit we can't avoid", responded Ricky.

Tyson and Ricky went over the rest of his work history as they both found out they had a lot in common besides the obvious gym life they shared. Ricky seen all that he needed to see and offered Tyson a spot on his crew as one of his bouncers when Marcus walked in to see the two powerhouses still talking. Ricky introduced Tyson to Marcus as one of the club's newest bouncers and the two guys started laughing, which caught Ricky off guard. Marcus explained to Ricky that Tyson is his little cousin that wanted to get a job with the club as he stated,

"I told him that he needed to come in and convince you that he could do the job, that I couldn't get him the position. My Lil cuz got a bad rap at the cabaret and very few clubs wanted to take a chance on him as a bouncer, but it looks like he convinced you that he could do it."

"Marcus you know how I am, you gotta prove to me that you can't do the job. I believe anybody can be a bouncer if they crazy enough, but it takes a different kind of dude to work in this industry and Tyson showed me that", responded Ricky.

Marcus poured up three glasses of whiskey as Ricky gathered up his resumes of the guys he selected for his crew. He was confident of the selection of men he put together, all having a specific quality that will melt good with the other.

Doris and Alisha just got home after helping Leslie with cleaning up her shop when they heard a knock at the door. When she opened the door there stood Doris' estranged husband Calvin, tattered clothes and all with the stench of spoiled onions. The smell pushed Doris back a bit as she covered her nose,

"Why you keep showing up to my house unannounced? What the hell do you want Calvin?"

"I was in the neighborhood and I wanted to know if you needed your grass cut", replied Calvin.

Doris just stood there wondering how her ex got to this point in his life, how he went from a very promising career to be a vagrant in search for hand outs. She just slowly closed the door and walked off but seen her teenage daughter just standing there with a saddened look on her face. Alisha always had hope that her father would come around, better himself and return back home but after seeing the shell of a man that was standing at their front door, she knew that notion was far from coming true.

"Mama, please don't take this as I'm blaming you at all because I know he's a grown man and made his own decisions. But how did you let him get that bad? He was your husband. You couldn't stop him, you couldn't control the situation?", asked Alisha.

Doris was thrown for a loop being asked that by her youngest because she has asked herself that several times over. She wanted to lash out being accused of not saving her marriage but instead replied,

"Baby you can't pull a person away from who they are. It only takes a person one moment for them to show you who they really are and it's up to you to accept it or not. Now can that person change who they are? Of course, they can but it's completely on that person and no one else can do it for them. Baby I loved your father with everything in me, but he chose being high over his family and I wasn't going to let him take all of you down with him."

Doris was never one to bash or talk down about her children's father in front of them or to them because she didn't want to sound like the bitter wife. But when it came to her kids, she held nothing back when it comes to protecting them, especially ever since Caleb's incarceration she's been extra protective. Doris was relaxing with her youngest, going over what they need to do before her oldest comes home when she got a call from one of her supervisors and Leslie's old school mate.

"Hey Doris, I know this is the weekend and I'm sorry for calling you on your off day, but I needed to talk to you before you come into the office Monday morning", stated Cedric Daniels.

Doris assuming it's another project the administration board came up with for everyone else to complete reluctantly listened as she replied,

"It's no problem, what's going on."

Cedric then informed Doris that she will oversee their whole department while he takes a leave of absence because of some family issues. Doris asked why her other supervisor, Kevin Talport, wouldn't oversee the department figuring, he should be next in line. But Cedric let Doris know she was the best selection for the role because everyone looks up to her already as a leader and that Kevin would be taking control of other departments in Cedric's absence. Doris hesitantly accepted the challenge but told Cedric she would do her best to keep the department running as smooth as always.

CHAPTER XII


Saturday morning finally came, and the Crawford household was wide awake with so much excitement.  The last time Alisha seen her big brother in person she was eight years old and she took pride in making Caleb's welcome home banner as she hung it up in the living room, so it could be the first thing he sees. Stephanie was in his room making sure everything was perfect, from the bed being crisp to the carpet being freshly cleaned. The week Doris found out that her only son is finally coming home she wanted him to have a fresh new start, so she went and bought him an all new wardrobe accompanied with all new matching shoes. Leslie even went ahead and contacted his parole officer to let them know Caleb would have a job as soon as he comes home. She was so ready for her nephew to get back on his feet and become a respected businessman. Doris couldn't keep still as she darted through the house, making sure everything was perfect for her son's arrival and patience was running thin waiting on her sister to arrive with the limo they ordered to pick up Caleb. Stephanie watched as her mother looked out the window for what felt like the 100th time and she had to comfort her anxiety,

"Mama sit down and relax, Aunt Lez will be here."

"I know she is baby, I'm just ready to go get my lil boy out of that place", replied Doris.

Stephanie laughed as she explained to her mother,

"You do know that's a grown man that's coming home and not that 17-year-old kid you remember, right?"

Doris knew her daughter was speaking the truth and was a little nervous as to what type of man she was going to encounter after spending 7 years in a maximum-security federal prison for a non-violent crime. Doris wasn't the only one nervous about the home coming as Caleb sat in the release tank waiting for one of the C. O's to call his name. He knew his family was so ready for him to come back home but Caleb wondered if he was ready himself. Stephanie and Alisha tried to keep him up to date on how things have changed since he first went to prison with their weekly letters. But nothing really can compare to actually being there versus reading it in a short letter. Caleb knew first he would have to change the crowd he use to run the streets with. He had no idea what his aunt Leslie had put together for them both, so Caleb's state of mind was to get a job and become a model citizen, but he knew that task would be hard as hell for an ex-con. Leslie finally pulled up, Doris shot out the front door like a track star, as Stephanie and Alisha followed suit to the limo. The driver let the ladies all enter, closed the door behind them and proceeded to drive to their destination, which was three and a half hours away, where Caleb was patiently waiting for them.

Levi was at the shop while Leslie and her family were going pick up Caleb when his old partner Mook showed up. Mook was dropping off some donated furniture his supervisor was giving Leslie to help start her business. Levi was surprised to see his former fellow street hustler but pleased to see him doing good for himself.

"Man, what are we doing? Back in the day we would be trying to see if this place had any security cameras", stated Mook.

The two old friends both smiled as they chuckled to one another,

"The more cameras, the more cash, get in there and rob they ass."

Their mentality back then was if someone would pay so much for multiple security cameras, that they are making sure no one is walking out with their money. Levi helped Mook roll in a few file cabinets and two large office desks as they talked about old friends from the neighborhood. With concern in his voice Levi asked,

"Say round, how ya son doing since he been out of the hospital?"

"I gotta say one thing, that boy makes me proud of him everyday", replied Mook.

He told Levi that his son is fastened to a wheelchair for the rest of his life because of the amount of damage his spine took in the attack. Mook even admitted that he knew his son wasn't the best kid on the street and have been arrested on several times for some petty crimes. Most people would have felt guilty being in the position that Levi was in, but he knew the fact that his old friend's son being fixed to a wheelchair for the rest of his life was the lesser of two evils. The two continued shooting the shit with each other when Mook mentioned that he was a little upset that the police closed the case on his son's attack, that they didn't have anymore information on who assaulted Mook's  son and that the incident felt gang related.

"Man, these little gangs have been getting out of hand lately but I can't see them just closing out the case with no suspects", stated Levi.

Mook just stood there silent for a minute and replied,

"Nigga I'm just glad my son is alive at this moment cause his potna ain't have a chance in hell, they put him down like a rabid dog in the street. But let me find out who did this and the old me coming out for real, ya heard me. I'm trying to slit both them niggas throats, ya heard me."

Levi figured as long as Mook was clueless to who did it, then they would all be good. Plus keeping Mook close would assure that nothing would point toward him or Leslie, being that the cops had no suspects. The guys relaxed for awhile after getting all the desks situated in the shop and then Mook left to head back to work. Levi was finally able to release his grasp from the .45 that was tucked in his waistband the entire time Mook was at the shop because he knew if his old partner knew the truth it would turn out bad really quick. He sat behind one of the desks and lit a cigarette to calm his nerves as he looked over what he had left to clean up before Leslie got back.


Ricky was meeting Marcus at the new casino and club ship to go over schedules when he got a text from Sunshine congratulating him on his position. He was kind of pleased that they were able to stay cordial with each other after the breakup as he texted her back thanking her. Ricky knew he would have to see Sunshine on a regular being that she's a main attraction for the company, but he tried to focus on doing what he does best and that's security. He walked into the casino for the first time in total amazement as the architecture and décor took him back. The old fashion New Orleans style scenic decoration covered every aspect of the city, from the brick layered streets to the gas fed streetlights of the city's old charm that attracted visitors for years. Ricky caught himself becoming a tourist as he gazed at how the walkways were named after popular streets in New Orleans and how some of the walls were fixed with Mardi Gras floats built right into them, the sight was simply astonishing.

"It kinda catches you off guard the first time you see it, the bitch pretty ain't it", stated Marcus as he walked up to Ricky.

The two men walked to the back as Ricky continued to be surprised at other magnificent pieces of artistry, heading to the club area. Marcus toured through the club section of the ship and at that point Ricky realized he had his work cut out for him. The club was in a word, huge but very manageable to secure. Stagelight was similar to The Rabbit Hole with its wide-open floor plan but the gentleman's club had three large stages, four fully stocked bars, a DJ booth that looked over the entire club and the same dazzling architecture as the casino. Ricky noticed there was just one way in and out of the club with the exception of employee access from the back. Security cameras canvassed the entire grounds which perplexed Ricky a little as he pointed it out to Marcus,

"I thought people like to be discreet in establishments like this. What's up with all the cameras?"

"The banks wouldn't agree to the loans if they weren't installed, protecting their investment", replied Marcus.

Ricky sat at one of the bars just visually scoping out the club going through his head where he would have bouncers stationed and the areas each bouncer would cover on a nightly basis. He handed Marcus the schedule he already had made up and told him that his guys would be ready on opening day which was a couple of days away. Marcus started talking about The Rabbit Hole and how he feels about their new headliner that's already making waves on social media.

"Melvin mention to me that Steph is putting her feet in the water. You think she ready for that kinda change? Being a waitress and being a dancer is totally different", stated Ricky.

Marcus looked at him with a devilish grin,

"Say round, they better be ready for her. You didn't see the audition, that girl got pure raw talent and if she keeps her head on straight, she can't do nothing but make big bags."

Ricky was curious at the fact that Marcus was giving Stephanie such strong compliments and he really wanted to see what the new dancer had. He compared every dancer to Sunshine because her shows were performances and not just any everyday strip tease, with some ass shaking.

Diamond was chilling at Spice's tattoo studio when two of his clients walked in. She knew the two guys had to be important because Spice opened his shop early just to work on them. One guy reminded her of Ricky because he was just a big massive muscular guy and the other guy was a well dressed calm mild manner gentleman, dressed in designer clothing. When Spice walked up to them, she knew he really knew the guys well as they all greeted each other with a hug like you would do a brother or family member. After the guys all stood there getting acquainted with each other, Spice turned around and introduced Diamond to them,

"This my girl Diamond. Diamond this my brother Devin and my cousin Khori."

Diamond just smiled with the cutest smile as she reached out her hand and shook theirs,

"Devin? You look like you should be on somebody's front four defensive line, like for real."

The guys all laughed at her comment as Spice replied,

"He is, he's one of Denver's best pass rushers ever."

Diamond was a little embarrassed that she didn't recognized the guy and apologized but Devin wasn't bothered by it one bit. Devin even cracked a joke that his cousin Khori was more popular than him and no one recognizes him. Khori looked over to his cousin as he laughed at Devin's remark,

"Semaj, can we go get our tatts now cause ya brother trying to clown me."

Diamond just sat back with Khori and watched as her beau started working on his brother Devin's forearm. She was curious as to what Devin meant by Khori being more popular than a professional football player and had to ask him what he does as a profession, his reply had her in awe. Diamond didn't know until just then that she was standing in the midst of a business giant in the Marijuana industry. She heard about a guy named Kush that came from New Orleans and started his own dispensary in Colorado, but she never figured she would meet him, besides Spice never mentioned he was related to him. Khori then asked Diamond what she does for a living and she replied,

"I'm an exotic dancer at The Rabbit Hole. Y'all need to come through cause my home girl debut is tonight, and she is the truth."

"My dawg Ricky works there, he's a bouncer. Yeah, we all may have to make an appearance", responded Devin.

Spice's brother and cousin continued getting themselves comfortable with the rare jewel named Diamond, as they shared embarrassing stories of when they all were little kids. They also filled her in on the tattoos they were getting and the heart felt meaning behind them as Khori pulled out his cell, scrolled thru his photo gallery and showed off beautiful pics of his little sister who passed away three years ago, like a proud father.

"I remember that horrible day because me and my mama was at that church festival when it happened. We even attended the funeral, I'm so sorry for all of your lost", replied Diamond.

Everybody kinda got a little quiet after that but Spice's animated character brought life back to the room with one of his stories as he told them about a crazy client, he had one day. The atmosphere was filled with laughter and jokes as Spice finished the artistic murals, he created for his family members.

Caleb was sitting in the release tank with his head down when he heard the C.O. shout out,

"Caleb Crawford, time to go! Grab ya shit."

The last time he was this nervous was when he first was locked up in a jail cell and the closer he got to the door the more the butterflies filled his stomach. Caleb had his one bag, with all his possessions, in his hand as he opened the double doors and as soon as he seen his lovely mother Doris standing there the nervousness simply vanished. Alisha didn't even wait for the guards to finish signing Caleb out of the system before she ran up to her big brother and wrap her arms around his neck. The sight of her brother was blurred with a collection of joyful tears as Stephanie just stood there silent, watching Caleb hug his mother and little sister. After receiving all the "miss you" hugs and kisses from Doris and Alisha, Caleb looked over at his sibling,

"Steph, you just gone stand over there or do I have to come over to you?"

 Stephanie rushed over to her big brother and hugged him so tight,

"I've missed you so much."

They all headed outside to leave but Caleb wasn't ready for the surprise of his aunt Leslie standing in front of a stretched-out Mercedes waiting for him to come out.

"Boy, if you don't get yo ass over here and give me a hug", shouted Leslie.

Caleb was completely overwhelmed with emotion as he just absorbed all the love he was getting from his family. He stood there taking it all in as the sun rays beamed down onto his skin and the fresh "free world" air filled his lungs. Right at that moment Caleb had finally felt relief, that everything is going to be alright and that he would never do anything that would jeopardize his freedom again. They all got into the limo and the driver started the four-hour drive back to New Orleans to the shop Leslie had created for them. Caleb looked over his shoulder to catch one last glance of the place he knew as home for the past seven years and Doris whispered in his ear,

"Never again baby. Never again will you have to deal with a place like that."

Caleb just nodded in agreement and laid his head on his mother's shoulder like he did when he was little. Alisha, being the teen that she is, started talking to her big brother about prison documentaries she's seen on TV and asking him if he ever been in a riot or prison fight like the ones from the shows. Caleb just chuckled and shook his head as he replied,

"It's nothing like that. True there's times situations come up but it's mostly just dead time of you being stuck in a cell 23 hours a day, only coming out to rec and shower."

"So, you never had to shank nobody", asked a curious Alisha.

Caleb burst out laughing with a definitive, "No!" and Doris cut the conversation short,

"Let's talk about something else and leave that prison behind us like it is right now."

Leslie was on the phone with Levi making sure everything
was ready for Caleb when they all arrived and got off the
phone after affectionately saying,

"See you in a few baby, bye."

A little shocked at hearing his aunt show affection to what
he could only imagine was a man on the other line, Caleb
had to ask after seeing this blushing smile on her face.
Leslie's answer stunned him even more as his mother
confirmed it and Caleb couldn't say anything but,

"Levi? Levi, Levi? Like Levi from round the way, Levi."

Leslie couldn't do anything but laugh at her nephew
because she never could have imagined that she would be
with someone like him either. Caleb knew Levi from the
hood and knew he was a man you didn't want to have as an
enemy but if he made his aunt happy, he was content with
it. As they all just enjoyed Caleb being back with the
family, Alisha whispered to her big sister,

"You still going to the club tonight?"

"You gotta go serve drinks tonight? I'm coming. I haven't
been to a strip club, like never", replied Caleb.

Doris just looked out the window of the limousine as she
stated,

"She serving something but it ain't drinks."

Stephanie's mother still wasn't comfortable with her
daughter becoming a dancer but after a long conversation
on the financial benefits Stephanie would receive from
being a dancer, Doris reluctantly complied to the idea.
After hearing her mother's comment Stephanie stared at her
with smiling embarrassment as she told her big brother that

her debut of being a dancer was tonight. Caleb sat silent for a minute as he attempted to let the information sink in and Leslie had to break the silence,

"Nephew, it's not what you think. She's not walking around completely naked with a bunch of guys groping all over her."

Stephanie could see all over her brother's face that he was totally against the idea of his little sister taking off her clothes in front of people. She explained to him like she did with their mother that she's dancing to pay for school and that she refuses to let anyone stop her from completing her goal of becoming a Physical Therapist. Caleb just listening to her plead her case and hesitantly acknowledged his sister's strategy to accomplish her goals but had one question,

"Isn't that the same club where those dudes got beat and killed? What if that shit happens again? I don't know about this."

Leslie and Stephanie just looked at each other, knowing that situation wouldn't occur again no time soon. Stephanie assured her brother that she would be and has been extremely careful ever since then. Caleb just shook his head as he looked down to the floor of the limo but knew his sister was set on being a stripper and nothing he say would deter her from that. Doris quickly changed the subject because she could see the situation was bothering them both,

"So, you ready for this dinner? I'm frying fish, shrimp, chicken and I'm making cabbage, white beans, cornbread, potato salad. Oh, and I'm making that cheesecake you like so much."

Caleb's eyes just got bigger and bigger as his mother continued to run down the list of foods, she was going to prepare for him, it really felt like a Thanksgiving meal but it was everything he asked for. The situation with his little sister becoming a stripper was pushed to the back and Caleb just sat back, enjoyed the ride and his family for the time being.

CHAPTER XIII

The Crawford family had all settled in after a spectacular dinner Doris had prepared for her son's home coming and it was time for Stephanie to prepare herself for her debut performance. She was a little nervous but knew this was the time to get all the nervousness out before she even stepped foot in the club. Caleb walked in her room as she was stuffing changing clothes in a duffle bag and just sat on her bed. He was awkwardly quiet as Stephanie was shuffling back and forth when she had to break the silence,

"Dude! You just gone sit there and not say anything? Just spit it out already. Not like I don't already know what you're gonna say."

"Really you don't", replied Caleb.

He sat there and told Stephanie how proud he is of her and how he understood that she had to do what she had to do in order to get where she wanted to be. The support from her brother was all Stephanie needed because her nervous chitters simply melted away after hearing his words. She sat down next to Caleb on the bed, laying her head on his shoulder and Caleb jokingly told her that she could come work at the shop with him and their aunt. A car horn was heard out front and Stephanie just laughed as she reached for her bag,

"No offense, but I don't think y'all can afford me."

Caleb walked with his little sister to the front door and noticed her best friend Keisha waiting outside for her.

Keisha seen Caleb's chiseled frame standing in the doorway and became instantly flustered as she whispered to herself,

"Shit! Prison has been good to this nigga."

Caleb walked out to Keisha as she was sitting in her car and at that point realized she wasn't the little skinny redbone he remembered. Resting in the driver seat was a honey caramel slim sexy frame, dressed in a short plaid "schoolgirl" skirt, accompanied with a white satin button down blouse and two pigtails to match.

"Now where do you think you're going dressed like this", asked Caleb.

Keisha eased her skirt up just a little revealing her long smooth mellow yellow legs as she arched her back pushing her perky "B" cup breast pass her low-cut satin blouse and with a giggle replied,

"I'm trying to find me a daddy."

Caleb was tempted to respond but held back as he just let the girls head out for the night,

"Y'all be careful out there."

"Why don't you join us? It could be fun", replied Keisha.

Stephanie gave her bestie a serious death stare after hearing her friend invite Caleb to tag along. But he declined the offer stating he is not ready or willing to see his sister on stage, even though hanging with the sexy Keisha would be a much needed treat. The girls backed out the driveway as Caleb stood there watching them pull off and Keisha couldn't help but to acknowledge Stephanie's older brother's features,

"Bitch! Caleb done got fine as hell! I know he yo brother and all but damn."




    Caleb sat with the lights off in the den just going over the events of the day when his baby sister walked in,

"Why you sitting here in the dark big head?"

"Enjoying silence for the first time in a long time", sarcastically replied Caleb as he gestured for Alisha to come sit with him.

She was eager to spend a little quality time with her big brother, being that the last time they ever were together was when she was in elementary. Alisha was like a motorboat just rambling on and on about her track meets, school and just everyday life as a teenager. Caleb was enjoying every bit of it, absorbing it all in when Doris walked in,

"Girl give your brother a break. He just got here and you're burning his ear off."

Caleb didn't mind the long conversation and was more than happy to hear everything Alisha had to talk about. What he really was concerned about was Stephanie taking the direction she was taking. Even though he had given her his blessings, being the big brother, he is, Caleb was a little uneasy about his little sister becoming a stripper. He and his mother talked it over, but Doris' comment put a different perspective on the situation,

"You and I both know your sister is strong willed when it comes to accomplishing something. She trained really hard for this and I myself never seen any of her dancing, but her friends said she's really good. This is what she wants to do, cause she refuses to take any handouts to pay for school and she's sticking with it. All I can do is pray and support her as much as I can."

Caleb listened as his mother went on about how Stephanie never missed a day of school or a day of work. Right then he realized, he himself has a lot of work ahead of him with the new shop he and his aunt will be running. Caleb promised to his mother that he will never jeopardize his freedom again with illegal shipments and Doris knew her son meant every word. Doris went off to bed while Caleb stayed in the den just relaxing on the sofa thinking about how he was ready to start back working.

Melvin was out front as always checking out the line of customers that were waiting to come in the club when he got a call from Evelyn,

"Hey, I just got a call from Lotus and she should be here in a few minutes. Is it possible that one of your guys meet her at the back door?"

Melvin was more than happy to do that for her as he told Evelyn he would be back there for her himself. Evelyn was the club's "Den Mother" and she made sure the dancers were always taken care of . She was an ex-exotic dancer herself, who knew the pressures of being a performer and whatever it took to just make their day go by smooth she tried her best to have it done. Now Evelyn catered to the dancers, but she wasn't a push over, if her "girls" were out of line or out of pocket in any way they had her to answer to and she had no problem cutting a dancer loose. Melvin waited at the back door with one of his bouncers for Lotus' arrival when he seen Keisha's car pull up. Stephanie stepped out with her bag and greeted Melvin with her usual hug,

"Hey, you big teddy bear."

"Hey girlie, tonight's the night. You ready", stated Melvin.

He grabbed her bag from her, gestured for Keisha to come in with them, told his bouncer to go park Keisha's car for her and escorted the girls inside. Melvin walked Stephanie to the dancers' locker room where Evelyn was waiting and had Keisha go take a seat at the bar so she could see the show. Diamond had just got back in the locker room when Stephanie arrived, and she was over excited to see her. Evelyn knew they were the best of friends so she brought Stephanie straight over to Diamond so that she could get herself ready.

"I have your music list and I'll give that to Felt-Tip. So just let me know when you're ready and I can get him to announce you. Now being that this is your debut, the club waived your house fee, so everything you make tonight is all yours. I can't wait to see you work baby, Diamond can't stop talking about you", stated Evelyn.

Stephanie just sat there listening ever so attentively making sure she doesn't miss one thing and Diamond eased her mind by joking around with Evelyn about the club waiving her fees also. Stephanie finally started getting herself together, pulling out the first outfit she was going to wear along with a bottle of cocoa butter scented baby oil and her high heel platform sandals or in other words stripper shoes.

She took all her clothes off while she sat at her dressing table and began oiling her entire body just like Diamond taught her. Stephanie couldn't help but to look over at the other dancers and wonder if they were as nervous as she was for their first time on stage. Diamond let her know that she got Spice to bring his brother and cousin to the club to see her perform,

"Girl one is a professional football player and the other one got that legal weed money. But they cool people though, I hung with them all day, laughing and shit."

Stephanie was listening to her friend but her main concern was making sure that her top was tied up right and that her heels were strapped on correctly. She stood there in front of a stand-up mirror looking over every inch of her body making sure everything was in place before she asked Diamond,

"Ok, how do I look?"

"The question is, would you fuck you? Cause bitch, right now I would fuck you. With ya fine ass", replied Diamond.

Stephanie took that as she looks good and went to go tell Evelyn she was ready.

Keisha was sitting at the bar waiting to see her friend step on stage when Quincy tapped her on the shoulder. She had been trying to ignore him the whole time she was there, but he made it his purpose to make his way over to where she was sitting,

"What you doing in here?"

Keisha really didn't want anything to do with Quincy after how the situation ended with him and Stephanie, but she told him she was there for her friend. No one really told Quincy that Stephanie was training to be a dancer and he had no clue that her first performance was tonight. He tried to make small talk, asking about how things are going with Stephanie and school but all he could get was a cold shoulder. Right when Quincy realized it was a loss cause in trying to talk to Keisha, her exotic friend Diamond rushed up to her, eyes as wide as ever and a joyous smile,

"C'mon! She's next."

The girls headed over to where Spice was sitting with his family. He had brought his brother Devin, his cousin Khori and his uncles Cedric and Kareem with him to see Diamond's friend appear on stage for the first time. Keisha sat down next to Spice as he introduced her to everyone, and Diamond sat on his lap waiting for the DJ to introduce their bestie to the audience. In all the excitement Keisha noticed they were missing a member and asked,

"Where's Smiley? She's gonna miss it."

"She's still not feeling 100% after coming back from Mexico but she told me to record it so that she can see her show", replied Diamond.

A spotlight came on and focused directly to the back of the stage and the DJ came across the speaker system,

"This ya boy DJ Felt-Tip and we have a special performance for you tonight here at The Rabbit Hole. Coming to you for the first time ever on any stage I'd like to introduce you to this chocolate diva and exotic flower, Lotus!"

The curtains parted with the artist Lotus standing there for all the audience to see the exquisite specimen of a woman, shining in the spotlight's glow. Her freshly manicured dreds draped over her chocolate shoulders, as the vibrant yellow and red two-piece bikini contoured her thick immaculate figure that demanded the eyes of everyone. The gentleman's club has seen it's share of sexy, fine, sensual and erotic performers but Lotus was all of that plus more, she was the definition of alluring. The music began to play thru the sound system, and it caught Cedric off guard because of the old school sound,

 "Say man, she is not about to dance to Silk Lose Control, what she know about that?"

Diamond leaned over by Cedric and told him that most of Lotus music selection is 90's R&B or Hip Hop,

"She said she really feels that style of music, old soul I guess."

As the music played on everyone's attention was glued to the stage, as Lotus jumped into a handspring, spreading her legs wide, slowly spinning around so that everyone could see her, and she did exactly what she was taught by her friend. Lotus found one client and focused completely on him, it was the familiar and kind face of Kareem that she danced for, keeping a strong sexual eye contact the entire time. Lotus climbed to the very top of the pole, locked her glistening toned legs around it, in a cross-ankle release and hung upside down as she slowly slid down with her arms spread wide open into an bowed handstand. The friendly pimp Memphis, Stephanie use to always take care of when she was a waitress, couldn't help but to walk up to the platform and throw a hundred ones at the new dancer.

Other guys in the club followed suit and began tossing money on stage as the exotic flower danced. Lotus got down on all fours and crawled to the edge of the stage, gesturing for Kareem to come to her. Resisting her command seemed ridiculous as he walked up to her and she wrapped her legs around his waist, pulling him closer to her. As she slow grinded to the music, staring Kareem deep into his eyes, Lotus pulled loose the string that held her top on, revealing two succulent chocolate 32D sized breast that screamed for attention and then she laid back onto the stage caressing her body in front of him. Kareem reached into his pocket and pulled out a small wad of cash, sprinkling it all over Lotus' sensual body. Right as the song was coming to its end, another pimp Stephanie use to always take care of, Lance walked up to the stage with his little crew and they tore the bands off of two stacks of ones throwing the money in the air on stage. Diamond was beyond ecstatic for her friend's first time on stage and shouted her name so that everyone knew who she was. But Lotus' performance wasn't done just yet when the DJ changed the tempo with an upbeat hip hop song. An old school Uncle Luke song blared through the speakers and the crowd went into an uproar as Lotus blessed the stage with a thunderous split that transitioned into some strong pussy popping. Keisha stood up and threw twenty ones at her and shouted,

"Face down ass up BITCH! That's my bitch!"

Lotus continued to twerk and execute acrobatic spin tricks on the pole, amazing her audience. The crowd cheered as Lotus finished her performance in another split and then stood up to drop in a curtsy with a smile. Devin was thoroughly impressed with Lotus' coming out performance that he walked up to the stage while she was collecting all of her money off the floor and placed two stacks of ten-dollar bills at her feet. But his cousin Khori couldn't be out shown so he pulled out three stacks of ten-dollar bills and handed it to the new exotic dancer. Khori smiled at her as he spoke,

"Baby girl, you are a beast on that stage. I couldn't take my eyes off you."

"Thank you", replied a blushing Lotus.

That comment alone was all the gratitude she needed to let her know she did a great job.


Leslie was home going over some invoices from different vendors she was working with to start up her shipping company when Levi came out of the bathroom from taking a shower. He wrapped his arms around her waist and began kissing her on the neck when she replied,

"Baby, I'm all dirty."

"Well let me clean you", responded Levi.

Those five little words put away all the paperwork Leslie was reading over and began unbuttoning her clothes as she made her way to the bathroom. Levi helped her remove the rest of her clothing, walked her into the shower and they both stood there in the warm spray of the shower head. The warm water seemed to just wash the day away as Levi caressed her wet body with a soapy towel. Leslie leaned back into Levi's chest as she could feel his masculinity press against her back and his manhood rest right in the crack of her ass. His arms wrapped around her as his hands cradled her soapy breast and he kissed her neck. She just stood there still while he wiped down every inch of her, only moving when he motioned for her to turn around. The whole time Levi hadn't tried anything sexual, even when he reached between Leslie's thick thighs to wipe down her plush pussy, but it all was extremely sensual all the same. Leslie had never felt a feeling like this before, of a man completely catering to her and Levi never knew he was capable of any of this but they both brought out something amazing when they're together. After her relaxing shower and Levi towel dried her off, they both went laid in the bed totally nude just enjoying one another's presence. The peaceful atmosphere was shattered with a bang on the door and the sensual relaxed Levi disappeared and a raging lion appeared with a .45 magnum attached to his hand. Levi rushed to the door, unfathomed by what may be on the other side of the door and shouted,

"Who is it!"

A quivering man's voice came from the other side asking for Leslie and at that point Levi swung the door open pointing the gun in the guy's face. Leslie stood at her bedroom door looking while Levi stood there completely naked in front of the mystery male but when she looked over his shoulder, she seen it was only Calvin, her drug addict brother-in-law. Leslie put on a robe as she walked up to the front door,

"What the hell do you want Calvin?"

"I would tell you if you get this big dick barbarian to get this hand cannon out my face", replied Calvin.

Levi looked over at Leslie and she nodded for him to let Calvin speak, so he lowered his pistol as he walked away to put on some clothes. Leslie asked Calvin again why he was at her house and Calvin began to cry stating that he wanted to go see his son. He began telling Leslie a drawn-out story of how he wanted to go see Caleb when he got home but he knew Doris wouldn't allow him to come to the house.

"That's my only son and he's finally out of jail. I just wanna see him", stated Calvin as he staggered back and forth at Leslie's front door.

Leslie was no fool and she could see that Calvin was high as hell, but she knew if she tell him no that she would never get rid of him. So, she told Calvin to come by the shop tomorrow and she'll see if she can get Caleb to come by. He thanked her but in Calvin fashion he began to ask her for some money but right then Levi came from the back room, gun pointing straight forward and ran Calvin straight out the house. Leslie couldn't do anything but cry laughing but Levi didn't think it was funny at all as he responded,

"Say man, that dude was tripping for real. He had to go, my bad."

"Well you come apologize to me in the bedroom, you big dick barbarian", replied a laughing Leslie as she dropped her robe to the floor.

CHAPTER XIV


It's been a month since the artist known as Lotus made her first appearance at The Rabbit Hole and the buzz was traveling through the industry that the reigning Queen of exotic dancing in the city may get dethroned. Stephanie knew she had a talent for seduction and performance, but she never looked at herself as being competition to Sunshine. Diamond on the other hand knew her friend was exactly the one that could dominate the stage to the point of taking the spotlight from the so-called diva. The exotic dancer with a 20th Century flare that brings life to "old school" music was exactly the refreshing feel the industry needed being that the company just opened its casino and gentleman's club on the lake. Caleb finally was cool with Stephanie dancing but couldn't be in the club when his sister was performing and purposely stayed clear from the clubs when his little sister was there. Marcus felt the time was coming to add Lotus to the roster of The Stagelight Gentleman's Club but didn't want to make Sunshine feel some type of way. He talked it over with Stephanie and she was semi excited about the move but her main focus was on her dear friend Smiley. She had been dealing with pains ever since she arrived back from Tijuana, a month ago. Stephanie was nervous that her friend had done some serious damage to her body and Smiley was scared that the entire surgery was all for nothing. Stephanie was sitting at the foot of the bed, with concern written all over her face, as Smiley laid on her stomach with ice packs laying on her ass and lower back. She sat there and watched as her friend flinched in pain, Stephanie knew something wasn't right.

Smiley kept saying she was okay, all the while chewing 800mg pain pills like they were candy and sweating bricks in a 70-degree air conditioned room.

"Baby, you need to go to the doctor for real", cried Stephanie as she reached and held onto her friend's hand.

Smiley just buried her face into a pillow in complete disgust with herself because she knew indirectly, she did this all to her body. Stephanie's encouraging to go to a hospital finally made its way through to Smiley as she peeled herself off the bed. The two headed to Stephanie's car when Smiley's mother scorned at her daughter,

"I told yo stupid ass not to do that shit, now look at ya."

"Mama, not now", begged a weak Smiley.

Stephanie ignored the dirty looks and frowned up face Smiley's mother was giving off as she helped her friend in the car. She sped off in desperate need to get her friend that much needed help but couldn't resist in asking why her mother didn't seem to want to help her. Smiley's response that her mother is only concerned with how much money Smiley can bring in the house instead of worrying about her wellbeing disturbed Stephanie to no end. She couldn't understand how a mother could put financial gain over her daughter's health. Stephanie was almost to the hospital when Keisha called her asking about Smiley because she knew Stephanie was going visit her. When Keisha heard that they were heading to the hospital she immediately said she would get in touch with Diamond and they'll meet them there. Stephanie was pleased not to have to tackle the task alone and welcomed the company as she told them she would be at the Tulane Medical Center. She pulled into the hospital garage, quickly parked the car and headed straight to the emergency room with Smiley. It was the middle of the week, so the nurses weren't super busy and were able to see her right away. Stephanie sat in the waiting area while the nurse conducted their first overall scan of Smiley's vitals and to ask her the exact reason for her visit. Sitting there waiting for her other friends to arrive Stephanie got another call but this time it was from an unusual number and when she answered she wished she hadn't. On the other end was Quincy trying to win his way back to her,

"Please don't hang up. I just wanted to hear your voice and ask you how you been."

"Q right now I really don't have time for your antics. I'm doing fine, you heard my voice, now goodbye", replied an agitated Stephanie as she added another number to the block list of numbers Quincy has called her from.

She sat there for what felt like two hours before a doctor walked out to talk to her,

"How are you doing ma'am, are you Samantha Mitchell's friend? I'm Doctor Stovich, in charge of her care."

Stephanie only knew Smiley by her stage name, so the name threw her for a loop but being that she was the only person in the waiting area she figured he had to be talking about her friend. She listened attentively as Doctor Stovich began telling her how Smiley would have to go through surgery to have some implants removed. The doctor informed Stephanie that the breast and gluteal implants were leaking into her body and they had to get them out before the foreign fluids get into her blood stream, causing serious damage or death.

"I'm sorry doc, what is gluteal implants", asked Stephanie.

The doctor explained that it's just another word for buttocks implants and the reason Smiley is in so much pain is because silicon is leaking out. Stephanie was terrified for her friend and begged him to save her life. The doctor was telling Stephanie that Smiley will be just fine when Diamond and Keisha walked up to them. Stephanie introduced them,

"Doctor Stovich, this is Samantha's very close friends also and they came out of concern for her."

"It's ok, she needs all the support she can get", replied Doctor Stovich.

Keisha could see the fear in her friend's eyes as the doctor told them that Smiley would have to stay in the hospital a few days and that she's being prepped for surgery as he speaks. The doctor explained that the procedure would take a few hours and he'll come out to talk to them as soon as he's done. The girls thanked him for his time and Doctor Stovich walked off through some double doors that read "Authorized Personnel Only." They all sat down in the waiting room, completely worried over the unknown and frighten to speak about it. Especially Diamond because she actually thought about having the same surgery Smiley had done and the thought of being in surgery again, close to death scared her to no end. Diamond hung her head down as she cried out,

"I told her don't do it. I showed her videos of how that shit can go wrong. Dammit Smiley!"

"She needs our help and support right now baby. We all make mistake. We just gotta be there for her", replied Keisha.

Caleb was at the shop going over some shipment orders that needed to go out when Levi's old partner Mook came by looking for him. Caleb recognized the guy from being one of his old friend's father when he asked,

"You're Spider's, I mean Jason's pops right?"

"You know Jason", replied Mook.

Caleb began to tell him that he and Jason use to always hangout before he went to prison. Mook could tell that Caleb hadn't seen Jason in a very long time and when he told him that Jason is in a wheelchair it hit Caleb like a load of bricks. Levi came from the back-loading dock when he seen Caleb and Mook talking. He overheard them talking about the incident that put Mook's son in the wheelchair and Caleb mentioned that his sister was there during that time. Levi knew it was time for him to intervene before the two start putting faces to names and inadvertently figuring shit out. He walked up to Mook with a friendly hand shack,

"Man, what you doing up here? You be around here much longer, I'm a have to talk to Lez about putting you on the payroll."

"Shid, you know I can always use a lil extra. But I came over to invite you and Lez to a barbecue slash birthday party for Jason. Caleb you come through too, I know Jason would appreciate you coming", replied Mook.

Levi was hesitant to answer but Caleb unknowingly answered for all of them, telling Mook they will be there. The situation was getting really sticky for Levi because he really didn't want Caleb associating himself with Jason but if he told Caleb the reason why, it might get worse. He knew Leslie was going to be pissed when she hears they may have to go to the party they were just invited to. Levi left Caleb up front and walked in the back-storage room where Leslie was taking inventory of stationary she need for the shop. He made sure to close the door as he stated,

"We may have a little problem."

" What now? Tell me that new driver not lost", replied Leslie as she thought Levi was talking about work.

But when she looked into his face, she knew it had nothing to do with deliveries. Levi ran the story down to her and gave her his views on it. Leslie being the strategic person she is simply stated,

"Hey, we gotta go but we definitely can't tell Caleb anything about his friend and why he's in that wheelchair. Cause if we do, Caleb would kill him, and I don't want that for my nephew. We just got him back."

Levi agreed and they carried on the rest of the day as if nothing was wrong but Caleb's curiosity of the event that partially paralyzed his friend Jason poked at him. He didn't want to upset Stephanie by questioning her about the incident but figured she's the only person that could answer his questions. Caleb called Stephanie's phone, but Keisha answered it, after hearing her voice the concerned brother forgot what he was calling for,

"Why you got her phone big head?"

"I know you not calling my head big, Mr. Jughead", replied Keisha.

She explained to him that they were at the hospital checking on a friend of theirs when Stephanie stepped away to talk to a nurse. They sat on the phone for a good while just talking, getting to know each other better, when Caleb stepped out on faith and asked Keisha to go to dinner with him tonight. She was truly flattered but a little uneasy about going on a date with her friend's brother. Caleb assured her that they were just going to enjoy a good meal and one another's company, but Keisha knew her weaknesses, which Caleb possessed everyone of them. He was tall, dark, built like a Greek God, chiseled jawline, loving eyes and a smile that would melt away the coldest winter, but the plus was he had drive to be successful with everything he touched. Keisha knew if she got close to him that she would fall for him and she didn't want to create any tension with her friend. She hesitantly responded to Caleb's invitation,

"We can hook up tonight for dinner but I gotta tell you one thing. I'm not a salad and crackers kind of girl, I eats."


Ricky hadn't had a chance to visit his favorite gym in a long time since he became the head of security at the gentleman's club. Getting under some heavy weights and pushing himself through the pain felt good but looking at the recent artwork he received from Sunshine on his arm reminded him that he hadn't talk to her in awhile. He wanted to call her but was unsure of what to say because the last time they spoke she seemed preoccupied with doing her own thing, like the interest in just being friends with him had left her. It wasn't like any animosity towards him in any way but more of she could be doing something more interesting than just holding a conversation with Ricky. So, he just focused on reaching his max on the bench press while he got his much needed gym therapy in. Ricky was almost done with his set when he seen Tyson walk in the gym,

"What's up Tyson? I didn't know you came to this gym."

Tyson told him that he just started coming to the gym because it was close around the club and that he could go straight to work after a good workout. He said he had to get some much-needed self therapy everyday just to keep himself together. Ricky remembered he use to do the same exact thing when he was just a bouncer but strayed away from it after he got the new position. Having the new position even affected his other job as a trainer because he filled up his time with the club. After thinking about it Ricky realized he needed to get back to how he use to be, workouts at the gym with his clients, meditation times to get centered and even getting back to writing poetry like he did back in college. Tyson could see the wheels turning in Ricky's head as he asked,

"Boss man? You in there?"

Ricky just nodded as he added some more plates to the leg press machine and thanked Tyson for bringing him back to what was important. After a few reps, it turned into a competition between the two to see who could pump out the most weight as Ricky started to struggle to push out his last set,

"Man, you trying to kill me."

"No pain, no gain old man", stated a laughing Tyson.

They finished their workout session and the two just hung around the gym having "shop talk" about the club as they watched novice stress themselves out over workout equipment. The sun was starting to set, and both of the guys knew it was getting close to the time to get ready for work, so they headed to the showers. Ricky had really bonded with Tyson that day, finding out they both had a similar mindset when it came to the job, he never really thought he would find a combo like he had with Melvin and that actually felt good.

Doris was heading home after work when she called to check on her kids. Alisha was home doing her usual teenager antics; Caleb was actually on his way home also but when she called Stephanie she could tell her daughter wasn't in a right place.

"Baby you ok", asked a concerned Doris.

When Stephanie broke down everything going on with her friend Smiley, Doris was lost for words because she never had to deal with someone going through a situation as such. She tried to console her worried daughter that the doctors are going to take care of her friend, but she could tell that the worry was too great. Doris asked Stephanie if she wanted her to come to the hospital and wait with her, just to be an added support system. Stephanie comfortingly replied,

"No mama, it's ok. I'm here, Keisha and Diamond's here. I'm fine. I just hope they able to take care of her."

Doris was curious to the fact that a lot of Smiley's friends were at the hospital but wondered where was the young woman's actual family. Stephanie's only response was,

"That's a whole other story mama."

The thing was, the only family Smiley had in the city was her mother because her only brother was in prison serving a life sentence, her son was with his father in Mississippi ever since she fell ill and she never knew her actual father. Smiley use to always make jokes that she would never give an old man a lap dance because she doesn't want to accidentally give her biological father a woody. She was the energetic bubbly one in the locker room with all the other dancers, but no one really knew the amount of pain and stress she was going through because she would never show it. Smiley had a mother that seemed like she refused to work, stayed on some kind of assistance program and always looked for a handout from everyone else. With fake ID's she had been dancing in strip clubs since she was 15, sold heroin with her brother at the age of 13 before he was arrested, molested by two different boyfriends of her mother at the ages of 11 and 9 but through all of that continued to carry a prominent smile on her face. If people only knew the amount of pain she was actually going thru mentally. Even though Diamond and Stephanie were really close to Smiley and pretty much the only sisters she's ever had she kept her secrets deep, refusing to let them surface for anyone. It started to get late and they still haven't heard one word from a nurse or a doctor in a few hours when Keisha told Stephanie she had an appointment to keep. Diamond followed right behind stating she had to go get ready for work but made it clear that she would be back afterwards. Stephanie understood that everyone had their own thing to do but just couldn't leave Smiley alone at the hospital. She waited a little longer hoping someone would tell her something but that's when Dr. Stovich had finally came from the operating room. The doctor informed Stephanie that her friend was in the recovery room and that they successfully removed all the implants that were virtually poisoning her. Dr. Stovich told her that they had to remove some damaged tissue in Smiley's buttocks that's going to need some plastic surgery later, but they want her to heal for now. Stephanie thanked the doctor for his help and made her way to Smiley's room to lay eyes on her friend. She was almost to the room when her high school ex Malcolm called,

"Hey you."

Stephanie hadn't talk to Malcolm in what felt like forever, so she never had time to tell him about her new venture at becoming the new upcoming main attraction known as Lotus. The thing was Malcolm was calling to confirm the social media post that featured the artist Lotus he had seen himself. Stephanie listened as Malcolm stuttered through his questions and found it funny that the only time she has heard from him in such a long time was because he seen some risqué pics of her on the Internet. He tried to be as understanding as he could but confused all the same as the girl he use to know was this seductive figure he seen on a web page. Malcolm went on and on about having to hear old school mates call him about his ex-high school sweetheart stripping at a club, how her actions are affecting him. Stephanie sat there and attentively listened to Malcolm ramble on about how shocked he was of her current career choice but not once did he say he supported her in whatever she does, like she has ever since he went to school out of state. She had had her fill of the unsavory inclinations that what she is doing is demeaning and cut Malcolm off with,

"Thank you so much for the call but I have more pressing issues to deal with in checking on someone that is not judging me right now. So, fuck you very much and you take care now. Please don't call me again."

Stephanie composed herself as she ended the call with Malcolm and entered Smiley's room. The low-lit room had the sound of an EKG machine filling the air as Stephanie's eyes fell upon her friend laying motionless in a hospital bed with an oxygen tube taped to her nose and an IV in her arm keeping her hydrated with fluids. She stood there silent in an attempt to not disturb Smiley's sleep as she just watched her chest go up and down as she breathes. Smiley slowly opened her eyes and seen a dark figure standing at her bedside, after recognizing it was Stephanie, all she could do was smile because the pain she was feeling had her wanting to cry.

"Well hello and how are you doing Samantha. Samantha Mitchell that is", jokingly stated Stephanie as she held onto her friend's hand.

CHAPTER XV

Caleb pulled up to the restaurant Keisha had chosen for their little date and the valet opened their doors to let them out. He wasn't expecting the full-service action for their first night out but didn't want Keisha to think he couldn't afford it, so he just went along with it. As they walked into the establishment the hostess greeted them and walked them to their table. Before he even took a glance at the menu, Caleb knew the bill for this restaurant was going to dig deep into his pockets. Keisha could see all over his face Caleb wasn't thinking they were going to an upscale place like this but that's when the Head Chef walked out from the back to greet them. It was Keisha's cousin Timothy in full chef jacket and all,

"Good evening and it is my pleasure to serve you all tonight. I'll start you off with my chargrilled oysters and stuffed mushroom caps for your appetizers. We will then carry on to…"

"Cuz can we just eat? You putting on a full ass show and a nigga hungry like a hostage outchea", stated Keisha as she cut Timothy off in the middle of his act.

Timothy just stared at Keisha with an evil look as he told them that the entire meal is on him and a waitress will be with them shortly with some wine for a starter. Caleb sat back and let out a sigh of relief after hearing that the whole meal was paid for and Keisha just laughed at his actions. She had told Caleb that she had asked her cousin Timothy to cook for them right after he had asked her out for dinner. Keisha smiled as she continued,

"So, I'm guessing you figured I was high maintenance after coming to the place I picked for our first date, huh? Now don't get me wrong a sister likes to enjoy the finer things but a fire ass shrimp po-boy, fries and a pineapple Big Shot is right up my ally."

"You know I haven't had a po-boy since I been out, it's been what a month now? My mama always cooking, saying she wants me to always have a home cooked meal", replied Caleb.

The waitress came to their table with two glasses of water with lemon, two glasses of sweet red wine, a basket of warm yeast rolls and a small tray of assorted cheeses. Caleb and Keisha were thrown back for a minute at the site of the arrangement not knowing what to expect next.

"Chef Warren said he was sending out oysters?", stated Keisha in an asking way.

The waitress smiled and told them that the chef likes to start his patrons off with a palate cleanse to prepare them for his entrées. Keisha laughed,

"This dude here is a mess, but I must say this cheese and wine is so good."

Caleb was enjoying the company, but he had a purpose for the entire meet and date as he began to ask Keisha about the night his friend Jason was beaten. He listened as Keisha gave her interpretation of what had happened that night that was burned into her memory. She told him how Stephanie was a little antsy about a guy that kept approaching her at the club, but she didn't know who he was. Caleb asked if the guy was talking to her when they went outside.

"Steph had started walking to the car and I was talking with the bouncers at the front door with Diamond when I heard the gunshot, it was so loud. And when I turned around, I seen one guy dead on the ground with the other one getting beat with a bat. They was relentless at beating that boy. I felt sorry for him cause they just kept hitting him over and over again but I was scared for Steph. Then as quick as it happened, they were gone", responded Keisha.

"So, they were by Steph the whole time? Were you able to see the people faces that did it?", asked Caleb.

Keisha explained to him that she really couldn't see their faces because of the hoods over their heads and the bandanas. Caleb's mind was just running all over the place trying to figure out why his old street running buddy was targeted and also why was he talking to his sister, something he didn't divulge to him at first. He left the subject alone for now and enjoyed Keisha's company as the waitress brought the dinner out the chef prepared for them. As they ate their food, Caleb couldn't take his eyes off her and Keisha tried to keep herself composed because the only thing running through her mind was how good his lips would feel on hers. The two had put themselves in invisible restraints, not realizing they both wanted the exact same thing but their desires for one another was strong, loosening those mental restraints slowly with every word of their conversation.

      The casino was gaining more and more publicity as word got around statewide about a casino boat with a luxury gentleman's club in it. Businessmen and women as far as Jersey made their way to the Stagelight Casino just to network and enjoy the newfound "Sin City" spot. The gentleman's club side of the huge casino boat kept Ricky busy with special events and the occasional private party. Tyson become his right-hand man when security had to be tightened up in the club. They both seen eye to eye when it came to protecting the interest of the club and the dancers. Ricky was cool with the pimps, like Memphis and Lance, that made frequent visits to the club, but they couldn't conduct any business in there even though some of their dancers arranged private parties with customers. Ricky made it evident to all the dancers that their outside business was their business, but it should not and will not affect the business of the club. Some of the performers thought it was strange that Ricky and the club's den mother Evelyn held a meeting right before the Grand Opening of the casino but Ricky felt that if staff meetings worked for corporate America, it should work for Stagelight. Marcus was so impressed with Ricky's work ethics that he was able to be more of a host to the "high baller" clients while his Security Supervisor handled the daily affairs. It all was meshing well together, the club was making money, the girls were making money and it all was moving really smooth. But Tyson got word from a few of the dancers that they've been targeted by some young purse snatchers. When Ricky found out about the incidents, he tried searching through camera footage to get a glimpse of the culprits. He had images of the aggravated robber's cars but after sending the pictures to one of his police friends, it all came back that the cars were stolen. Looking at the videos of the criminal acts upset Ricky because every incident got more and more violent, where it first started off as a simple snatch of a purse on a females arm to them pushing the dancers to the ground and taking everything from them forcefully. Tyson had gotten to the point where he wanted to take the law into his own hands, by setting up an ambush, using a dancer as bait and catch the criminals in the act. But Ricky advised against it because he didn't want anyone getting hurt,

"You know these youngsters don't respect life. Shit, if we corner them, they gone shoot they way out."

Tyson was pissed but he understood where Ricky was coming from but still needed to make it clear that the Stagelight and its employees are off limits. He called in a favor from a few of his old neighbor friends who never mind getting their hands dirty. Without Ricky knowing of the plans, Tyson had some true goons stationed at all four corners of the parking lot waiting on any sign of a prowler on the hunt. They all kept in touch with each other through text messages and Tyson was confident that all the dancers would be completely safe when they left for the night. Ricky was watching over the club floor when Sunshine walked up to him, she smelled like a delicious fruit salad and glistened like a radiant star. Her smile pierced through him like a hot knife would butter as she placed her soft hands on his chest,

"You always working, eyes scanning back and forth, when are you going to relax and just enjoy the moment?"

"I relax when the club closes. But how is Stagelight's headliner doing? You know everybody here for a Sunshine performance", replied Ricky.

Sunshine was about to ask Ricky would he like to go get something to eat after hours when one of her apprentice, Essence, walked up and told her that a group a customers wanted time with them in the "Champagne Room".  Ricky let the ladies walk off to their business as he continued to conduct his business at watching the floor.


Stephanie was sitting next to Smiley's bed, looking at TV with her and listening to Smiley tell old strip club stories. Smiley had been an exotic dancer for so long that the wild stories seemed endless as she told countless events of her time on and off stage. Some of her stories were funny, some were downright terrifying, and some were complete "what the fuck" moments. Smiley was telling her friend about one time she did a party for a well known rapper at his new house, with a few other dancers. The night was going good, she was making crazy tips on top of the money she was already being paid to do the party and then things went awfully wrong. Smiley said she was giving a guy a lap dance by the stairs when they seen water running down the steps onto the floor. Another guy seen all the water and ran up the stairs to investigate but when he got to the upstairs bathroom, he found one of the dancer's bikinis stuck in the sink. Someone had left the faucet on, with clothes in the sink, it filled up and flooded the entire upper level of the house. The guy who the house was for was so pissed and out right started blaming every dancer that was there, threatening them with a crowbar he had picked up out of his garage. Smiley said she ran out the house barefoot with just her two-piece bikini on to get away because the guy was walking up to her,

"As soon as I seen him look my way, I got the fuck out. Bitch I was booking up the street, titty out and all, that nigga was mad mad. Muthafucka threw a champagne bottle at another girl that ran out after I did.”

“Damn, did they ever find out who clothes was in the sink?”, asked Stephanie.

The giggling Smiley told her that it was one of Lance’s girls Mercedes, who was washing her clothes out in the sink and forgot them in there. Stephanie couldn’t help but to laugh at the story thinking about Smiley running up the street with her breast flopping in the wind. Smiley herself knew the story was funny,

“Girl, I can laugh at it now, but a bitch was scared, hiding behind a damn bush with my ass out for the world to see. That nigga was mad behind his house getting fucked up and I couldn’t blame him, water was everywhere.”

Stephanie laughed with her friend over other stories she told as they chilled in Smiley’s room. Stephanie being new to the industry only could imagine the stories she would have as time goes on, but it was all exciting to her right now just experiencing it all.


        Caleb was walking Keisha to her apartment reveling in a great dinner date with her as they laughed over how her cousin Timothy performed like he was hosting a chef show at the restaurant. They got to her door and Caleb thanked Keisha for coming out with him for the night but as much as he wanted to ask to come in, he began walking back to his car. Keisha stopped him in his tracks when she invited him in for a late movie and drinks,

"I got a cold bottle of Moscato and a bootlegged Web browser to look at some movies, if you want to come in."

"Hell yeah I want to", replied Caleb.

She walked him in and told Caleb to make himself comfortable while she go get them two glasses of the wine promised. Keisha came back from the kitchen to Caleb sitting upright and stiff on the sofa,

"Dude I said make yourself comfortable not sit there like you're in a church pew."

Caleb had to laugh at himself sitting there like a statue, but his nerves had him nervous as hell, sitting with such a sexy woman. Keisha was nervous herself because Caleb looked so good, with his strong masculine frame, but she didn't want to rush anything and mess up the good vibe they were having. She placed the wine glasses in front of him on the coffee table and went to her room to change clothes, talking to herself the whole time,

"Girl do not molest that man. Damn, he fine. Stop it! We just gone chill and look at a movie. That's it, just chill."

Keisha didn't realize the comfortable outfit she chose to put on was so sexual and completely see through, but it was her "hang around the house" clothes. Caleb sat there and instantly began sweating bricks, preaching to himself,

"Do not try to fuck her on the first night, play it cool."

Just like the restaurant they both wanted the same thing but held back in fear that the other wouldn't return the same feelings. They sat there watching a movie Caleb had picked out and laughing at the bad quality but also the occasional shadowed figure standing up in front of the camera. They were enjoying the movie and Keisha got really comfortable, laying across Caleb's lap. He was doing good at controlling himself, in not doing anything that could be perceived as making a move. But when he felt her soft body against his it was no stopping his dick from getting hard and Keisha could feel his manhood harden as it reached down his leg. It felt as if it was about to touch his knee when her hand glanced over it and she judged the thickness in the palm of her hand. Her mind raced with images of how it may look, and the curiosity was killing her as she began to stroke him through his pants. Caleb wanted to stop her, but it felt too good to stop because he hadn't had a woman touch him in a long time. Keisha slowly rubbed her hand up and down his shaft as she closed her eyes, imagining him deep inside of her. Caleb's hand carefully reached down into her white cotton "Boy shorts" to her plump waxed pussy and his fingers found Keisha's moisture filled lips. Her fluids seemed to surround his fingers as he rubbed her clit bringing her to an ecstasy filled brink of explosions. Keisha had had enough of the fondling and took it upon herself as she straddled Caleb on the sofa, took her top off revealing her perky honey colored breast and they engaged in a passionate kiss. She could feel his meat pressing up against her throbbing pussy as she rotated her hips and he found her weak spot behind her ear as he kissed her. Keisha wanted him so badly that she reached down into his jeans, wrapped her hand around his massive muscle of a dick and eased it out of its hiding place. It sat there resting on his stomach, hard as a steel pipe and she wanted every inch of it, but she knew she had to be careful,

"Please tell me you have a condom."

Caleb let out a heavy sigh as he put his head down on her breast and Keisha took that as a defining answer that he doesn't have any. He told her that he wasn't expecting to do anything with her, that it was only supposed to be a dinner date and packing a contraceptive for the night wasn't in the plans. Keisha looked down at the tube steak she so wanted to devour that night and reluctantly whispered to Caleb,

"You gone have to put him up."

Keisha got up off Caleb's lap, put her top back on and headed to her front door. Disappointed with himself, Caleb knew it was definitely time to go because they both knew if he stayed, they would end up jumping each other and unprotected sex was not on the menu. He stood in front of her, softly kissed her on the lips and told her they will finish up where they left off on his next visit. Keisha smiled as she reached down to grab a handful of semi-hard dick and replied,

"You just make sure you bring some XL's cause a regular size condom is not gone fit this motherfucka, I'm just saying."

Tyson was out front of the casino with Cashmere, one of the dancers of the Stagelight, when he got a call from one of his partners that were out in the parking lot. The guy told Tyson that he seen a car full of youngsters driving around the far west end of the parking lot and that they looked like they couldn't get into the casino. Tyson figuring that those are the ones they been looking for told his friend to just keep a close eye on them. Another dancer by the name of Tipper came out to leave, Cashmere went with her, as Tyson said bye to them and watched them walk away. It wasn't shortly after that; he heard a woman's scream and Tyson looked in the direction of the two dancers that had just left his side. But it wasn't them as they looked back at Tyson with fear in their eyes. He ran towards where the screams came from to find Luscious, another one of the club's dancers, on the ground and a teenage boy standing over her, pulling at her purse. Tyson scanned the scene and noticed another teenager running away between the cars in the parking lot. Right when he was about to shout for the runner to stop, he seen one of his friends that been outside tackle the guy and they fell to the ground between two cars. Tyson looked at the teenager in front of him and stated,

"Say man, whatever is in her purse is not worth the ass whooping you gone get if you try to run. You already see yo potna down."

The teen smiled and the statement that Ricky made earlier all came true as the barrel of a .38 Special stared Tyson in the face as the teen asked,

"Nigga, who is you?"

The thing that made the teen a little uneasy was that Tyson didn't look scared or shocked that a gun was pointing at him. See the teen didn't know the rest of Tyson's neighborhood goons were closing in on him, from behind, with semi-automatic rifles aimed at his back. Tyson slowly helped Luscious up off the ground and the teen cocked the hammer back on the pistol, as to say,

"Don't move."

Tyson motioned Luscious to get behind him for protection and the teen turned around to run off with her purse but came face to face with three assault rifles pointed at him.

"I told you son, it's not worth it. Gone put the purse down and walk away", stated Tyson.

The teen dropped the purse as he started to walk away but then the night air was filled with red and blue police lights. Law enforcement cars came from all different directions and Tyson looked over to his friends gesturing for them to lower their guns. The teen boy darted through the parking lot in an attempt to get away from the police but just like his co-conspirator he was tackled to the ground and arrested. Several officers cautiously made their way to Tyson and his buddies with guns drawn because they seen the fire power they were carrying. One officer, in a stern voice, instructed the three gunmen to lay their weapons on the ground and they did exactly that. Tyson walked up to the officer to explain to him that all his people were licensed carriers and working for him. The officer looked Tyson in the eyes, asked the three men for their identification and stated,

"You must be Tyson. Well see, we are working a detail for Ricky Boyd, the Head of Security, he told us you would have yo people out here playing cops and robbers. While y'all was dealing with these two we grabbed the other three in the car around back but thanks for the assistance."

The officer had informed Tyson that Ricky had ordered a police detail unit for the parking lot as soon as he heard about the purse snatchings but didn't want anyone in the club knowing because he had a feeling it was an inside job. Tyson was confused at the "inside job" statement because he never figured someone that works at the club would be setting up the dancers to be robbed. After all of Tyson's friends were checked out, the officers let them go and they left the parking lot. Tyson walked his buddies to their cars, thanked them for all the help they did and headed back inside to address Ricky about the police detail he knew nothing about.

Between all the commotion going on outside the club and her friend being in the hospital, Diamond's mind was all over the place, but she didn't show it while she was at work. The sexy vixen mesmerized her audience as she danced on the stage, pulling off acrobatic pole flips and spins with erotic innuendos. Diamond was finishing her set on stage when the young obnoxious pimp Lance walked up to her,

"Say lil mama, when you gone give me some time?"

"Time equals money Lance or do you not know that", replied Diamond.

She was gathering the blanket of ones that were sprawled all over the platform floor when Lance asked her to meet him in the VIP Room. Diamond knew Lance was going to do his usual one song one dance routine and then try to convince her to join his team. She's heard his spill time and time again but knew he would slide a C-note in her bikini just for sitting with him. As she headed towards the VIP Room, the always pleasant to talk to Memphis grabbed her by the hand,

"I've been knowing you for a minute now Shawty and that cat can't be trusted."

"I'm a big girl Memphis, I think I can handle little Ole Lance", replied Diamond.

Memphis told her he doesn't trust Lance because nearly every girl that has been to the VIP Room with him has been robbed when they leave the club. Diamond figured it was just an old school pimp being suspicious of everybody, she smiled at Memphis and kissed him on the cheek as she left to meet up with Lance. She was almost to the area where Lance was sitting when Memphis words kept ringing in her ear,

"A wolf can show you his teeth even when he's dressed like a sheep."

Diamond ignored the speech from the flamboyant procurer as she sat next to the flashy Lance all decked out in designer clothing, chugging from a 200-dollar bottle of champagne and puffing on a Cuban cigar. She giggled to herself because he just looked silly to her, a person who was trying too much to be something he's not built for. Lance father was a street hustler and Jack of all trades, he did everything possible to have Lance in the best schools and best programs. But Lance's attraction to the grime of the street life was more to him than following his father's instructions. Girls seemed to just fall at his side because Lance always was covered in the latest of fashion, drove top notch cars, bands of money and his mouthpiece was wicked. He had the gift of gab and could convince the weakest of minds to follow him through fire if he wanted them to and it didn't help either that Lance was extremely handsome. Lance was what you call passé blanc or what people would call a real light skin guy with charcoal black soft curly hair, hazel green eyes and a persuasive personality. It was as if he was destined to be a pimp, working girls to the bone to benefit him but Diamond wasn't falling for the flashy glamour. She did what she would do to all her customers, rub their ego and make them feel like a king for the moment. Diamond knew how far to take any situation, be it on stage, during a lap dance or even casual conversation with a potential human ATM, getting the bag was always priority. Even though the client felt they were in control, she had full control as she made calculated moves like a chess game. She knew subtle touches, eye contact, innocent smiles and fragrant body scents could pull any man into her web, to give her what she wanted. Diamond understood that Lance had a way with words, his charm was captivating, and his seduction level was professor worthy but the sensual dancer had a certain set of skills. Counting back to when Diamond was a pre-teen, she has always been able to get people to do for her. Just like Lance, she had a very persuasive personality and the fact that she was undeniably gorgeous didn't help but she didn't use it to manipulate anyone that didn't deserve it.  She found out then that men and sometimes even women were easily moved by her. Back when Diamond was a freshman in high school, she had a male gym teacher that was a borderline pedophile. He would always find the weak-minded little girls that had a crush on the handsome gym coach and coddle them with inappropriate touches and conversation. Diamond used his predator mentality against him with her own charm but always kept him at arm's distance which in turn held his attention. She used to get him to leave the other innocents alone because they weren't strong enough to keep him at bay like she could until he was eventually caught for having inappropriate conversations with a minor. Diamond realized then she was able to use men for her gain and Lance was no different, she just had to use his own arrogance against him. So, she listened to his rambling of growing an empire, just the two of them taking over and how he could make her into a main attraction but she knew it was all a smoke screen. Just like her high school gym teacher, Lance was a predator but on a different level. After the one-sided conversation was done Diamond thanked Lance for the time and went on her way to leave for the night but noticed his friendly demeanor turned aggressive. Lance seen he wasn't getting anywhere with Diamond and she wasn't budging with her decision to not join his entourage. Diamond smiled as she looked in Lance's eyes,

"Looks like that wolf is finally showing his teeth."

"Fuck that mean? I'm sitting here offering you an opportunity to make some real money, have the right protection you need and you around here turning away from me like you better than me", replied Lance.

Diamond knew the conversation was lost because of the attitude Lance was holding and if the conversation was gone, so was the flow of money. She got up, walked away comfortable knowing she made enough ends for the night and headed home.

## CHAPTER XVI

Ricky was standing at the front entrance of the club, looking over the crowd, accompanied with four uniformed NOPD officers when he seen the person, they all were looking for. The officers began to fan out as Ricky made his way towards a female dancing on one of the mini stages that were stationed throughout the club. The customers around the stage knew something had to be wrong and began to move out the way as Ricky asked the dancer Mercedes to step down off the stage. Mercedes looked confused as she asked,

"Ricky what the hell is all this? What the fuck I do?"

"Ma'am we just have a few questions for you, but we need to ask you in private", responded one of the officers.

They were escorting her to the back-dressing room when Lance darted through the crowd to see what was going on because Mercedes was his main girls, his bottom bitch and the main source to his income. Ricky stopped him in his tracks before the police could even tell Lance not to come any closer, but the pompous pretty boy tried to push his way pass the head bouncer. One officer walked up to Lance face to face,

"Unless you want to be hogtied in the back of my squad car and dropped off at Orleans Parish prison, I advise you to back the fuck up."

Lance was hesitant in listening to the law man but one of his buddies tugged at his arm to pull him away from getting arrested, all the while Lance shouting,

"What the fuck she do? You wrong Ricky bruh!"

The group made it to the dressing room and asked Evelyn
to get all her girls to leave for a moment. As Mercedes sat
there still questioning why they pulled her to the back,
Ricky assured her that the officers just had a few things to
ask her. The young dancer began to get agitated that they
were keeping her from making anymore money and even
stated that they will have to pay her for her time. After all
the other dancers finally exited out the lead officer in
charge calmly walked up to Mercedes and showed her a
picture of a young guy he had in his top pocket. With
nothing but attitude spewing from her lips, Mercedes asked,

"So, who the hell is that suppose to be?"

"You don't know who he is, cause he really knows who
you are", stated the cop.

Mercedes looked at the picture again, shook her head no
and sat there silent with a face of disgust. Ricky tried to
convince her to tell the police what she knows but the
disgruntled stripper refused to talk to them. The officers
were done trying to talk to Mercedes, they started placing
handcuffs on her wrist and was about to start reading her
Miranda rights because she was being arrested for
organized crime involving assault. When she felt the cuffs
tighten around her wrist, Mercedes started flooding them
with information of how she didn't like that Lance kept
bringing dancers in the VIP Room without her. Ricky and
the officers were a little confused of what she was talking
about, so they asked her to fill them in on what she meant.
Mercedes stated that Lance would always bring a different
dancer in the VIP Room, give them money, talk to them in
private for several minutes and not tell her anything about

it. She told them that she was tired of being disrespected and that the dancers should pay Lance for his time instead of the other way around. With the most serious face Mercedes stated,

"So, every time one of them bitches come out the back, I sent my lil cousin to go get that money from them. Them hoes owe my daddy for his time."

"Wait one damn minute! Because you didn't like yo boyfriend talking to other strippers you had them set up to be robbed? You gotta be fucking kidding me?", asked one of the police officers.

Ricky had no words for what he just heard and asked the officers to take Mercedes away as he headed straight to have a word with Lance. The law men didn't want to walk the suspect through the crowded club, so they made their way to the back-exit doors that lead outside. Mercedes tried to explain that she was just making Lance his money back, but no one was trying to hear anything she was saying. The officers were completely baffled that she was that brainwashed to believe that she was helping her man and didn't do anything wrong. Ricky was standing on the main floor looking for Lance when the hot head young pimp saw him first, making a beeline straight towards him. Before Lance could get one word out about Mercedes, Ricky asked in a demanding voice,

"Nigga tell me you didn't know anything about what was going on. Lance if I think you lying, I'm a take all yo damn fronts out."

"Hold on my nigga, first off who the hell you think you talking to? I ain't one of them damn scary ass tourist that see the big black man, yo muscles don't scare me playa", responded Lance as he stood toe to toe with Ricky.

At that moment Ricky was still furious but didn't want to make a scene, even though he knew if he was to get into a fist fight with Lance it would be a total disadvantage for the young hustler. He then composed himself as he explained to Lance that Mercedes was arrested for organized criminal activity and that she was the reason that the dancers were being targeted outside of the casino. Lance didn't know what to say because he truly had no idea that one of his girls would have done such a thing. Ricky then dropped a bombshell when he told Lance that he and all his girls are banned from the clubs the Stagelight own. Lance started to get loud, drawing attention from anyone that was in ear's reach of them and Ricky attempted to calm the situation, but Tyson had had enough. Snatching him up by the back of his designer shirt and 500-dollar belt, Tyson showed Lance the exit faster than he could reacted. A line of bouncers stood at the entrance of the club as Lance shouted repeated threats to Ricky that it wasn't the last time, he would see him. Before Ricky had confronted Lance about Mercedes, Tyson had already instructed Evelyn to gather all the dancers Lance had on his team. The girls were allowed to empty out their lockers and pack their things up so that they could leave. One of the girls even stated with frustration,

"This is messing with my money; I could do this by myself for all this."

Listening to the girl gripe about the situation Evelyn wondered herself why would a dancer even have a pimp to begin with. She usually stays out of the girl's personal lives but she couldn't help but to ask,

"What good was he anyway? You did all the work, you promoted yourself, you talked to every Tom, Dick and Hakeem out there on the floor, but you had to give him the money you made, for what? To say you had a man you had to share with five other bitches? Oh, my bad, he was suppose to be your protection and lover. Baby girl, a stripper is an entrepreneur, a trendsetter, a talented and powerful woman that uses her skills to get paid. Don't you EVER listen to a fuck boy, selling you some pipe dream. That's for them slow bitches, are you a slow bitch?"

The young dancer stood there, letting every word just sink in as her mentality completely changed and she realized that she didn't need Lance anymore. It was easy for her to stay behind and let the other girls leave with Lance because everything she owned was in her carrying case. Evelyn was pleased that her speech reached one of them and went to tell Ricky that they had to find her a safe place to stay for the night.

Levi was laying on the sofa with his head resting in Leslie's lap as they watched TV when he received a call from Caleb. Thinking it's a normal call from Leslie's nephew he answered,

"What's good with ya boy?"

Caleb switched the whole conversation to Levi calculating his words when he started talking to him about the night Stephanie was approached by those guys at the club. Caleb told Levi that he found out that his friend Spider was one of those guys talking to Stephanie when they were attacked and wondered if his buddy Mook told him that bit of information. Levi knew then that Caleb knew a little too much about the incident and if he kept digging that eventually he would find out what really happened. He tried to brush it off as coincidence,

"C'mon now round, you know how small this city is. Everybody knows everybody some kind of way."

"Nah, them two hung in two totally different crowds bruh", replied Caleb.

Levi then stated that Stephanie is a very attractive female and that Spider was probably just trying to shoot his shot outside of the club. Caleb wasn't really trying to hear that the whole situation was coincidence and that his lifelong friend just so happen to try at his little sister but he left it all alone for the night. Leslie was quietly listening to the whole conversation, confident that Levi was able to steer it clear of any assumptions but knew Caleb was just as nosey as his mother. She knew she would have to fill Stephanie in on Caleb's questioning of the incident, so that she wouldn't be caught off guard. The story had to match up at least on their end so that Caleb doesn't get wind of the truth about his now handicap friend. Leslie texted Stephanie,

"I'm a need to talk to you in person real soon, Caleb suspicious."

After he got off the phone Levi went back to his relax mode and continued to look at his show. Leslie asked him if he thinks they need to have a sit down with Caleb and explain the who situation with him. Levi advised against it because if Caleb found out that Spider was actually trying to hurt Stephanie that night, he would slaughter him and that wouldn't be good for any of them. Leslie agreed, knowing her nephew and knowing his capabilities when it comes to protecting his siblings. Caleb once beat his own father unmercifully for stealing and selling Alisha's game console when he was a teenager. This situation would turn out very bad if Caleb found out about Spider and Stephanie, but deep-down Leslie was getting tired of all the cover up. She wanted to just tell her nephew about the whole situation and that they took care of it, trusting Levi's approach was the only thing that was holding her back. Leslie wasn't interested in watching TV anymore as she headed to the bedroom to call it a night, leaving Levi in the living room to himself. Levi knew his woman was frustrated over keeping everything on the hush, but he figured it would be better for everyone to keep that information from Caleb for his sake. Leslie laid in bed as her mind rambled on and on of "what ifs" about the Spider episode that just don't seem to ever end. She wanted to just get it out and let Caleb know that it all was taken care of but that scary "what if" of Caleb losing his shit kept nagging at her. Leslie knew her nephew, the young man before prison and the man that came out of prison still had time to prove to her he wasn't a hot head like she used to be. So, she decided to hold it all in for the time being.

Smiley woke to Stephanie asleep in the chair next to her bed as Diamond and Spice stood in the doorway of her room. Still in a little pain she let out a smile as she gestured for them to come in to visit with her. Diamond came in and immediately hugged her friend laying in the bed as Spice walked in behind her. The laughing between the girls woke Stephanie as her blurry vision focused in on Smiley and

Diamond looking over at her giggling. Spice just sat back and watched as his girlfriend did what most young women do when two or more all link up, gossip about everything. Diamond filled the girls in on the craziness that took place a few hours ago with one of Lance's girls and the police in the dressing room. Stephanie made it known that even when she was a bartender that she always kept the pistol her aunt gave her close at hand when walking to her car. Especially ever more so after the beating incident that took place right in front of her, even though secretly Stephanie knew those people. The girls started talking about different situations they've encountered being a part of the industry but how those instances haven't detoured them from pushing forward. Smiley told them how once she was followed by a stalker from the club who was persistent at finding her no matter where she went until she filed a restraining order on him. Diamond talked about her time getting into a physical altercation with a female who thought Diamond was messing with her husband.

"But my question is, bitch was you", asked a laughing Smiley.

Diamond gave her the serious evil eye as she answered no and explained that the guy would always give her money for videos on her website. The wife seen the payouts on his credit card statement one day and confronted Diamond about it and they got into a fight. Stephanie hadn't had any crazy stalkers or disgruntled wives approach her but stated she always kept an eye out for anything strange when she was in the club. Spice just sat there amazed at the stories they would tell of thirsty fans, horny stalkers and females that thought every stripper was a money greedy nympho that was trying to take their man. He went to take a walk to give the girls some time alone but seen a whole other side of the life that wasn't all the glamour, that wasn't showers of money and some times the risk reward factor is a little slanted in the wrong direction.  The girls understood the pros and cons of the industry but the pros more than some always seemed to outweigh the cons every time. Just from practicing they knew physically the job wasn't going to be easy, sometimes family would look at them different and a lot of times the money won't always be there to make. The girls laughed about the crazy stuff they had to deal with on a daily and it all kind of hit home with Smiley as she looked at herself laying in the hospital bed bandaged up. She looked at how she drastically altered her body, in a botched surgery, to cater to the image that drew in more money. The big breast accompanied with the huge ass and small waistline was becoming the standard that almost killed her.  She tried to keep herself from tearing up, but the emotions took over as she softly cried out,

"Damn, I'm stupid, I really messed myself up y'all. Diamond you told me not to do that shit and I wouldn't listen. I could've kilt myself."

The girls sat there consoling Smiley as the tears just continued to roll down her face as they continuously told her that she will get back on her feet. The whole time Smiley was trying to figure out what will she do after the hospital because no one wants a dancer with surgical scars all over her body. Diamond and Stephanie knew the same thing but refused to say anything to their friend about it because they wanted her to focus on getting well soon before thinking about money. Smiley has been a dancer for so long that she doesn't know how the working class operates and that part scared her. She had her moment and was desperate to get out of the funk she was in so Smiley asked about Keisha's whereabouts.

"That thang went on a date and didn't want to tell me who the guy was, but you know I'm a find out", responded Stephanie.

Diamond knew who the guy was but promised Keisha she wouldn't tell because they didn't know how Stephanie would react to it. Smiley not knowing any of the details was just happy they weren't talking about her recent surgery and her mind could relax from that stress for a minute. Stephanie started to notice the sun peaking through the blinds in Smiley's room and realized she has been with her friend for almost 24 hours straight. She told her that she'll be back later, but she had to go home, shower and get some sleep. Diamond told Smiley the same as she began to collect her things. They both gave their recovering friend a kiss on the cheek before walking out of the room to head home. Smiley was back to thinking about what she's going to do next but knew she had friends that would support her in this new journey.

Tyson walked into his apartment after a long night and all he wanted to do was collapse in his bed, but he had unexpected company with him this time. The young dancer, Allure, that decided to leave Lance and go on her own didn't really feel comfortable staying at a hotel by herself. Only because Lance was cool with a lot of the hotel staff in the area and they would let him know where she was, Allure felt more comfortable staying at someone's house instead. She didn't want to inconvenience Tyson but asked him if she could spend the night until she could figure out her next step to getting herself on her feet. Tyson didn't mind helping her out, in fact the Bachelor welcomed the guess with no intentions of taking the friendly relationship any further than it already is. He told her to make herself comfortable in his bedroom while he got a pillow and blanket for himself to lay down on the sofa in the living room. Allure never really had a guy be nice to her without wanting sex in return and it felt so securing to her. She was laying in his bed, in a fetal position, sheets pulled up over her shoulders when the smell of bacon tickled her nostrils. It was as if the smell pushed the sheets back off her and eased her out of the bed as Allure peeked out of the bedroom to see Tyson cooking in the kitchen. She walked up to the waist high marble countertop as Tyson looked over his shoulder,

"I knew that bacon would wake you up. I'm sorry, I gotta have breakfast. You hungry?"

"If you cooking, I'm eating", replied Allure.

Tyson put together a Southern Soul food breakfast for the both of them as they sat down to eat at the table. Allure kept thanking him for his hospitality while she indulged herself in the belly busting breakfast of scrambled eggs, bacon, grits, pancakes, thin pork chops, strawberries, orange juice and coffee. They knew each other from the club and were very cordial with each other but the time alone gave them time to actually get to know one another. Tyson had realized that he had been knowing Allure for a month or so, never knew her real name and there was no time like the present to find out being that she's sleeping under the same roof as he was. She smiled at the fact that someone wanted to get to know the person and not just the stripper as she answered,

"My name is Mary-Ann Wallace and I'm from Odessa Texas. Moved here two years ago to finish school but ended up in this situation you see here."

Tyson couldn't help but to laugh when he repeated here name imitating a country accent. They laughed together as they sat at the table and talked most of the morning away. Allure helped Tyson clean up the kitchen after breakfast and then went to the bedroom to lay down. She felt more and more comfortable with Tyson as she offered that he come sleep in his own bed with her. As much as Tyson wanted to sleep in his comfy plush bed instead of sleeping on the couch, he declined the offer while he let Allure go to the bedroom alone. The young dancer sat on the side of the bed baffled that a man would turn down an offer to lay in bed with her, but she wasn't offended by it. After a few minutes Allure finally laid down and fell asleep with visions of stacking her money to get herself straight. Tyson on the other hand laid on the sofa thinking about how easy it must have been for a city boy like Lance to take advantage of a country girl like Mary-Ann. He thought about the endless cycle of girls that fall prey to guys like that, believing they are in love, thinking the guy is there to take care of them and not realizing they're the victims. The more Tyson thought about it the more pissed he got because his little sister fell in that trap years ago but wasn't as fortunate as Allure to get out. Tyson still remembers the call from the police like it was yesterday stating that they found an "overdose" in a hotel room in Dallas of a young female that state ID had their address on it. His little sister, who was 17 at the time of her death, had been missing for 3 years after meeting a guy on the Internet and running off with him. Tyson's family later found out that the guy had a string of young girls working for him in a sex trafficking ring, he would get them strung out on heroin or pills and use them until they were no more good for him. The ordeal took its toll on Tyson to the point where he would go out of his way to help any female that wants to get from under a predator like that thumb. He couldn't help his sister before it was too late and knew most of those girls were so brainwashed to the point where they wouldn't listen to reasoning. So if a female showed him that she wanted out, there was nothing that would stop him from helping her to the best of his ability and giving Allure a safe place to rest her head for the time being was just a small gesture to him.

CHAPTER XVII

It's been 4 weeks since Smiley's emergency room visit to the hospital and she's almost 100% back to normal, minus the physical therapy along with the ever-piling hospital bills. Stephanie tried to help her friend out as best as she could by getting her a job as an assistant for Caleb at the shop to make some sort of currency. But nothing was going to stop her from seeing her friend Lotus perform on the Stagelight's main platform tonight. Stagelight Gentleman's club was packed with customers and not one seat in the club have an ass in it. Everyone there was patiently waiting for the dual performance from the Diva Sunshine and the Seductress Lotus because they've never been on stage together before. Two weeks before the event was Sunshine's very first-time seeing Lotus in action, beside the day of her audition. They both wanted to practice together to get a feel for each other's style so that the collaboration went seamless. It felt like endless hours of training until the two seemed to know each other like twins, the two were devastating together. Lotus learned some tricks from Sunshine and vice versa as they worked out the finishing touches of their performance. They were packing up for the day when Sunshine asked,

"So, who's your front man or hype man when you hit the stage?"

Lotus not knowing what she meant held a surprisingly confused face at the question she was just asked. Sunshine laughed at the fact that Lotus had no clue as to what a "front man" was and explained that a front man or hype man does exactly what the word says. Customers or onlookers usually don't like being the first one to throw money to a dancer unless they're a high roller, celebrity or dope boy, that just want to show off how much money they got. So, some dancers get them a front man to start the money flow on stage and the person is usually in on the act. The front man would wait for the opportune time when all eyes are on the dancer, walk up to the stage with a wad of money and throw it in the air, letting it rain down on the performer. That one little act would usually coast the other customers to follow along and do the same because they seen the attention that one customer got from the dancer on stage. Lotus only knew how to make money the normal way by just enticing her customers and not using psychology to trick them into trying to prove who has the bigger dick. After listening to Sunshine's explanation, she had a person in mind but had to ask,

"So who do you use as yo front man?"

"Girl my cousin is always my front man because one he not always in the club, so no one really knows his face and second I can trust him with my money", replied Sunshine.

The girls were ready, the crowd couldn't wait any longer and the anticipation seemed to fill up the room like a dense fog. The DJ got on the mic and it was as if he was introducing the headline performance of an R&B group to the stage,

"Y'all know this ya boy DJ Felt-Tip and I've had the pleasure of seeing both of these women rise to the stardom status you know and love. One the dynamic diva known as Sunshine and the other the sultry seductress named Lotus but both are Queens of the Industry. Stagelight

Gentleman's club happily welcomes you to the dual performance of the Black Asian Queen Sunshine and the Chocolate Exotic Flower Lotus!"

The lights went low with one spotlight fixed on the large curtains at the back of the stage but the only thing that came from the curtains was thick smoke from under the bottom. The heavy mist had the appearance of walking straight down the stage until it rolled off the end and then the sounds of a marching band cadence began. Smiley heard the music and instantly recognized the music as one of her classic entrance songs, but she wasn't ready for when the curtains opened up. Lotus had been studying and practicing Smiley's routine for a minute because she wanted to pay homage to the now young retired dancer. The curtains parted and the silhouette of a woman's frame could be seen in the fog as strobe lights blinked and flashed over the stage. Emerging from the mist was the sensual Melanin Queen Lotus dressed in a one shoulder shape fitting short red dress with a split on the side. The dress literally accentuated every curve Lotus owned as she marched toward the front center pole on the stage. When she was just arm's length from the pole, in Smiley fashion, she launched in the air, grasping hold to the pole and spun around in a "Teddy Cleaver". Smiley seen it and instantly jumped up in excitement because her friend started accomplishing athletic feats that took Smiley years to perfect. Lotus did a few more spins and flips on the pole in mid air but as the music began to slow down, so did Lotus. The lights dimmed down once again as Lotus slowly dropped to the stage floor in a "Box Split" and the marching band cadence changed to an R&B slow jam, the Queen of Exotic performance Sunshine blessed the stage. Dressed in a bright yellow matching dress like her counterpart, Sunshine slowly walked on the platform to the front pole where Lotus was waiting. The two stood there like a powerhouse duo at opposite sides of the stage as they danced, twerked and grind for their audience. The dresses found their way to the floor as Lotus seductively undressed Sunshine and she did the same to Lotus. Sunshine's thick honey toned thighs just shined in the lighting, the large koi fish tattoo on her leg seemed to dance itself as she twitched the muscles in her thighs. Everyone's attention was glued to the stage as both women showed off their talents and Ricky wasn't exempt from that group. It was his first time seeing the artist known as Lotus on stage performing and she didn't disappoint not one bit. He was trying to do his job at security and watching the club floor but the pure sexual sensation pouring from the stage called for his eyes to glaze over to those performers. Lotus was slowly spinning around on the pole, while Sunshine had her legs wrapped around one of her customers, when she seen Spice walk up to the stage and she knew it was time for a shower. She crawled to Spice, laid on her back with her long dredlocs hanging off the stage, her face inches from his dick and he sprinkled 500 ones on her like it was seasoning. Sunshine's cousin followed suit as he ripped the band off a stack of ones and threw them in the air at his dancing cousin. The "front man" trick worked like a charm as audience members began tossing ones, fives, tens and even twenties onto the stage to the girls. The money simply carpeted the dance floor from front to back as Lotus and Sunshine acted out their final performance. The chocolate colored Lotus laid on top of the lightly caramel complexion Sunshine, their bodies seemed to melt together like an ice cream swirl. Sunshine's thighs wrapped around Lotus' waist, their breast pressed together, Lotus fingers walked through Sunshine's long black hair and the two locked lips in a passionate kiss as the music stopped with the crowd cheering, throwing more money on them. The girls stopped kissing and looked at each other as they smiled that they pulled off a great performance. They got up from the stage floor and in Lotus fashion, they both posed in a curtsy for the audience before collecting all the money on the stage.


      Caleb didn't attend the "Queens of Exotica" but he was in the casino playing some blackjack with his buddy Jason. The only reasons Caleb came to the casino was to meet up with Keisha, because she was going to see her friend perform and to get some bro-time with Jason at the casino. The two friends chilled at the table losing chips to the dealer when Keisha walked up behind Caleb and kissed him on the cheek. He turned to her,

"Hey you. How you find me in this crowd?"

"You forgot? You told me you always liked playing 21, so this the spot I went to. But hell, with that, you should have seen your sis. She was amazing, the crowd couldn't get enough of her and Sunshine on stage", replied Keisha.

Caleb knew seeing his little sister strip on stage was one of the last things he wanted to witness and was comfortable in the spot he was in. His friend inquired about the dancer because he hadn't been to a strip club in a very long time since he been in a wheelchair and didn't know Caleb's sister was a stripper. Keisha instantly pulled out her phone to show off her friend's social media page "Chocolate Lotus". Caleb focused on the playing cards that was in front of him while Jason looked over the picture roll Keisha was showing him. Caleb's buddy instantly got nervous when the dreadloc princess' face rung a bell in his memory. Jason didn't want to see anymore pics as he gave Keisha her phone back and sat there silent, but his fears all escalated when the images he seen on the phone walked up to Caleb at the table. Quietly standing behind the two secret lovers, Stephanie stared at Caleb as Keisha sat on his lap, affectionately rubbing his head. She let out a little smile as she stated,

"So, this is the mystery man you been keeping from me? Y'all could have told me."

Jason turned his chair away from Stephanie so that she couldn't view his face as Caleb and Keisha was caught in stutter mode trying to explain themselves to her. Stephanie really didn't mind her best friend connecting with her big brother and laughed at them try to tell her why they hid their relationship from her. After the relief of his little sister's approval Caleb introduced Jason to Stephanie and the facial expressions, they both held was evident that they recognized one another. Stephanie's heart raced in fear as her eyes gazed at the Spider tattoo on Jason's neck and the images of him chasing after her at the convenience store sped through her mind. Jason in return mentally went through every minute of the beating he received that night in front of the strip club. They both had some PTSD issues that messed them up over the past that still haunted them today.

"Say my nigga, you good", asked Caleb.

Jason looked over at his friend trying to gather himself as he nodded his head yes and keeping from looking

Stephanie in the eyes. Keisha changed the subject and began praising her friend on a great show, bringing Stephanie back from the terrifying memory she was stuck in. Caleb didn't say anything but just from seeing both of their reactions when they met, he knew something wasn't right and he knew he had to get to the true answers. Caleb's whole reason for coming to the casino was to try and get the two to meet so he could watch their reactions, his intuitions didn't fail him. Jason made up an excuse that he was feeling tired and wanted to go home but when Caleb got ready to take him Jason replied that he will have his father come get him. Caleb didn't want to hear the nonsense as he began to bring his friend to the exit explaining to him that it is no problem and that they rode there together so they will leave together. Jason tried to insist that Caleb stay at the casino with Keisha and Stephanie, but the request was ignored, Caleb kissed Keisha telling her he will see her later tonight.  When Caleb got to his car, he helped his buddy out of his wheelchair to get in the passenger seat and noticed Jason had an accident in his seat, the entire cushion was wet from piss. He didn't say anything because he didn't want to embarrass Jason but to Caleb there was only two reason that would happen to someone. Caleb knew either Jason had a weak bladder, or something literally straight scared the piss out of him and he knew from the few talks they've had that Jason doesn't have bladder problems. The investigating big brother was intent on finding out what was going on between them two but knew Jason was good at keeping his skeletons hidden deep. Caleb attempted to make small talk while they were heading to Jason's home, but the passenger was awkwardly quiet, answering in short statements or just one word answers. Jason knew he had truly fucked up going after the girl from the convenience store that night in more ways than one and knew he had to cut all ties in an attempt to preserve his own life. Jason seen Caleb in action before when he was mad, when they use to run the streets and that kind of smoke Jason didn't want any part of.  As Caleb pulled up the driveway to the house, Jason thanked him for the night out and Caleb grabbed the wheelchair as he helped his buddy get to his front door. Right when Jason unlocked the door he stated,

"It was nice meeting your girl and your lil sister, she really grew up, I didn't even realize that was her."

"Yeah, can't say I'm cool with her choice of profession right now and like you say she grown but I'll protect her til the end, ya heard me. She still my baby sis", replied Caleb.

Jason went inside as Caleb got back in his car with all intent to just meet back up with Keisha and put all his inquiries on the back burner until he had some solid evidence.


        Tyson was getting ready to leave for the night when his cousin Marcus called him to the office to talk about Allure. Marcus understood his younger cousin's reason behind housing the young dancer at his home but was concerned that it would be an issue because the club manager didn't know the girl that well.

"Cuz I know you just trying to do right by her and that's all noble and shit. But you know these females that get caught up with these pimps ain't working with a full deck. I need you to watch yaself round her", stated Marcus.

Tyson admired his cousin's concerns and told him he has everything under control when it came to Allure. He even told Marcus that they are in the process of moving her in her own apartment in a few weeks but that she could take as long as she wants until she's truly comfortable being on her own. Marcus was relieved that Allure wasn't trying to make Tyson's place her permanent residence and had to clown with him,

"Nigga you done taste the pussy, huh? How many times she done let you hit? You ain't gotta lie to me."

Tyson shook his head as he laughed at his cousin while they walked out of his office right into Allure waiting with her duffle bag standing in front of the dancers' locker room. Marcus smiled as he patted Tyson on the shoulder, greeted Allure and walked them to the back-exit door of the club. Ricky was outside getting some fresh air after he had walked two dancers to their car. He seen the two cousins with Allure and made his way to them but was stopped by a man shouting his name, Tyson heard it too. When Ricky turned around, he found Lance walking towards him with his small entourage of followers close behind. Ricky was annoyed with Lance's numerous attempts to get back in the club, but everyone knew the ban was irreversible. Tyson and Marcus walked up to assist Ricky with any problems that might arise, but Lance didn't want any of that smoke until he seen Allure close behind them. With fire in his eyes and fist clinched,

"Oh! So, I'm banned from all y'all clubs but you can keep one of my hoes? Bitch, bring yo ass over here."

Allure's denial infuriated Lance to the point that he lunged toward her with his hands stretched out in an attempt to snatch her to him, but Ricky's open palm shoved him back on his heels. Lance was a raging bull as he reached in his waistband to pull out a shiny black .38 Special pointing it at Ricky's chest. Tyson reacted without thinking of his safety and clubbed Lance in the face with a crushing left hook, but the firearm discharged anyways striking it's victim. Before Lance could hit the ground, Tyson was already on top of him pounding his fist into the downed pimp's face and daring anyone to stop him. Lance's small group scattered after the gunshot and Tyson wasn't letting up until he heard a frantic scream from Allure along with Ricky tugging at his shirt. When he turned around, he seen Allure on her knees with Marcus resting in her lap with a single gunshot wound to his neck. She was trying her best to keep pressure on the wound but the blood was pouring out faster than she could handle. Tyson rushed over to his cousin's aid as Ricky held a battered Lance to the ground, kicking the pistol away from him. The overwhelmed little cousin called 911 as Marcus laid bleeding on the concrete in Allure's lap blaming himself for the catastrophe. Marcus grasped Tyson's shivering hand in a last gesture to calm him down before the grip finally loosened to a limp hold and the inevitable was clear that he was gone. The mountain of a man stood up, walked over to where Lance was laying, pushed Ricky out of the way like he was a rag doll and wrapped his large hands around the shooter's neck. Lance was fighting to get a fraction of air to fill his lungs, but Tyson's grip ceased any of those attempts as he tried to choke the life out of him. Ricky pleaded with him to stop as he pulled at Tyson, Allure begged him to let Lance go but the angered cousin only let go when he seen the flashing red and blue lights coming up towards him. A hard gasp of air could be heard over the police sirens from Lance as

Tyson stood up from the kneeling position he was in. Close behind the police cars was the screeching sounds of an ambulance as it pulled up to the scene. Ricky was oh so familiar with the scenario of police and paramedics after such a horrific act that it had taken him back to the incident that took place in front of the Rabbit Hole. He knew Tyson was in no way ready to talk to police about what just took place and Allure, with blood stains all over her, was still visibly distraught over what she just seen. Ricky calmly walked up to the police officer that was first on the scene and began telling him in detail what had just occurred with his co-workers. One medic looked over Marcus assessing the damage caused by the gunshot wound as he pronounced the time of death while the other helped Lance off the ground as the arresting officer placed handcuffs on him. Lance wasn't in a standing position for 10 seconds before Tyson launched another attack, this time striking his cousin's murderer in the jaw with a thunderous right cross, breaking bone in the process. Lance fell to the ground once again and the arresting police officer tackled a non-resisting Tyson to the ground as the other officer that was talking to Ricky shouted,

"It's okay! That dude just killed his cousin in front of him. Let'em up."


After the main event was over Spice left his sexy date to have some girl time with her besties, he kissed Diamond, told her he'll be waiting for her to get home and told Smiley to stay out of trouble. Smiley laughed as she replied,

"I can't promise that."

Diamond and Smiley met up with Stephanie, who was still in the casino chilling with Keisha at the roulette table. The girls were enjoying themselves with a few celebratory tequila shots after Stephanie's big performance and Keisha was her loud self as usual letting everyone in the casino know that her bestie had a great show. Stephanie started noticing a lot of extra movement from staff officials and security guards when her curiosity had her ask a passing guard what was going on. When the guy told her that all he knows is that the police was out back, Stephanie knew it had to be something that involved an employee of the club because they were the only ones that went out the back doors. She told Diamond and Smiley what she heard, and the girls all went back to the club to see what was going on. As they were trying to enter the club the bouncers were escorting everyone out, including dancers and other employees. Diamond knew something had to really be bad for them to close the club down early and they have all the employees leave. Stephanie tried to get one of the bouncers to let them in to speak with Ricky or Marcus, but all the bouncer would say is,

"Ricky told us everyone has to leave, and no one comes in, I'm sorry."

They all found it weird but left it at that as they headed back to the casino to leave for the night. As Diamond made it to the exit door, she could see police checking all the patrons walking out of the casino, she knew something just wasn't right and called Marcus' cell. She didn't get any answer so Stephanie tried Ricky's cell, but she got the same results. Stephanie was a little nervous cause the last time anything like this happened one man was dead laying in the street in front of her and another was beating to a pulp. Keisha went with Diamond to go get her car while Smiley and Stephanie waited out front, but Stephanie wasn't one to idly sit around waiting for something to come to her. She walked up to a young police officers that was standing in the parking lot directing traffic and asked him what was going on. The officer's reply was vague as he knew as little as Stephanie did, but he did know that someone was under arrest and another person needed medical attention. Keisha pulled up to the girls and Diamond opened her door with tears in her eyes as she told her friends that Marcus was killed. She told them that she kept trying to call Marcus' phone,

"The phone would just ring and ring and then Tyson answered. He told me Lance tried to shoot Ricky but shot Marcus instead. Him and Ricky still out back. This shit don't make no sense."

Stephanie knew she had to get in touch with Ricky some how just to hear his voice, just to know he was okay. She called one more time to only get his answering machine again and left a message for him to call her as soon as he can. The car ride home was quiet with faint sounds if sniffles as Diamond cried the whole time. They all were hurting behind the loss of a co-worker and friend like Marcus, who never had a violent bone in his body.

## CHAPTER XVIII

Caleb was at the shop going over some invoices with his aunt and Smiley of the day's shipments that had to go out. Smiley was getting really good at keeping track of everything that came in and out of the shop, Leslie really liked her organization. The three were in deep conversation about a large shipment that had to be at The Audubon Zoo by 11 o'clock in the morning that they didn't see Levi walk in. Levi just finished dropping off a shipment himself because one of the drivers didn't show up for work that day. Leslie was a stickler for all her shipments to be on time or early and she didn't want to hear any excuses why. Caleb and Levi were a little more lax on the issue but kept the orders on time because no one wanted to feel the wrath of Leslie's anger. Levi joked with them as he watched them map out delivery routes,

"Why it look like y'all planning the perfect bank robbery?"

"Hey baby, just making sure this truck gets to the zoo administration office on time. We do this right and it will open more doors for the shop. More customers, more deliveries, more money", replied Leslie.

She was always chasing the bag ever since she made her first delivery from years ago and now running the shop on all cylinders is a must for her. Smiley loved the fact that Leslie was so determined to make the shop more money because more money for the shop meant more money in her pocket also. She worked hard everyday trying to prove to Leslie that she was an asset to the business and Leslie noticed the hard work. Smiley had become her favorite employee and Leslie knew she could count on her to do the job needed to keep things moving. Smiley was printing out the labels for the big order when Mook had stopped by to drop off a shipment of packages that his office needed delivered with his son Jason in tow. Mook had told Caleb that Jason was outside in the van and Caleb had to go out to go see him. Jason was looking down at his phone when Caleb walked up to the passenger side window,

"Wha cha ass doing nigga!"

"Dafuck man! Runnin' up on a nigga like that", blurted out a shaken Jason.

Caleb apologized for startling his buddy as he told him he just came out to check on him after their night out at the casino. Jason was a little offish with the conversation as if he didn't want to really talk and Caleb noticed it but before he could excuse himself from being the unwanted guest, Leslie walked outside with instructions.

"I'm a need you and Levi to head out with the truck. I want that order to be at their doors on time. Am I understood", stated Leslie.

Those last three words said by Leslie sent horror through every inch of Jason's body because that was the last words he heard from his assailant. Caleb walked off, leaving Jason to his own thoughts and fears as those three words kept ringing in his head constantly because it sounded exactly like it did that night. Before Caleb walked back in the shop Jason asked him who the lady was and when he heard that Leslie was his aunt a lot came rushing to him all at once. The fact that the girl he was chasing after was Caleb's sister, the person that beat him near to death with a bat sound just like his aunt Leslie and all of it was too close for comfort for him. Jason blew the horn for his pops to hurry up because he desperately wanted to get away from Caleb and Leslie as quick as possible. Caleb noticed the fear in Jason's face and was fed up with the secrecy. He got into the truck to head out with Levi and figured there was no better time than now to find out what he needed to know. When Caleb started with his questioning Levi darted around with his answers, not giving confirmation of Caleb's accusations. Just from what Caleb was saying about Jason and Stephanie, Levi knew the young man was connecting the dots, but one thing was missing from his inquiries. Levi had had enough of playing "cat-n-mouse" with the questions and figured Caleb was strong enough to know the truth about it all,

"Look here, after we drop this shit off at the zoo, we gone have a sit down and clear a bunch of shit up cause it's time that you know. Hell, with your aunt feeling you not ready."

Caleb felt like a weight was removed off his chest after hearing Levi speak those words and he rushed to the Audubon Zoo so they could make the delivery.


Diamond was beyond devastated as she laid in bed with Spice as he tried his best to console her about losing her co-worker. She hadn't had a chance to stop crying because all she could think about was how kind of a man Marcus was, his wife and his little boy that would never have the chance to know his father. Marcus wasn't just the club manager to Diamond, he was a good friend, a levelheaded word of wisdom, someone she could always go to in a time of need and never looked for anything in return. Numerous girls would try to get at Marcus because he was model status handsome, well dressed at all times and very well off. Not to say the temptations wasn't there but he would always stand his ground that his wife was all the woman he needed and that was so admirable to Diamond. She seen men firsthand lie to her as well as their wives about extramarital affairs because they wanted some new pussy, spent money they didn't have and was willing to jeopardize it all. Diamond applauded the fact that Marcus was never one of those men even though he worked in an industry that sometimes catered to those factors. She seen the same qualities in Spice and kind of felt that was one of the main reasons she was with him. Spice tried to get her to get out of bed but with no success as Diamond told him,

"Baby I really appreciate you just being here cause I know you have things you have to do but I'm okay, I promise. I just need some time to get myself together."

Spice headed out after kissing Diamond on the forehead and ran into Stephanie coming up the stairs to their apartment. He told her Diamond was in there and pleaded with her to encourage his lover to get out of the bed, Stephanie complied and headed to the apartment door. After knocking on the door for what felt like two or three minutes the door opened to Stephanie's friend standing in front of her with blood shot swollen eyes and the two just clutched each other in one another's arms. Stephanie could feel the pain in Diamond's body as she cried some more but then pulled herself together as they walked into the apartment. Diamond went to the kitchen and poured up two glasses of red wine as she commented,

"Steph it's 12 o'clock in Rio de Janeiro, so drink up."

Stephanie welcomed the drink as she needed it just as much as Diamond did as the two went down memory lane of Marcus' moments. They laughed as they talked about the first time they met and how Marcus tried to save Stephanie from Diamond's antics. Diamond said she thought Marcus was making a mistake in hiring such a "greenhorn" to be a waitress at a strip club but seen that she was completely wrong. Stephanie was weak laughing at how her friend thought she wasn't ready for the club life and that she wasn't going to make it as a waitress. Diamond started feeling better as she commended Stephanie,

"Now look at cha bitch! You done passed me up, headlining the clubs and shit. I'm so proud of you but don't get it twisted, you better have yo ass in class Monday morning."

"And you the same! I have no problem dragging yo short ass by the back of your head if I have to", replied Stephanie.

Marcus always drilled in them if they were going to school that they stay with it and not let the fast money they made at the club deter them. He always said that a sexy body can fall out of shape and a pretty face will get wrinkled, but a strong mind stays strong. When it came to dancers that Marcus knew had drive to do more or do better, he always looked out for them and he made sure they were reaching their full potential. Marcus encouraged all his employees to use the club as a stepping stool, Diamond and Stephanie was more determined than ever to fulfill that request. Diamond asked Stephanie if she heard from Tyson or Ricky since the shooting, but Stephanie hadn't heard from either one of them, except for a text from Ricky that read,

"I'm a hit you up later."

Stephanie wanted to call him, but she didn't want to feel like a nuisance if all he really want is to be left alone. So, she stayed with Diamond for the time being as they brought each other's spirits up.


Allure had just come out of the shower after one of the longest nights she's ever experienced in a long time as she wrapped herself in a short pink Terry cloth robe. Even after a hot shower she still felt like she had Marcus' blood on her, but she knew it was all in her head. Tyson was still sitting on the patio of his apartment in the same clothes he had on from the night before when Allure came out to check on him. Allure had never been in a situation like Tyson, losing a close family member, except for grandparents because of old age and she really didn't know what to do. She eventually got him to get up from the patio chair to get out of his clothes and go clean up. Tyson made his way to his bedroom as he began to take off his blood-stained shirt, kicking off his shoes and making his way to the bathroom but images of his cousin wouldn't leave his memory. He turned on the shower and just stood there staring at himself in the mirror thinking that his cousin's death was all his fault. Tyson had put in his head that if he wouldn't have reacted with a punch that Marcus wouldn't have been shot in the first place. The tears began to well up in his eyes as he thought about how Marcus' wife was crying uncontrollably when he went to the house to tell her with the police. To Tyson it was all his fault that Marcus was dead and the pain of that was ripping him apart from the inside. He attempted to pull himself together when Allure walked in the bathroom to check on him. She took him by the hand as she walked him to the shower,

"C'mon, you can't just stand there. It's time to get in baby."

Allure took off her robe and pulled Tyson in the shower with her. He stood there under the shower head with his head down and hands against the brown marble stone shower wall as Allure wiped his back down with a washcloth. The hot water felt good hitting his shoulders and running down his spine as Allure rubbed him down with a soapy towel. She wasn't trying to make any of her actions sexual in any type of way, but Tyson's masculine muscular frame aroused her so that she lightly kissed him on the back. The affection felt good to Tyson, but he wasn't responding to it at all because his emotions were all over the place with hurt, anger and despair. Allure just continued to wipe him down, washing away all his negative energy as she continued to whisper to him that everything is going to be alright and that they will get through this. It was as if she was a voodoo priestess because her constant chanting started to work as is felt like the hot water just washed it all away. Tyson turned around, pulled Allure to him, wrapping his massive arms around her and their bodies seemed to just melt together in the water spray. He didn't know that the embrace from Allure would be what he needed to feel better and held onto her while the water covered them. He held onto her as she continued to tell him that he's going to make it through this ordeal and it finally sunk into the point where he actually believed her. The two got out of the shower and while Tyson was drying himself off Allure made the comment,

"If you wanted to just take a shower together all you had to do was say so, now you done got me all wet and I took a shower already."

Tyson let out a little chuckle but didn't know Allure was really referring to sexually wet. Just watching Tyson stand there completely nude had her to the brink of just attacking him in the bathroom and giving him every bit of her. Ever since her first time spending the night at Tyson's place, she's never really looked at Tyson in that way but Allure was finding herself becoming very attracted to the gentle giant. Comforting him in his time of need elevated that attraction and seeing his demigod physic didn't help any either. After getting dressed Tyson went sat at the kitchen table and Allure went to grab a drink but Tyson made her feel amazing when he stated,

"Mary, I always put myself out there to help people as best as I can, being that shoulder, they could cry on, never looking for anything in return. But today you were my rock and I just want to thank you for that. I couldn't have made it without you baby girl, thank you so much. Marcus was like my big brother and watching him pass away in front of my eyes was just a little too much for me but just hearing your voice calmed me. As horrible as the night was, coming home with you was a blessing because you held me together."

Allure sat across from him silently and just smiled as she slid him a glass of iced tea, her pretty light brown eyes simply replying,

"Your welcome."

They chilled the rest of the day as Tyson told funny Marcus stories of their childhood and they became closer every minute.


Caleb was heading back to the shop after their delivery when Levi told him to stop at a near by corner store where they grabbed some po-boys for lunch. Caleb was anxious to hear what Levi had to tell him about his assumptions but didn't want to press the issue in fear of Levi shutting down. Levi had him drive to City Park where they got out to sit and have a serious man to man talk about everything because it was time for Caleb to know the truth. They sat at a nearby picnic table, close to one of the many duck ponds in the park to enjoy their lunch, Levi was cool with the spot because it was early in the day and City Park pretty much is empty around that time. With no prying eyes to spy on them or wide-open ears to hear any of their conversation Levi broke the whole situation down starting with the convenience store. Caleb took a bite of his sandwich when Levi began,

"Look, first off your aunt Lez didn't want you to know because she was looking out for you. You just got back from doing a joce and she didn't want you going back on some dumb shit. But ya sister was making a run for her at this convenience store uptown and when she was in the back the shop got robbed. Steph hid in the back, but the dudes started chasing her when she ran out the back door. Me and Lez went looking for the dudes cause Steph said one of them was a white guy with braids and the other was a skinny black dude with a Spider tattoo on his neck."

When Caleb heard the description, he instantly knew who both of the guys were they were talking about and his nerves started bubbling in him. Levi continued telling him that they kept an eye on Stephanie the whole time and got her the job at the club as a waitress. The manager was a good associate of Leslie and made sure Stephanie was protected in or out of the club. Caleb listened as Levi told him about the night of the attack,

"So, Steph was celebrating her Bday at the club but she seen the Spider tattoo guy and the white dude walked up to her trying to talk. She called your auntie and we headed out there to make sure nothing happened. We got to the club, Steph came out with her friends, walked to her car and the guys she described was walking behind her. An example had to be made that your sister was off limits and the points was made clear to anyone around. I didn't know that lil dude was my homeboy's son until Mook came walking up on me at the shop and mentioned he was in a wheelchair. But I kept him close so I can make sure he doesn't suspect anything, that everything is 'copastetic'. You were the one that really started snooping and I figured it was time for you to know before you said or did the wrong thing. I know you ain't no kid and you won't go running at the mouth about this, but it was time you knew the truth. Like I said, your auntie only was keeping it from you because she knew how protective you are when it comes to your sister and she didn't want you to do anything to end you back in jail. Shit is taken care of."

Caleb sat there quiet for a minute as he went over in his head what he had just heard and how his so-called friend Jason had been acting. He trusted his aunt's decision and believed Levi knew what he was talking about but didn't have faith in Jason keeping silent. Caleb was pissed that his so-called friend would try to hurt his sister in any way and held onto the anger with a vice grip as he made the comment,

"People go missing from this city every day, one mo' won't make a difference."

"Say man, Atchafalaya River always have openings for a new resident. But I'm a tell you this, once you go down that road there's no coming back from it. Yo sister is safe, ain't nobody fucking with her. You done found you a girl already and you got a pretty good gig here running a company with your family. We got a good thing going here, let's keep it like that. But if you must, to make yourself feel better about it, I got ya back at all times. Just give me the word and it's as good as done."

Caleb thought about it and came to his own conclusion as to what needs to be done as he finished off the last bite of his sandwich. He thanked Levi in believing in him enough that he would keep their conversation between them and that he won't do a thing without consulting with him first. They headed back to the shop talking about what they had planned for the rest of the day and left the conversation about Jason at the table.

CHAPTER XIX

A few days went by and the Stagelight Gentleman's Club stockholders were ready for the club to open its doors back up. Ricky was second in command and he wasn't ready for the responsibility or confident enough to run the business how Marcus did. But the guys with the big money wasn't trying to hear any of that when they had a conference call with Ricky, telling him that he will be the manager. Ricky sat in his condo contemplating resignation just to get away from all the unnecessary rhetoric of the show must go on. He felt like the company didn't care that he just lost a close friend to a senseless crime and they wanted him to get right back to making them money. Frustration filled his veins because he knew that quitting would put him in an unpleasant place and state of mind but going back without a care in the world would be a spit in the face of everybody affected by Marcus' death. Ricky did the one thing that always pulls him back into focus and that was hit the gym. He made his way to his car and got a call from Tyson, they hadn't talk since that horrid night. When he answered the phone, he could hear the grievance in Tyson's voice as he raged,

"Dawg, these muthafuckas want me to show up for work like ain't shit happen! My cousin funeral in two days and y'all want me to act like it's just another damn day, the fuck!"

"They called me too. Meet me at the gym", replied Ricky.

The ride to the gym wasn't long but long enough for Ricky to get a calm head but it wasn't the same for Tyson as he walked up still furious at the company wanting them to show up for work. They walked in the gym, went straight to the bench and started pushing weights up to get rid of both of their anxieties. Ricky started to tell Tyson that because they put him in charge of the club, he will give him as much time as he needs to get himself together. Tyson appreciated Ricky's concern for him but was still pissed that he was called by some businessmen that he didn't know, that didn't know him and demanded in so many words that he get back to making money for the club. The more weight they put on the bar the better they started to feel as they began to talk about more than just the club. Tyson started joking with his gym partner,

"Nigga you snatching this bar like it owe you money, Ole cock-strong ass. You need to get you some pussy, Mr. Dry Dick."

"Everybody don't have in house pussy like Allure fine ass walking around", replied Ricky.

The new manager was surprised to find out that it wasn't the case with them two, that in fact Tyson still sleeps on the couch while Allure sleeps in the bedroom. Ricky was completely taken off guard when he heard that they never had any sexual contact. Tyson explained that he is starting to have feelings for her especially after the shooting and it got even more confusing for Ricky when he was told about the shower incident. Ricky had put the weights down with a puzzled look on his face as he asked,

"You mean to tell me, you was in the shower, she was as naked as the day she was born, wiping you down and you ain't fuck?"

"Nigga I thought about it but at the time my mind wasn't in the right place, shit", replied Tyson.

The two laughed at Tyson looking confused himself after saying he didn't try to take the relationship further. They worked out a little longer as they talked more about Tyson's roommate, where they wanna be as a team with the club and laughing about finding Ricky a woman. Tyson thanked Ricky for the convo as they headed out of the gym because usually the person he was always able to talk to about anything was Marcus. Ricky was honored with the comparison as he got into his car to head home.

 

Stephanie was just leaving class and looking over some pics, in her phone, she had taken for her social media pages. She got a call from her friend Diamond about the club wanting all their dancers to report to work tonight, for the reopening. The girls really didn't feel like being there but understood that it was their means of funds if they wanted to get paid. Ever since Lotus' appearance at The Stagelight, her paid sites gained followers and bookings for special events or promo appearances at night clubs grew also. The money was pouring in with the minimum payout playing around two thousand a night just to walk in a club, taking a selfie ranged from 20 to 30 dollars a head and Stephanie wasn't complaining one bit about it. But going into the gentleman's club without Marcus being there just didn't feel right to her or Diamond as they discussed their next move. Diamond wanted to stay home but if Stephanie was going than she would too as she stated,

"I'm only doing this because it's you, anybody else would have got all kinds of cussed out."

Stephanie let her friend know she would be at the club as she made her way home to get her mind right for work that night. While she was driving home a news report came over the radio about Lance's court appearance and it frustrated her to hear the reporter talk about what they considered a bad element. Instead of discussing the senseless murder of a good man, the person who committed the crime, the reporter began bashing the gentleman's club stating that the types of people that frequently visit the club are mostly criminals and that the casino/club is bad for the community. Stephanie was furious that the media made such a drastic spin on a horrible situation and that her co-worker's memory is now stained with bad media press. She wanted to get "their" side of the story out but just didn't know how because she felt it would get turned around just like this story was. Stephanie was livid because the reporter didn't once mention how Marcus was a family man, how Marcus use to put together car wash events to make money for back to school drives and how 15% of all the profits made in the casino/club was donated back into the community. The reporter didn't mention all the jobs the casino/club created in the city but was quick to mention a few incidents that occurred which heated Stephanie even more. Already agitated she had made it home to see an unwanted site sitting on her mother's front porch as Malcolm stood up with a smile on his face. Stephanie got out of her car with pure annoyance in her spirit because of the last time her and Malcolm had spoken,

"What are you doing here, you just gone sit on my porch and stalk me?"

"Well damn, hello to you too Steph", replied Malcolm.

Stephanie didn't even put the keys in the door to open it as she stood there on the porch wondering why Malcolm was at her home. She poised there silent just staring at him with nothing but disgust in her eyes as Malcolm made a defense case for himself and his actions. He told her he was in town for a few days for a game and wanted to apologize for how he handled finding out that she was a dancer. Stephanie just listened to Malcolm's blank confession of how he was disturbed that the girl he still had feelings for would dance at a strip club, taking off her clothes for strangers. Then he stated that he understood her life choices are solely hers and that he supports her decision to pursue the life of a stripper. She couldn't believe the pure audacity of Malcolm, like she needed his approval to be an exotic dancer, that he was doing her a favor and she ripped loose with her reply,

"First off, please don't ever show up at my mother's house without calling. Second, your lame ass apology and approval for my career choices are completely unwanted and definitely were never needed because you sir were never a factor in my decision. Lastly, please leave cause I need to finish my paper for school and get some rest before work tonight, I got some strangers that wants to see my titties. Oh and good luck on your game, hope ya team wins. Fuck outta here."

Malcolm got the picture that his presence was truly unwanted when Stephanie went inside and closed the door behind her, leaving him on the porch speechless.

Leslie was sitting in her little office going over her books with a fine-tooth comb, making sure all the numbers added up right because she wanted the business to be spotless if she was ever called to be audited. Her nephew going to jail behind her previous workings shell shocked her into wanting this business to be completely on the up and up. Leslie knew Levi still had his connections with the underbelly of the city and that Caleb still associated with a few of his old partners, but she made it very clear that none of them were allowed in the shop. The guys honored her wishes and besides neither of them wanted any trouble coming to them or the shop. Leslie was about to go on some errands when Smiley walked in with two well dressed gentleman, she knew from The Rabbit Hole. Smiley got in contact with two of the investors of The Stagelight Casino and handed them a proposition to work with Leslie's delivery service. Leslie's confidence in Smiley grew as Alex and Luca discussed having the shop make 50% of the deliveries for the casino. She couldn't believe Smiley had the savvy to pull off such a lucrative deal with some prominent men, but Leslie found out that her Administrative Assistant was way more than just a pretty secretary. Smiley had the same hustle that drove Leslie to always be better than any of her competitors and the business owner seen it firsthand. The suave Latin Luca had nothing but wonderful things to say about Smiley's business proposal to have Wilson & Crawford Shipments handle their orders. The lustful attraction he still had for her kind of swayed his decision also, but he wouldn't say it though. Alex was all about the books, the numbers and after looking over the account books Leslie just finished examining, he felt really good about doing business with them. While Smiley was printing up a contract, Leslie showed the gentlemen around the shop and explained to them their process. Caleb had just got back from a delivery when he seen Alex and Luca sitting in the back with his aunt when he asked Smiley about the suits.

"They work with the casino and we are just about to close a deal with them to start making shipment orders", stated Smiley as she handed Caleb the contracts.

He wanted to go to the office and meet the new customers, but Caleb had some pressing issues he needed to clean up first. While Leslie was preoccupied with her new clients, Caleb headed over to have a talk with Jason. He tried to let the situation be and trust that everything would be fine, but it bothered him knowing the truth about Spider. Caleb had all intentions to talk and he promised himself that it was the only thing he would do but the closer he got to Jason's house the madder he got. The fact that a guy he considered a friend would attempt to harm one of his family members was complete disrespect and Caleb had to address it. Caleb had talked it over with Levi earlier that day and explained that he had to confront Spider about both incidents. Levi felt it was a bad idea but understood if Caleb didn't face Jason that he could end up doing worst, so Levi did what he does best and that's search for an upper hand in the situation. He called around, looking under some old rocks, when an old associate of Levi had some news for him. Caleb had made it to Jason's house to find the wheelchair bound man sitting on the front porch getting some of that New Orleans humidity on his face. Jason looked with suspicion as he asked,

"What's up C? What you doing here?"

"Just came over to check on ya and holla at you for a sec", replied Caleb.

The two sat there just beating around the bush, making small talk but Caleb had had enough and went right to why he was really there. Jason sat there with anger in his eyes as Caleb ran it down to him of how he knows that he was one of the men that chased Stephanie through the back of the store. He told Jason that he knows exactly who the attackers were that night in front the strip club and that he has no problem reenacting that day again. Jason told Caleb that he's crazy if he believes he won't go to the police with what he just heard, especially now that he knows the voice he heard that night was Leslie's. Caleb was nervous for his family but pissed all the same when he stood up,

"You can try to go that route, snitch on all of us and I end up back in jail but trust me when I tell you. What happened to you in front of that strip club ain't shit compared to what I'll do to you before they get close to arresting me. Please don't think just because I'm doing shit by the books now that I can't get gully. I'm still that nigga, split yo shit and let the white meat show."

Spider was done talking and plotting his next move in his head when Caleb received a text from Levi stating he found something really important. It was the video footage they all thought was gone from the convenience store robbery and Jason's face along with his tattoo was crystal clear on the screen as the store clerk was shot by him. Caleb released an evil grin as he turned his phone screen to Jason so that he could see what he was smiling at.

"You cute, you won't make it in prison playa. Kinda hard keeping a nigga off yo ass if you can't run. Open ya mouth and watch what happens. Remember I still know niggas in there and they would be more than happy to run through them ass cheeks of yours", stated Caleb to a now scared Jason.

After making serious eye contact to let Jason know he means business, Caleb walked off to his car to head back to work and confident that everything is in the clear now.

Tyson was home watching Allure get her stuff together before it was time for her to leave for the club. She didn't want to leave him home alone, but Allure knew she needed to make some money because the savings she did have wasn't enough for her new apartment. Tyson understood she needed to go but he just wasn't mentally ready to deal with the club scene just yet, himself. Allure was in the bedroom sorting out her different outfits in her suitcase, making sure she had everything she needed when Tyson walked in and sat on the bed. He looked over the clutter of multi-colored string bikinis, neon colored stockings, 6-inch platform clear heels and was amazed at how much it took for a dancer just to get themselves ready to perform. Tyson began to feel really comfortable with his roommate as he held up one of her bikini tops to his chest, laughing,

"I did not know you did all this just to dance on stage. Do you need all these outfits?"

"This not even half of what I should have, I gotta re-up. You lil boys like big titties wrapped in bright colors so I gotta make sure I'm prepared", replied Allure.

Tyson smiled cause her statement was true and that the bright pink bikini set was his favorite color on her. He watched as she sat on the floor in her grey boy shorts and hoodie crop top, going over what she wanted to take with her. Allure could feel his eyes just gazing at her as he sat there silent and she joked with him that it's rude to just stare. Tyson's reply made her blush as he told her that it was hard not to stare at something so beautiful. She resisted getting up off the floor and kissing the gentle giant sitting in front of her, but it didn't stop her from telling him how beautiful a person he is to her. The two sat there while Allure finished, closed her suitcase and made a mental inventory of everything that was in there. She got up off the floor as she made her way to the bathroom to take a shower before heading out and Tyson took her hand pulling her to him. The two engaged in a passionate kiss that pushed them both onto the bed as Allure straddled Tyson's lap. The kiss was something they both wanted as Allure pulled his tee shirt over his head and Tyson's hands rubbed up her back under her top. His massive muscles seemed to flinch at every touch it received from Allure's soft hands, her fingers following the grooves of his chest. Their eyes met after Tyson pulled Allure's top over her head revealing her voluptuous breast with hardened nipples and she could feel his manhood press up against her through his jogging pants. Earlier all Allure had on her mind was racking in as much money as she could but at the present time all she wanted to do was take in all his dick. She laid Tyson back onto the bed, pulled his jogging pants off and his large phallus stood at attention for her as if she was it's commander. Allure wrapped her hands around the stiffened tube as she parted her full lips, inserted him into her mouth and gave an oral pleasure that was borderline magnificent. It was as if she was sucking out his soul, the more her head bobbed the weaker he got until he couldn't take it anymore and pulled his meat from her lips, Tyson had to take a breather. He sat up on the side of the bed as Allure stood in front of him and he slid her shorts off her letting them fall to the floor. Her pristine plump freshly waxed pussy already moist with its juices begged for Tyson's attention. His mouth engulfed her nipple as he picked her up effortlessly, laid her on the bed and began traveling down her soft frame with his tongue. Two fingers reached inside of her as she arched her back in pleasure pressing herself onto his hand. Tyson could feel her walls grip the more he slid his fingers in and out. He finally was face to face with a gorgeous thumping clit, after he opened her lips and he knew he just had to suck on. His tongue flicked against her clit and the taste was delightful, like candy pineapples and he went in for a deeper taste as his tongue twirled around her clitoris. The movements of his tongue worked like a whirlwind, sending shivers up Allure's spine as she reached down and grabbed his head. Tyson's licking, along with some deep finger penetration, brought her closer and closer to a monstrous orgasm that caused her to squirt out her first orgasmic encounter with him. Still shivering from the electrifying feeling going on with a dripping juice box, Allure remorsefully apologized for the uncontrollable splash Tyson received. He smiled and replied,

"Oh, you can't put the toothpaste back in the tube. I'm trying to make it happen again, so buckle up."

Tyson laid Allure on her back, opened her legs and teased her wanting pleasure pocket with the head of his dick right before filling her up with his massive meat. The gasp saturated the air in the room as his large hands clamped around Allure's hips pulling her closer to him. He slow stroked his pipe, going deeper every time he went in, until he was balls deep inside of her. It felt as if he was touching her stomach with his staff and Allure couldn't fathom why it took so long for her to fuck Tyson in the first place. His stroke was feeling too good, small squirts coming out with every thrust, she started pushing back trying to get some leverage and the skin slapping echoed thru the apartment. Her juices surrounded his appendage and the tingling feeling rushed to Tyson's manhood as he snatched himself out of her pulsing box, creaming all over Allure's stomach. Allure, still reveling in pleasure, laid there heavily breathing right along with Tyson stated,

"Now I really gotta go take a shower, nasty boy."


Ricky was getting "Seersucker Suit" sharp as he got dressed adding the finishing touches with a pocket square. He was heading out of his condo, looked over to his blue steel 9mm sitting on his dresser and images of Lance pulling out a gun went through his head, he tucked the gun in his waist. Ricky was getting in his car when Stephanie called him,

"Hey you, I'm sorry that I haven't called you in awhile. Just been trying to get my head straight. I'm a see you tonight?"

"Yeah, I'm grabbing my stuff now. I just needed to hear your voice. My brother is on 10 right now because I'm going to the club, I told him I will be okay", replied Stephanie.

Stephanie's brother Caleb was not happy at all that his little sister was going back to the club that just had a murder occur a few days ago. He strongly defended his decision that she shouldn't go to the club and that she needs to find another line of work. The two argued for almost an hour with things being said that would hurt the weakest of people. Their mother Doris had finally had enough of the sibling rivalry and shut down the argument, but the damage was already done. Stephanie knew she wouldn't talk to her big brother for a very long time after what he had said to her and Caleb felt it too. As Ricky was talking to Stephanie, he could hear the pain in her voice and being an only child, he didn't know what it was to have a fight with a sibling. But he did know how to console a friend as he just let Stephanie vent on the phone about how her brother called her a "gold digger", a hoe and even accused her of selling ass. Stephanie was truly hurt at the fact that her own flesh and blood would think of her that way. She prides herself on being the best exotic dancer she could be, without settling for sex to make extra money no matter how much is on the table. Stephanie pushed herself to make sure she goes to school no matter what, to keep her head in her studies and for her brother to accuse her of performing sexual favors for money hurt her like no man has ever hurt her. Ricky had heard of family members disapproving of a female becoming a dancer and he understood some of their quarrels with the profession, but he also knew it took a certain type of talent to be an exotic dancer. He knew that a dancer wasn't only an athlete because of the feats and stunts they could accomplish with their bodies, but Ricky knew that a true exotic dancer carried multiple hats to fulfill their job. They were therapist, listening to every gripe or groan from their client and just being that ear. They were teachers, showing other females' things that may make the bedroom more exciting to them and their man. But most of all they were magician, being able to blur the lines between fantasy and reality, making a customer believe the sexual attraction is there all the while keeping it completely professional. Stephanie had all of those traits from the first time she stepped on the stage as Lotus but her brother looked at her different and that was the pain she had to carry. Ricky continued to talk to her as he got closer to the casino, comforting her over the phone and reassuring her that she is a strong woman he admires. Just hearing Ricky's warming voice helped Stephanie get through her little trial of the night. She thanked him for listening to her vent the whole drive to work and it was a little healing process for Ricky too because he didn't have to think about how he's going to become the new manager of the club. By the time he pulled up to the employee parking lot he realized the thought hadn't crossed his mind one time talking to Stephanie. Ricky told Stephanie he would see her in the club later, got off the phone with her, got out of his car and put his game face on as he buttoned the jacket to his tailored suit.

CHAPTER XX

The club was running like a well-oiled machine, everything that Marcus had put into place before his demise worked like a charm and all Ricky had to do was make sure it stayed going. The mood in the club was a little somber because everybody was looking for a glimpse of the man, they all came to respect and love. Ricky could see that most of the dancers were just going through the motions and weren't really into performing at the caliber that the club was accustom to though. He took it upon himself to bring some energy back into the scene when he got on the microphone,

"Check one two one two, what's up Stagelight? This ya boy Ricky, Pretty Ricky what they call me. Well, no they don't. But anyway, first off, I want to thank y'all for coming out and right now I need to ask all my dancers to report to the main stage, all dancers please."

The crowd didn't know what to expect, the dancers, along with Lotus and Diamond were puzzled too about why Ricky had them all on the stage. Once the stage was packed with 50 plus dancers on it, Ricky started to explain himself,

"The Stagelight Gentleman's Club is more than just a strip club; we are like a family and as you all know we lost a valuable piece to our family a few days ago. He was so many things in this club besides the club's manager. He was a father figure, a cousin, a protector, a supporter, a motivator, a disciplinarian and he became my brother. Tonight, we are going to celebrate the man that helped build this grand casino and gentleman's club from the ground up. Tonight, is for Marcus. Now ladies, as for you on that stage, I need you to show up and show out cause Marcus always wanted nothing but high energy. Oh, and for the next 30 minutes, all drinks are on me, pour one out for my nigga."

DJ Felt-Tip instantly started playing some hype music that got all the ladies dancing and twerking on the stage. The little speech from Ricky seemed to work because the sad faces were replaced with big smiles and the club was getting back to the electricity filled atmosphere it always had. Ricky came down from the DJ booth and just began walking through the audience as they watched the stage full of dancers perform for them. He saw Memphis waving for him to come over to his table, Ricky knew the old school pimp was going to have some elaborate play on words for him. Ricky made his way over to Memphis and was applauded for his uplifting words that got the club started up,

"Say lil fella, I likes that. Keep that same energy no matter what. You doing real good."

The new manager was a little proud of himself that he was able to motivate them because the direction it was going would have been detrimental to everyone. If the customers don't feel the excitement, they don't spend and if they don't spend the club nor the dancers make any money. The dancers started coming off the stage after the hype song ended, their customers started pulling them for lap dances, the waitresses were moving non-stop selling drinks and Ricky took that time to take a break in his office. He was sitting at his desk trying to gather his thoughts when there was a knock at the door, Ricky opened the door to a smiling Lotus waiting to come in. She walked in, closed the door behind her and wrapped her arms around Ricky,

"You just don't know how much that meant to everybody. Some of the girls were really thinking about leaving before you got on the mic. Looka you, from bouncer to manager, Marcus would be proud."

"I know you not talking. From waitress to headliner, C'mon now. I been meaning to tell you about your show last week, you killed it baby girl. I couldn't take my eyes off you", replied Ricky.

The two talked for a minute before Lotus headed back out to entertain the audience and Ricky got back into manager mode as one of the bartenders came for some help. He went on about his night but couldn't get the ex-waitress and now prime time dancer out of his head.


Keisha was completely naked on her back, legs in the air wide open with Caleb's hand around her neck and his engorged tube steak pounding away at her juicy pussy. The erotic asphyxiation brought Keisha to another level of orgasm, as her lover dripped sweat onto her and punished her vaginal walls with his swollen sword. Without pulling himself out of her deliciousness, Caleb spun her around on her knees and slammed his dick in as deep as it could go, Keisha couldn't do anything but hold onto the sheets. She could feel every inch of him glide in and out of her, filling up every part of her, every muscle tissue and vein rubbing up against her insides. The sounds of syrup being stirred was accompanied with the occasional grunt from Caleb and moans slipping from Keisha's lips. Right before Caleb felt like he was about to end their slam session with a nut buster, he pulled himself out and got acquainted with Keisha's clit again, sucking her into another spastic orgasm. After cumming for the third time, Keisha laid there limp as Caleb had full control over her body. He put her on her side, climbed between her legs and slid his massive log deep into her plush moist lips, all the while rubbing her clit with his thumb. The strokes got faster and faster until the large snake released its load. Caleb collapsed on the side of Keisha as they both laid on the bed tingling from head to toe after such an amazing session. Keisha got up from the bed, went to the bathroom and came back with a warm washcloth as she pulled away Caleb's condom and began wiping him off. She grabbed hold of the still stiff shaft, wrapped the towel around it and washed all the excess juices off but she couldn't help herself as she began sucking him off.

"Don't you get him hard because I have no problem burying your face into the pillow again", stated Caleb as he looked down into Keisha's big brown eyes.

She got up to take a shower and Caleb happily joined her as they cleaned each other off. After the hot shower, Caleb laid in the bed looking through the menu on the television and Keisha nuzzled herself next to him. She mentioned Stephanie telling her that the gentleman's club opened back up and Caleb's hostility towards his sister going came out in a huff. Keisha knew her lover had some discomfort in his sister being a dancer, but she didn't know that they got into a heated argument over it. When Caleb spilled the news to her, Keisha was caught between a lifelong friend she loved like a sister and the man she just began to grow to have feelings for. Caleb wasn't ready for all the valid points Keisha laid out for him as she told him that Stephanie only started dancing to pay for school, that most of her payouts online go straight to their little sister Alisha's schooling and that Stephanie hadn't been with a man sexually since Quincy broke her heart. Keisha went on to tell Caleb that Stephanie has always held a standard when she's dancing to never degrade herself in anyway,

"She is a performer and a damn good one I might add. But Steph is a boss too, handling going to school, passing with high grades, managing her own paid sites and not one guy can say they fucked her for money. Her being a dancer is a means to an end and instead of being mad at her, you should be proud of her."

Caleb sat there and listened to every word Keisha was saying, realizing he was wrong for all the horrible things he said to his sister that night. He thanked Keisha for standing up for her friend and getting him thinking on the right track, but he still had an issue with Stephanie working in a dangerous environment. Keisha agreed that sometimes the club does have some unsavory characters in them but also clarified,

"Baby in these days and times, you can get shot just going to a convenience store."

That little statement hit harder than anything Keisha said earlier because it hit home with Caleb knowing what Stephanie went through months ago. After their talk, Caleb got up to get dressed and told Keisha,

"C'mon, we going to The Stagelight. But I'm telling you now, if she gets on stage I'm not watching, I refuse."

Leslie and Levi were just finishing a late dinner when Levi told her about Caleb confronting Jason. Being pissed was an understatement of the feelings Leslie was going through as she shouted,

"I told you, you shouldn't have told that damn boy about what happened! But no, you wanna go head and run ya damn mouth! What if this nigga goes to the police about what we did to him? I'm just getting the shop off the ground and I don't have time for this shit, Levi!"

"Are you finish? Are you finish", asked Levi as Leslie paced in the house?

He then handed her a CD and his phone with the video playing of the convenience store robbery Jason was involved in. Levi told her that Jason won't be saying anything to anyone in fear of going to jail himself. Leslie couldn't believe that the dilemma was solved between them and Jason that quick. Levi put the CD away for safekeeping and Leslie had to eat a lot of humble pie because of how she blew up on him as she sat in the living room quiet. The silence in the house was broken with Levi bursting out laughing at Leslie,

"You a mess. You was on 100, going off on me about everything being my fault and look at you. So stubborn you can't even say I'm sorry or my bad."

"You already know I go from zero to 60 really quick but I'm a be the bigger person and apologize for your actions", replied a smiling Leslie as she gave her man a big kiss on the lips.

Levi just laughed it off as they watched TV and Leslie told him about her meeting with the businessmen from the casino. Alex and Luca were really impressed with the company that they told Leslie if she does a good job with deliveries to the casino that they may use her with other companies they are involved in. Levi just listened to Leslie go on about the meeting and the potential of the shop but her drive to succeed was what kept his attention the whole time. He seen that she was determined to make the Wilson & Crawford Deliveries a household name with big companies. Besides her exquisite thick chocolate frame, her ambition and hustle was what drew him closer to her. Levi knew this was his chance to turn it all around, stay away from the street hustle lifestyle and live like a normal human being, without having to look over his shoulder. Leslie also seen the change in Levi to where she knew she could count on him for anything and he would always put her first.

Lotus was on stage entertaining her audience as always and when she came out of a spin, she noticed her bestie Keisha standing in front of the platform, with the biggest smile on her face. Keisha walked up to the exotic lily with three singles in her hand and placed them in Lotus' garter, but the dancer got a shock of her life when she seen her brother standing behind Keisha. Lotus was pleased to see her sibling there even after the heated argument they had a few hours ago. Just knowing he came to see her was all the apology she needed, and all was good between them two in her eyes. Her set was finished, and Keisha met Lotus at the steps of the stage,

"Caleb actually suggested we come tonight and girl you know I'm always up for a good turn up."

Lotus seen Caleb had went to the bar and was talking with Diamond over some drinks, as a treat she told Keisha to bring Caleb to the VIP Room for a lap dance. When Caleb and Keisha got to the room, they found two extremely sexy dancers Lotus had set up to give them both a personal dance. An almond complexion, sensationally sexy, half Spanish and half black dancer by the name of Cashmere took Keisha's hand, sitting her down on a plush red sofa. While an athletic but sexy framed milk chocolate toned dancer named Essence sat Caleb on the sofa across from them. The music was playing, and the beautiful Essence was doing her best to entice Caleb but he was too occupied with not looking aroused in front of his girl across from him. Keisha on the other hand was all into her lap dance caressing thighs, breast and enjoying every inch of Cashmere's soft skin. Caleb caved in, grabbing a handful of titties, when Essence sat on his lap and her fluffy ass rubbed up against his wood. The couple was relishing their dances, but Lotus had another surprise for them when two more dancers walked in with her,

"This is Joy and Chocolate; they'll be joining you for one more dance."

Caleb's eyes got big when, the cute schoolgirl uniform dressed, Chocolate started walking towards him because he literally had his hands full with the sensual Essence perched in his lap. Keisha was on full "turn up" mode as she reached out for Joy to come sit with her and Cashmere on the sofa. While Caleb and Keisha enjoyed their treat from Lotus, she sat at the bar with Diamond appreciating a glass of wine with her friend. The melanated exotic dancer was really pleased with how the night was going, they both made above their quota, her brother finally accepted her exotic dancing career and things were flowing smooth. Quincy walked up to them and instant annoyance came across Lotus as he began talking,

"Hey you, I guess this the only time I can actually talk to you, superstar. How have you been baby?"

"Diamond, why is this fuck boy talking to me? Dude maybe you didn't get it the first time you tried talking to me. I have nothing to tell you, you truly don't exist to me, if you was the only bartender behind the bar I would rather go thirsty than to ask you for a drink of water. Ain't you married nigga, where yo wife? Please stop talking to me before I lose the last bit of composure I have left", replied Lotus.

Diamond escorted Quincy away from her friend as Ricky walked up to the agitated dancer wondering why she wasn't carrying her usual pretty smile. After hearing about the encounter Ricky suggested they all hook up after work like they use to do when they worked at The Rabbit Hole, with the exception of the unwanted bartender. Lotus was pleased with the idea and agreed to meet up with Ricky at a bar they would always go to after the club closed.


        Tyson waited outside of the casino in his car for Allure to come out when he seen one of his co-workers out front. The bouncer walked up to the car, happy to see Tyson in good spirits and told him about how Ricky had a performance done in honor of Marcus. The story made the cousin pleased that the company would keep Marcus' memory alive after he was gone. He knew he had to get back to work soon but the bad memories were still too fresh in his mind to face everyone. Allure had come out to the car, loaded her bag in the backseat and as she sat in the front seat she gave Tyson a loving kiss on the lips, confirming to the bouncer that they were a couple now. Tyson smiled and pulled off,

"So how was tonight, tips was good?"

"After Ricky gave his little speech it turned into a true Hot Girl Summer, niggas was throwing money on the stage like it was Mardi Gras beads", laughed Allure.

She told Tyson how a lot of the dancers and employees were going to meet up at Gabby's bar-n-grill for an after-hour session. Tyson kind of missed everybody at the club and was more than welcoming to see his crew outside of the casino atmosphere. They headed to the bar as Tyson reached over and affectionately held Allure's hand telling her that her presence truly blessed him. The two never realized how much they both needed one another but right at that moment the peaceful silence brought it all in perfect perspective for them both. Except for her father, Allure never had a man care about her wellbeing like Tyson did and even before their relationship gained ground, he always looked out for her. She felt like she really found a genuine one in him and to find a man that was comfortable with her being a dancer was a plus. He encouraged her to get back into school, get her degree and push to become whatever she wanted to be because being an exotic dancer didn't last long. They parked in front of the bar and Tyson seen Ricky walking in with Lotus. Gabby's Bar-n-grill was like a rest haven for the dancers, a place where they can go, relax and didn't have to deal with guys hovering over them like sweet dessert dishes. The bartenders treated them friendly like normal customers and even listened to them fuss about the night they had at work. The bar would have karaoke along with open mic nights for their customers and the cooks made the best bar food you could imagine. It was a spot that Marcus had picked out and it was truly a place to wind down after being at a fast pace all night. After two Jägermeister shots, Diamond and Keisha were all ready to get on the karaoke machine, while Ricky and Stephanie sat at the bar enjoying some nachos and beer. Even Stephanie's brother Caleb found himself enjoying the bar and the company of the club employees. Tyson walked up behind Ricky with Allure right on his side,

"So you wasn't gonna tell me everybody was hooking up at the spot tonight? I thought you love me man."

The new club manager turned to see the new couple holding hands and couldn't do anything but smile as he gave Tyson a hug that you could only compare to brotherly love. They all sat at the bar while Diamond and Keisha had everybody in stitches laughing at them on stage singing. Stephanie and Ricky had a little time to themselves where they complimented each other on how good they both are at their jobs. Ricky couldn't help telling Stephanie about the first time he seen her walk up to him that night at The Rabbit Hole and how she had him flustered. Stephanie laughed as he told his version of the story and she shocked Ricky when she told him that for a minute, she had a crush on him until she saw he had a girl in Sunshine. The two sat there just done with themselves because they both were feeling one another but fear of rejection kept them from pursuing a relationship. The night was going good,

everybody was enjoying the complete fellowship and
Diamond went to the mic, calling out Ricky to get on the
stage. Some of the veteran staff knew of Ricky's poetic
talent but Stephanie never experienced it and was
pleasantly surprised when he reluctantly walked on stage.
Ricky let out a nervous smile as he tapped the microphone,

"Ok, since Diamond's loud ass called me out. I have this
piece I wrote a long time ago for a beautiful woman that I
was scared to share it with, but I guess I have no choice
now.

It's called Taste You.

I need to taste you, not just in a physical way but I wanna
taste you deep.

I can only imagine how succulent your spirit would
actually be.

Most guys just wanna find your spot, touch it a lot and get
you hooked.

I wanna find your light, open you up and not just gaze but
take a deeper look.

I don't think you understand how bad I wanna taste your
everything.

From when you sit in the corner and cry, to when your song
comes on and you sing.

I wanna lay my tongue against your supple lusciousness
just to quench my thirst.

But I want to get to know your worth instead of your
physical first.

I want you to taste me tasting you so you could experience the gratification.

I want to fellatio your inner thoughts with a missionary position of satisfaction.

You got me begging like I'm your lowly servant and you're my priestess or oracle.

Girl I just wanna taste you, it really can't be that hard to do."

After the poem was done the entire bar gave Ricky a standing ovation and he walked off, going outside for some fresh air to collect himself. While he was outside the ever so clowning Keisha went to Stephanie telling her,

"You do realize that poem was about you, right? Girl if you don't give that fine ass man a chance or at least just get you some good dick out of it."

"Go yo ass somewhere, I think my brother looking for you", replied Stephanie as she headed outside.

Levi got a late-night call at 4 in the morning from Mook that he needed to see him, the call sounded very important and he had to go. Leslie didn't want Levi to leave but he felt really confident that the meet up was on the up and up. He met Mook at a parking lot by the Riverwalk that was pretty well lit with streetlights, so Levi had a good feeling about everything. Still on guard though, Levi tucked his chrome .45 in his waist as he walked up to Mook's car parked across from him. He looked in the car and noticed Mook in the front driver side, but Jason was sitting in the back-passenger side seat. Levi knew he wasn't getting in the car with them in that position, in fear that something wasn't right and stayed outside of the car while he talked to Mook. Levi's old running partner explained to him that trust was the biggest thing they had between each other and that if they couldn't trust each other there was no need for the friendship. Right then Levi took that as his cue to go back to his car and leave the scene before anything took place he didn't want to happen. As Levi made his way to his car, Jason pointed a pistol out the window firing it and striking his target in the back of his leg. Mook rushed out of his car and ran up to the grounded Levi with a six-inch serrated tactical knife grasped in his hand. With five quick jabs Mook pierced through Levi's upper as well as his lower back and then turned him over to finish off the onslaught but wasn't ready for the muzzle of his victim's gun pointing at him. Levi pulled the trigger of his .45, the bullet found its place in Mook's neck and exited out the back but with one last jab the knife pushed its way into Levi's stomach. Jason helplessly watched as his father collapsed on top of Levi and the only movement, he seen was Levi crawling away to his own car. Levi made it to the driver seat, blood was pouring out of him with every beat of his heart and he knew he didn't have long. He started the engine and drove off as Jason sat in the other car angrily screaming as he tried shooting but missing Levi. The street started getting blurry and the white lines on the road just disappeared when Levi picked up his phone to call Leslie. When she answered Leslie didn't know her world was about to change when Levi said,

"Baby I'm so sorry, I…I won't be able to make it home to you. It…it went really bad, but you and the fam are safe."

Leslie cried out Levi's name as she heard car horns blow and tires screeching but then the call dropped as if he hung up the phone. Leslie knew he was gone but also knew that the CD Levi hid away was her insurance policy that no one would come for her. Jason on the other hand was in a lot of trouble as NOPD officers pulled into the parking lot he was in, literally paralyzed in the backseat with an emptied gun at his side and his father dead in front of him.

OUTRO

The artist known as Lotus raised to a level of "Main Attraction" in the city, as she filled up clubs and made a lot of money in the process but Stephanie never loss her true purpose as she continued to finish school. The one difference now was that she had her entire family, friends and her new lover Ricky backing her the whole way. Ricky soared as the manager of The Stagelight so well that the company made him their General Manager over several other night clubs they had throughout the city. Diamond retired as an exotic dancer, started up her own pole dance studio and got engaged to Spice. Keisha and Caleb's love grew to a status of living together and they couldn't be any happier. With Ricky stepping up to be the GM, Tyson stepped in as the manager of the club and Lotus took Allure under her wing and trained her. Leslie didn't let Levi's death go without her having the last word. After he was buried next to his daughter, Leslie only needed two cartons of cigarettes and 100 dollars in someone's commissary to have a rope find itself around an incarcerated Jason's neck. She found peace in the fact, but she found blessings in the bump growing in her belly. With the help of Smiley, Wilson and Crawford Shipping became a household name and a rehabilitation second chance business for recently released ex-cons, looking for a new beginning.